BLOOD TiES

LORi G. ARMSTRONG

Gold Imprint
Medallion Press, Inc.
Florida, USA

Published 2005 by Medallion Press, Inc.
225 Seabreeze Ave.
Palm Beach, FL 33480

The MEDALLION PRESS LOGO
is a registered tradmark of Medallion Press, Inc.

Printed in the United States of America

Library of Congress Cataloging-in-Publication Data

Armstrong, Lori, 1965-
  Blood ties / Lori Armstrong.
    p. cm.
  ISBN 1-932815-32-5
  1. Women private investigators--South Dakota--Fiction. 2. Indians of North
America--Crimes against--Fiction. 3. Murder victims' families--Fiction.
4. South Dakota--Fiction. I. Title.
  PS3601.R576B585 2005
  813'.6--dc22

                        2004030265

ACKNOWLEDGEMENTS:

Thanks to everyone at Medallion Press for believing in this book.

The authors who generously granted me their time, enthusiasm and expertise.

The Rapid City Police Department, Pennington County Sheriff's Department, and the local FBI office for keeping suspicions to a minimum at my barrage of questions. Any technical/factual/procedural errors are mine alone.

To Brian Schnell, of Professional Investigative Resources, for sharing the details on making a living as a "real" PI in western South Dakota. Again, any procedural embellishments are purely fictional.

Daughters, Lauren, Haley and Tessa: Thanks for reminding me on a daily basis what's really important in my life. And for not complaining about popcorn for dinner (again) when I'm writing. You rock! Now, go clean your rooms.

Mom and Dad, for being proud of me, no matter what crazy stuff I attempt. Brett: You are the best brother and friend on the planet. PS— I got here first, Bud.

My critique partners and members of my local writing group for their support.

Lastly, and most importantly, thanks to my husband, Erin, for not having me committed when a bumper sticker changed the course of my life. Love ya, babe.

AUTHOR'S NOTE: For those unfamiliar with South Dakota, I've taken a few liberties with the Black Hills. Although Bear Butte is a real landmark, Bear Butte County is entirely fictional.

BLOOD TIES

PROLOGUE

DEATH HAS NIPPED AT MY HEELS like a disobedient dog since I was fourteen.

A drunk driver killed my mother the autumn of that year. She was hit head on. The extent of her injuries, including massive head trauma, excluded the option of an open casket.

I felt cheated. I believed then, if I'd touched her hand or stroked her cheek one last time, acceptance of her death might have offered me comfort or closure. It didn't ease my pain that she didn't suffer. It didn't ease my sense of injustice that the drunk also died upon impact. And it didn't ease my father's rage that the man responsible was Lakota.

After my mother's death, my father's hatred of Indians deepened, spreading wide as the Missouri River which divides our state. He'd never hidden his prejudice, but in the aftermath, the racial slurs flew from his mean mouth with regularity. *Prairie niggers* and *gut eaters* were flung out heedlessly. In those public moments I cringed against his harsh words. In private I fumed against him. I found it puzzling that a man with such a deep-seated loathing for an entire race had sired a son with the same blood.

Apparently my father believed he was absolved of his part in the creation of that life when he signed away paternal rights. The child's mother believed the boy would never know the truth about his white father.

They were both wrong.

My half-brother, Ben Standing Elk, arrived on our doorstep shortly after he'd turned nineteen.

When my father leveled a look of pure disgust upon the Indian darkening his door, I was horrified, and demanded an explanation for things I didn't have the ability to understand. His stony silence mocked me. I expected him to yell back. I expected to be grounded for showing disrespect. But the last thing I expected was the hard, stinging slap he delivered across my face.

We never spoke of that day. By some miracle, probably of my mother's making, I forged a relationship with my brother.

Good old Dad was conspicuously absent whenever Ben came around. I'd gone beyond caring. I loved Ben without question. Without boundaries. And without clue to the consequences. With him I found the bond I'd been lacking. A bond I counted on years later when the tenuous one with my father finally snapped.

Blood ties are strong. But the strands can easily be broken, whether tended with love or ripped apart by hatred. My father chose his means, fate chose mine.

Fate and death seem to be intertwined in my life. After recent events, I realize nothing about death ever offers closure, regardless if it is accidental or premeditated. I still feel cheated. But I'm older now. Wiser. More determined that justice will be served, even if that justice is a brand of my own making. I won't blindly give in to acceptance until I know the truth. Even then, I doubt it will bring me peace.

Ben helped me deal with my mother's death. I grieve that there is no one to help me deal with his.

The dog is quiet once again, sated somehow. But I know it won't last. It never does.

Three years later . . .

CHAPTER ONE

"ALMOST, JUST A LITTLE LOWER. Right there. Oh, God, yes, that's it."

I'd shamelessly splayed myself over the filing cabinet, but the warm masculine hands caressing my vertebrae froze.

"Knock it off, Julie. Sheriff hears you moaning like that, he'll think we're doing it on your desk."

"Al." I sighed lazily. "If I thought you could find my G-spot as quickly as you zeroed in on that knotted muscle, we *would* be doing it on my desk."

"Smart ass. Don't know why we put up with you."

I twisted, heard the satisfying crack and pop of my spinal column realigning itself. No more sex on the kitchen table for me.

"You put up with me because I file, but I'm not dedicated enough to devise my own system."

My blond, waist-length hair curtained my face as I

slipped my heels back on.

"Besides my pseudo-efficiency, I look a damn sight better manning the phones than Deputy John. Admit it, tiger," I added with a snapping, sexy growl.

Al colored a mottled burgundy, a peculiar habit for a forty-five-year-old deputy. He adjusted his gun in a self-conscious gesture, which made me wonder if he'd finger his manhood in front of me as easily. In law enforcement the size of your gun was closely related to the size of, well, your gun. Hmm. Was Al's private stock an Uzi? Or a peashooter?

"Regardless," he continued, unaware of my questioning gaze on his crotch. "If my wife heard me trash-talking with you I'd be sleeping in the den for a month."

I set my hands on his face and slapped his reddened cheeks while I maneuvered around him.

"I've seen your den. And your wife . . . Wouldn't be much of a hardship."

Light spilled across the mud-crusted carpet when the steel front door blew open. All five-foot-one inch of Missy Brewster, my 4:00 relief, sauntered in.

My tolerance level for Missy was lower than a stock dam during a drought. She embodied the skate-by-with-a-minimum-amount-of-effort civil servant attitude, versus the work ethic my father had literally pounded into me and which I couldn't escape, no matter how menial the job. Lazy, whiny, and petty were Missy's least annoying characteristics.

I guessed she'd compiled her own list of my irritating quirks: punctuality, humanity, a stubbornness born of desperation.

Her crocheted handbag thumped on the filing cabinet. She peeled off her NASCAR jacket, and slung the silver satin over the chair with a loving touch before adjusting her cleavage with a slow overhead stretch. A haughty look followed.

"Hey, Julie. Stud boy is waiting. Said something about you getting your ass out there pronto."

I watched Al's gaze linger on Missy's mammoth breasts, crammed tightly into a pink t-shirt. My eyes followed his, but I refused to glance down at my own 36C chest in comparison; there was none.

"Stud boy? You call him that and flash those boobs in his face?"

Her lips, the color and consistency of candied apples, turned mulish.

"I didn't flash him."

"But I'll bet he looked."

"Honey, they all look." With a fake sigh of resignation, she squeezed her big butt in my chair and swiveled toward the computer to clock in.

She reached for a pencil, deigning to answer the phone on the fifth ring.

"Bear Butte County Sheriff's office." Her tone oozed

sweetness. "Hey, Gene."

Yuck. I added disinfecting the receiver with Windex to my list of duties for tomorrow.

"Yeah, I just came on."

Missy flicked an irritated glance my direction.

"No, she's still here." Pause. "He's probably messing with his computer. Want me to ring him?" A minute of silence followed; her false eyelashes batted with apparent panic.

Al, sensing Missy's damsel-in-distress signal, stepped forward.

I stayed put.

"Well, glad it didn't happen here." She muttered a bunch of "uh-huhs" before adding, "No problem. I'll tell him straight away. Bye, now."

"What's up?" This from Al, the brave, blushing warrior.

Missy's shifty gaze wavered between Al and me. "Nothing in our neck of the woods."

Skirting the desk, she hustled down the hallway, Al hot on her Ferragamo heels as she rapped daintily on the sheriff's door.

I got the distinct impression Missy wanted me to leave. So, naturally, I followed the merry little band into the inner sanctum of Sheriff Tom Richards' office.

He didn't respond immediately to our interruption. His back, roughly the size of a Cadillac hood, greeted us, a constant *click clack click clack* echoed from the keyboard. The plastic slide-out tray bounced, and although I didn't see his hands, I knew they fairly danced over the keys. My typing skills are half-assed on a good day. It amazed me thick fingers could be so nimble when it came to office drudgery.

"Sheriff?"

His acknowledgement was a harsh grunt.

"Gene Black called."

"Yeah? What did he want?" *Tap, tap, tap.*

"They found a floater."

His movement stopped; his spine snapped straight as an axel rod. He turned. "When?"

"This morning. Some fly-fishermen hooked it in Rapid Creek."

He scowled at the clock. "He's just calling me *now*?"

Missy's fleshy shoulder lifted; the gesture a nervous twitch, not a casual shrug. "Wanted to give you a heads up before the media did."

"Whereabouts was this?"

She plucked a loose paperclip teetering on the desk edge. "Up in the Hills, off Rimrock." Her pudgy fingers twisted the metal into a caricature of modern art.

"Pennington County claimed jurisdiction, but Rapid City PD was on scene as a courtesy. Then a whole mess of people showed up."

The sheriff chugged his coffee, gorilla hands dwarfing the cup.

Being around him every day makes me forget how immense, how out of proportion he is with the rest of the world. At six-foot nine, he has the distinction of being the biggest sheriff in the state. His arms, legs, and torso are perfectly balanced, but his huge head isn't: It resembles an overgrown honeydew melon with ears.

His button nose is centered in a grayish face; his coffee-colored eyes withhold any trace of softness. Spikes of black hair protrude from his head and chin, reinforcing the ogre-like image from a fairy tale. The knife scar connecting the right side of his mouth to his jaw line creates a constant scowl and discourages most comments, either about the state of the weather up high, or whether or not he plays basketball.

"Gene said they weren't allowed to move the body right away," Missy continued. "They called in the DCI from Pierre. Which also caught the interest of the Feds."

"The Feds and DCI? Why not the NPS, too? Who the hell did they find up there?"

Don't go there, my brain warned, but my mouth ignored the plea. "With that much manpower?" I said. "I'll guarantee it wasn't another Indian."

Ugly silence followed, thick as buffalo stew.

In the past two years, five transient Lakota males — varying in age from thirty to seventy — had become life-sized bobbers in Rapid Creek, which twists from Pactola Lake and zigzags through Rapid City before dumping into the Cheyenne River. Despite the toxicology reports of the drowning victims, which revealed blood alcohol levels approaching blood poisoning range, cries of outrage among the Sioux Nation and resident supporters fell on deaf ears. It seemed neither local law enforcement nor federal agencies were spurred into action, especially the FBI, still smarting from Yellow Thunder Camp in the 1980's and the controversy surrounding the 1972 siege at Wounded Knee. Not even the appearance of Native American activist/ Hollywood actress Renee Brings Plenty, who'd lodged a protest march down Main Street to the Pennington County Courthouse, had changed the status quo.

The "so-what" local attitude remained: Another dead, drunken, dirty Indian out of the gutter and off the welfare rolls.

Who cared?

I did.

Three years had crawled past since the discovery of my brother Ben's body in Bear Butte Creek. Unlike the other Native Americans, Ben hadn't drowned, no alcohol or drugs showed up in his tox reports. With his throat slashed, his body discarded like garbage, he'd washed to the bottom of Bear Butte Creek, an area the Lakota consider sacred.

And like my mother's death, I hadn't gotten over it, I hadn't moved on. In fact, I'd moved *back* to South Dakota from Minneapolis for one specific purpose: to find out who had killed my brother and why.

Probably masochistic to abandon a promising career

in the restaurant industry to apply for a secretarial job in the miniscule county where Ben had been murdered.

In my pie-eyed state following his funeral, it'd made sense. With unfettered access to legal documents, I suspected I'd uncover a secret file on Ben — like on those TV detective programs — detailing why, how, and whodunit, and I could get on with my life.

There wasn't any such file. So, here I am, years later, stuck in a rut that's developed into a black hole: a dead-end job, sexual flings that masquerade as relationships, and the tendency to avoid my father and his new family like Mad Cow disease.

No one understands my anger, frustration, and the sadness wrapped around me like a hair shirt. Some days, I didn't understand it. Time hadn't healed the wound of grief; rather it remained an ugly sore, open for everyone to gawk at and for me to pick at.

In the immediate silence, Missy's globes of cleavage turned into blushing grapefruits. She avoided my eyes, but her clipped tone was the voice of authority. "They prefer to be called 'Native Americans'."

I snagged the mangled paperclip and pointed it at her, hating the saccharine tone she bleated in the presence of testosterone. "No, they don't. Most of them prefer their tribal affiliation. Native American is a politically correct term."

"Whatever," Missy said with a drollness she'd yet

to master.

"So, fill us in," I said. "What color *was* the body they found?"

Al shifted toward the fax machine, away from me. Missy furnished me with a view of the bra straps crisscrossing the folds of her back. "White. Young, female, about sixteen, fully clothed. The body wasn't decomposed, according to Gene."

"Suicide?" Tom asked.

"Didn't say. They're keeping the details quiet."

A disgruntled sound cleared my throat before I stopped it.

Missy whirled back to me, coquettish manner forgotten. "Don't start. This doesn't have a thing to do with your brother's case." She whined directly to Al. "See?"

Hands shoved in my blazer pockets, my fingers curled longingly around the pack of cigarettes stashed there. Damn those crusading non-smokers.

The sheriff shot me a withering look, but asked Missy: "She been identified yet?"

"They notified next of kin."

"What else did Gene tell you?" His gaze swept the bulletin board overwhelmed with official notices and the never-ending explosion of papers on the desk. "I don't remember seeing any reports of a missing local girl."

In a community our size, a missing dog is big news. A missing child is tantamount to calling out the National

Guard.

"That's why they're keeping it low key. The girl was a minor living in Rapid City, but for some reason her parents didn't report her missing."

Again, my mouth engaged before brain. "Well, lucky thing we've got local law enforcement, the Feds, DCI and everybody and their fucking dog concerned about this one dead white girl."

The sheriff gaped, hooking his thumbs in his gun belt loop. His sigh was a sound of utter exasperation. Touchy, feely crap was not his forte' but I didn't give a damn. Let him flounder. God knows I'd done more than my fair share.

"Aren't you off shift now? Go home. Forget you heard any of this."

"I think that's why Gene waited to call," Missy offered slyly. "He knew *she'd* react this way."

Again, my reputation for resentment had eclipsed the real issue.

"This case doesn't affect us," Sheriff Richards said. "Ben's death is irrelevant."

"Irrelevant to whom? Not to me." My thumb ran along the grooves of my lighter. In my mind I heard the click, watched the orange flame fire the tip of my cigarette. Mentally I inhaled.

"Surface similarities, but we don't know the details. Besides, your brother's case is cold, so I'm missing the connection."

"Come on," I intoned, rookie teaching a veteran a lesson. "A death in *any* local creek is a connection. Maybe now that one with the right skin color has surfaced, Ben's case will get the full investigation it deserved."

The ogre in him bellowed, "Julie, will you stop? Jesus! We did a full investigation. Everybody and their fucking dog — as you so eloquently put it — busted ass on his case."

Paws slapped his desk, sending a family picture snapped at an old time photo studio in Keystone crashing to the carpet.

"You know the BIA and AIM still sniff around, so don't give me that 'we don't care because they were Indian' line of bullshit."

So much for the short-lived touchy, feely crap. I struggled not to flinch under the discord distorting the airless room.

He sighed again. "Take the weekend to clear your head; get drunk, get laid, whatever it takes to get you out of here until Monday."

His finger shook in the same manner as my father's. I braced myself for the slap that wouldn't land, waited for the invariable *but*.

"But I hear one word you were up there playing PI at the crime scene, or asking questions of any agency involved and I'll suspend you without hesitation and without pay, got it?"

In my mind's eye, I zoomed inside the safety of my TV

screen, a cool cat like Starsky, blasé about getting my ass chewed. There, in the perfect fictional world, the stages of grief were wrapped up within the allotted hour. I wished it were simple. I wished I didn't live every damn day with sorrow circling my throat, choking the life out until my insides felt raw, and hollow, and left me bitter.

So, for a change, I didn't argue with him, press my viewpoint or try to change his; it was useless. Recently, even *I'd* grown weary of my combative stance and reputation. Unfortunately, my uncharacteristic silence didn't help the sheriff's disposition. He'd brought meth-crazed bikers to tears with his practiced glower, which quite frankly, right now aimed at me, tied my guts into knots that would make a sailor proud.

"Get some help," he said. "Grief counseling, anger management, whatever. Deal with your loss and stop making it some goddamn," he gestured vaguely, plucking the appropriate word from mid-air, "*soapbox* for racial injustice."

Neither Al nor Missy spared me a glance. Wasn't the first time he'd broached the subject, nor would it be the last. At this point it wasn't worth my crappy job. Playing PI indeed. I *was* a PI — albeit part-time. Although Sheriff Richards disapproved, legally, he couldn't do a damn thing about it.

I smiled pure plastic. "Fine. I'll drop it. As far as grief therapy? I'll be doing mine at home, in my own way, but gee, once again, thanks for your overwhelming concern."

Self-indulgence aside, the door made a satisfying crack as I slammed it on my way out.

CHAPTER TWO

MY HAND AUTOMATICALLY BLOCKED the sun's intensity when I shuffled down the buckled concrete of the sidewalk. A cool breeze softened the flush on my cheeks, yet inhaling a breath of clean spring air had no immediate calming effect on me. My mood, like the South Dakota weather, could change rapidly.

The outlook for mood enhancement remained grim when I caught sight of Ray's rattletrap Dodge pickup parked next to the Dumpster again. I held my breath against the stench, guessing I'd have to hold my tongue too.

His blond head leaned against the back window, his calloused fingers tapped on the steering wheel in time with the radio. Ray is good looking in an unpolished way. With a construction worker's build and swagger he rates a second glance from other women. He's not particularly bright, exactly the type of guy I want warming my bed at this stage of my life: young and virile. A man with simple goals, nothing beyond collecting a weekly paycheck and someday owning a vintage Corvette.

At first the change was good, hanging with a man who wanted me for no other reason besides I was around.

Lately, Ray's become a possessive asshole, apparently smart enough to recognize my restlessness and the impermanence of our relationship. It's a classic dilemma in reverse: The more he wants from me the less I have to offer.

He grunted and gunned the truck after I'd slammed the door. "What the fuck took you so long? Been sitting out here for twenty minutes."

My hand shook with residual adrenaline as I torched a cigarette. After the first blessed nicotine hit, I said, "Something came up."

"Well, I don't like waiting."

I blew a stream of smoke in his direction. "So, don't."

"Next time I won't." His meaty palm batted the smoke aside, then he threw the truck in gear. "Where to?"

ZZ Top blared through the tinny speakers until I switched it off. "Home. I need a beer."

His suspicious glance moved over my clothes. "You gonna change before we head to Dusty's?"

"Something wrong with what I've got on?"

"That suit makes you look like a damn lawyer." He tossed a cursory look over his shoulder before switching lanes. "Put on that black beaded number you wore last time. Man, you looked hot."

Ray's comment threw me; my fashion sense is as immaterial to him as my political views.

"Forget it," I said, picking a chunk of sheetrock off my Anne Klein blazer and knocking a wood shim to the tool-cluttered floor. Riding in his truck was hell on my wardrobe. "After working a ten-hour shift I'm not changing into slut clothes to please you. Besides, I'm not going to Dusty's." Idle chatter with any of the wives or girlfriends at tonight's league pool game sent a shudder of revulsion rippling down my spine.

"Jesus, you're in a mood." He punched the clutch, shifting to third. "What is your problem?"

His petulant, little boy expression didn't hold its usual charm. "Did you tell Missy for me to 'get my ass out there, pronto'?"

"I was kidding, Julie. Lighten up."

I leaned forward, kicking aside the Thermos leaking black goo on the toe of my leather pump. "Don't pull that macho bullshit on me, Ray, even in jest."

"You pissed off at the world in general *again* today?"

"Never mind, just drive, okay?" After the last stellar moments of my workday I'd prefer to sink into my couch and drink alone. Berating Ray for his overnight stay and his insistence we share transportation this morning stuck on the end of my tongue. I swallowed it back and turned my attention outward to the same scenery zooming past like a *Flintstones* cartoon.

Spring. The season of rebirth. Newly planted fields zipped by, a black blur. The furrows would sprout new growth in another week; now the barren mounds of earth were eerily reminiscent of freshly turned graves. Why did my brain attach a gruesome meaning to everything today?

I stubbed out my cigarette at the same time Ray flipped on the radio. Our hands brushed, our eyes met. He locked his fingers around mine and set our joined hands on the bench seat between us.

"Bad day?"

The constant caress of my knuckle soothed me a bit. "Turned out that way." Carlos Santana crooned "Black Magic Woman."

"You playing pool tonight?"

Ray nodded. He released my hand when he shifted, turning down the rutted, muddy road that led to my house.

The sight of a familiar black SUV parked in my drive, and the body lounging on my front steps was as effective as a Band-Aid on my soul. My mood improved instantly. I grinned and jumped from Ray's truck.

"Hey, gorgeous," Kevin said, saluting me with a Diet Pepsi.

Why didn't I feel the same punch of pleasure at the sound of Ray's voice? A question for another day, or another lifetime perhaps. "When did you get back?" I said, reaching for his outstretched hand.

"Tuesday night." Kevin ignored Ray as Ray crowded in behind me.

I turned slightly but Ray's furious eyes were fixed on Kevin. Kevin's grip tightened when I tried to pull away.

Kevin and I have been inseparable since seventh grade, but Kevin's disdainful once-over wasn't winning him any best friend points. Kevin detested Ray. Again, no big surprise. Some stupid male pissing contest occurs whenever Kevin and Ray cross paths. I chalked it up to a hormonal thing and returned the favor by hating Kevin's current squeeze, Lilly.

With deliberate provocation, I slid my palm up Ray's bicep. "Game starts in fifteen. You'd better get going. Come by later if you want."

Ray kissed me hard, his hands wandered. If he'd had a branding iron handy, no doubt he'd have seared my ass with his initials. God save me from territorial men.

"Maybe I will," he spouted cockily, turning to Kevin. "Later."

Kevin's curled lips in no way resembled a smile. "Most definitely later."

Neither of us spoke until Ray's pickup peeled out of sight.

"All right, Kev, what's up? You are acting weirdly proprietary."

"What's weird is the fact you're still boning that idiot."

I chose to ignore his comment. "Want a beer?"

"Sure." Inside the house I grabbed Ray's leftover six-pack from last night, an ashtray, kicked off my heels, and shed my hose.

On the porch, Kevin hadn't moved. I handed him a can of Pabst Blue Ribbon. He snorted, "I'm gone a week and you resort to drinking this crap? What? Is pretty boy on a budget?"

"Pretty boy may be hard up for cash, but he stays hard in other, more impressive areas." Kevin scowled and I laughed that I so easily provoked his scorn. I really had missed him.

Lines of fatigue were etched around his eyes. I flopped next to him and cracked the seal. "Anyway. I'm glad you're back."

He took a drink of beer. "Feeling's mutual."

We stayed silent, secure in the comfort of old friends.

"Well, Detective," I said after a while. "Did you solve the case?"

"Yes and no. That's partially why I'm here." He measured me with a tiny smirk. "Called the sheriff's office but you'd just left."

I reached for my smokes. "I imagine Missy told you where I'd gone?" He nodded and I moved the ashtray next to my hip. "What else did she tell you?"

He didn't answer right off; he shrugged, but his eyes never moved. "You were pissed off at the sheriff and went home in a huff."

I laughed, choking a little on the exhaled smoke. "Yeah, I guess that about covers it."

"She told me about the floater." Kevin sipped his beer, adding nonchalantly, "Course, I already knew."

That superior tone of his irritates the hell out of me. "How could you know? We only found out half an hour ago."

He picked up my lighter, flicked it a couple of times before aligning it perfectly on the center of the pack. "Remember the missing person's case I've been working on?"

I nodded.

"Guess you could say when they found the body today, my case sort of solved itself."

"That your smug way of telling me that the body in the creek was the missing person you'd been hired to find?"

"One and the same." Kevin leaned back, cocking his head sideways. "You're a quick study. Sure you don't want to quit your lousy day job and come to work for me full-time?"

He grinned in that slow, wicked way that had most women dropping to their knees in front of him. I played it cool. "Do you have a decent dental plan?"

"Hell, no. I don't even offer health insurance."

"Then, no way." I flicked an ash. "Seriously, why are you here?"

"Can't I have a drink with a friend?"

"Yeah, right." I rolled my eyes. "You're here on a Friday night after you've been out of town for a week? I imagine

Callous Lilly has her Liz Claiborne pantyhose in a twist."

"Lilly has a cold or some damn thing. We're meeting later." He frowned, drained his beer. It hit the redwood decking with a thud.

Evasiveness is Kevin's premier trick, and the fact he hadn't bothered with it bothered me. "Kevin, what's wrong?"

"This damn case is wrong." He shoved a hand through his hair, disheveling the sleek style. "I'm missing something."

"Besides me?" I batted my lashes.

"God, you *are* morphing into Missy." He gave a mock shudder. "I could use your help on this case."

His wasn't an odd request. Kevin's PI business is a one-man operation. Since South Dakota is one of the few states where you don't have to be officially licensed to be a PI, I'm a legitimate investigator whenever I work for him.

On the occasions he needs extra help, I'm happy to oblige. He trusts my gut reactions and it's a valid excuse to spend time together. Besides, the benefits are two-fold: Lilly hates it and the pay rocks. I think he overpays me with visions of me quitting my job and forming a partnership. After a day like today I'd jump at the chance. "What do you need?"

"Another pair of eyes and ears. My client will be in the office tomorrow morning, and if he agrees, I'd like for you to listen in."

"But you said the case was solved."

"I can't get into it right now."

"Can't or won't?"

He shook his head. Now that I thought about it, even his teasing had been half-assed. Kevin wasn't just frustrated. He was disturbed.

He unlatched his briefcase and pulled out a picture of a young girl. "She look familiar?"

Sweet smile over straight teeth, wide blue eyes, light auburn hair. She might've been any girl I'd seen giggling in the food court at the Rushmore Mall. "No. She the one they found today?"

"Yeah." Kevin reverently ran a fingertip over the picture. "Do you remember Shelley Macintosh? Graduated two years ahead of us?"

"Sure." A memory flashed of Shelley and me standing in front of a roaring bonfire, an autumn chill in the air, drinking warm beer from plastic cups and laughing in the way of teenage girls. She'd been older, cooler, and I'd considered myself lucky that she'd chosen to hang out with me that night.

"She married Dick Friel. This is, or was, her daughter Samantha."

The horror on his face matched my own. My earlier flip comments to the sheriff brought shame to my soul. "Jesus."

"I told you this case sucked."

I glanced at the picture again, then back at him. "But how . . . ?"

Kevin stared through me, absentmindedly sweeping a tangled section of hair over my shoulder. "Not tonight."

"You can't just drop this into conversation."

"Sure I can. That's why I'm the boss." His beer-cooled lips touched my forehead. "Eight o'clock tomorrow morning, okay?"

When he pulled away, I focused on his eyes, wanting reassurance. I found none. The last thing I needed was the image of a sweet-looking dead girl floating around in my head all night along with the other dead people already clogging my nightmares. I followed him to his driver's side door to tell him so. "Thanks a whole fucking lot. Just how am I supposed to get to sleep tonight?"

"I think the better question, Jules, is, 'How is Shelley supposed to sleep tonight?'"

As he drove away, a bad feeling coiled in the pit of my stomach, and it had nothing to do with cheap beer.

CHAPTER THREE

ACCORDING TO THE NEWSPAPER, the body had emerged miles from where he'd abandoned it. Memories from that day fluttered to the surface like aspen leaves caught in a windstorm, only to decay, rotten and dank, in the badlands of his mind.

Her hair, a dull, mousy brown, had shimmered beneath the silvery water. In death she'd possessed purpose she'd lacked in life.

Yet, he'd taken no joy in killing her. Unlike the others, the end result fell short of his sportsman's sense of fair play. Skill hadn't been required; no negotiations for cheap booze, no pledges of monetary compensation; usually he broke these promises as easily as long-ago treaties. Although, he had granted himself bonus points for stealth when faced with her distrustful youth. Despite her adolescent pleas, one clean slice under the soft meat of her chin and she'd bled out as neatly as last season's antelope.

Icy water had purified the gash discoloring his knuckle. The little whelp had lashed his skin in a final, desperate act. He'd worn the mark with pride; worthy prey often scarred him as reminder of a hard fought victory.

A splash and shove later, she drifted away like she'd never been.

Disposing of the body hadn't been an issue. The ebb and flow of the cold creek, coupled with runoff from spring snowmelt, would sluice the carcass downstream. Someone would discover the corpse, or it'd become prime pickin' for buzzards. Either way, he'd washed his bloody hands of the matter and nature would take its course, as it should have years ago.

In the fading sunlight, he'd surveyed his handiwork, cockiness a given; he, a hunter without equal, he, a man who lived by his own rules. God might be in the details, but He wasn't in the bodies. After nineteen kills, he hadn't witnessed a diaphanous soul soaring from the discarded shell, but he had seen plenty of blood, piss, and shit soaking the ground. His afterglow wasn't attributed to outsmarting anyone, but in proving to himself again that religious platitudes and assurances of eternal reward had been, and still were, the world's biggest con game.

He'd crossed himself then, as he did now, and got back to work.

CHAPTER
FOUR

THE SHADOWS IN MY ROOM gave no indication of the hour. I groaned and cracked the shades open, noticing fat raindrops glisten, then slither down the foggy windowpane. A rainy Saturday. *Burrow under the covers, sleep till noon,* my lazy thoughts insisted. Pure indulgence to spend the day making slow, lazy love, preferably with a partner. Ray hadn't dropped by last night. No blame there; my "Miss Congeniality" sash was gathering dust rhinos under my bed.

Red numbers on the clock held steady at 7:05. If I flopped back in bed for another fifteen minutes, I'd give up shower time. Kevin wouldn't care; we'd been stinky together for days during surveillance and he hadn't complained.

Half an hour later I tossed back the star quilt, slipped on my toasty moccasin slippers, and shuffled to the kitchen like an old medicine woman for my morning fix.

Coffee is a necessary evil. I'll resist the showering ritual on occasion, but never coffee. The sad thing is I don't even *like* coffee. A friend once referred to it as hot dirt water. However apt that description, I don't bother doctoring the taste. I drink it quickly and hope the caffeine kicks in before the flavor does.

Chilly air bit my ankles as I retrieved my newspaper. Shorts, skimpy tops, and opened-toed sandals were off the wardrobe list again today. I'd been stuck with the same damn wool clothes for months.

Winters in western South Dakota are erratic. Temperatures range from sixty degrees above zero to sixty degrees below. I've barbequed steaks in my bare feet in February only to be slapped in the face a day later with wind chills dipping to the thirty-below-zero mark. The constant freeze-thaw cycle wreaks havoc; from roads and sidewalks to the premature budding of trees and flowers. Potholes and cracked concrete are first true signs of spring. But spring is as fickle as winter. Balmy spring days blossom into heat as effortlessly as they turn ugly with unwelcome snow flurries.

The story about the unidentified victim was not the headline, but figured prominently on page one, overshadowed by early projections for the upcoming agricultural season. Seemed Samantha's demise *had* rated the same level of coverage as the Native American drowning deaths.

Hair combed, teeth brushed, dressed in flannel-lined jeans and a sweater, I was ready to rock-n-roll. My Nissan Sentra didn't warm up until about halfway into the twenty minute drive into Rapid City. On Main Street, I whipped into the first open parking space.

Kevin's business is nestled in one of the historic buildings downtown. Around here, historic can mean anything from buildings built during the 1876 Deadwood gold rush, to ones erected in time for the 1941 completion of Mount Rushmore. Architecturally the building looks Russian, with a spire resembling a jumbo Christmas ornament. It doesn't have that slightly seedy look I associate with fictional PI's. The rent is cheap, probably because the owners haven't updated the plumbing or electrical since the 1930's.

The narrow staircase in the back led to the third floor. The door to Kevin's suite was closed against the rank smell of permanent wave solutions drifting up from the downstairs salon.

I crossed the reception area to Kevin's office and left the door ajar.

Kevin sat at his desk, phone glued to his ear. He motioned me to a brand-spanking new chair before refocusing on the conversation. My hand caressed the buttersoft yellow arm. Buffalo skin. It figured. Not that I could afford the indulgence. The PI business pays better than lowly secretarial work; consequently Kevin has the money to back up his great taste.

My opportunities to study Kevin the way he likes to scrutinize me are limited, so I reckoned that entitled me to a little open leering. Pathetic, I know, but what else was I gonna do to kill time without a TV?

Dressed in casual clothes today, he seemed approachable, the kind of guy you'd share a beer with, not the attractive, professional-looking type of man I avoid like church.

In junior high, my girlfriends labeled him cute, with his unremarkable brown hair, mossy green eyes, and easy smile. As a man, "cute" no longer applies. Quite simply, he's striking. Tall, muscular, and confident, he's grown into his angular features, pumped up his once-slight frame, and success fits him as well as the double-breasted suits he favors. His smile, no longer quick and easy, is more potent because of its rarity.

He favored me with one of those smiles after he'd hung up. "Morning, beautiful. You look chipper for a rainy day."

I decided showers were overrated. "I assume everything with your client is A-okay?"

"Yep, he'll be here any minute." He reached in the small fridge behind him and tossed me a Diet Pepsi. "You ready?"

"For what?" I popped the top, slurping foam from around the rim.

"You are leading the interview." Kevin's eyes searched mine. He started to add something else, but a soft knock had him looking away.

The client wasn't what I expected. A young man, nineteen or so, an unshaven baby-face marred by black smudges of grief. That same look stared back at me in the mirror most mornings, and my sense of unease rose accordingly.

"David LaChance, my associate, Julie Collins. Julie works for the Bear Butte County Sheriff's office. When I'm lucky, she also works for me."

I pumped David's hand and skipped the usual "nice-to-meet-you" bullshit, reluctantly offering him the deep-cushioned chair. Cold metal stung my behind as I settled into the cheap folding variety shoved against the wall. "LaChance? Any relation to Charles LaChance?"

"My father. Mr. Wells said you know him."

"Yes," I said, keeping my face neutral.

With grace born of athleticism, he slid into the seat I'd vacated. "You don't like him, do you?"

Charles LaChance had repulsed me long before he metastasized into a personal injury attorney. Five years older than Kevin and me, he'd skulked around with high school kids long after he'd graduated. He had no friends; a weasel like him rarely did, but he'd provided a useful link to local liquor stores. During his senior year, Chuck knocked up a fifteen-year-old cheerleader from the Catholic high school. Rumor: Her father threatened a charge of statutory rape unless Chuck married the girl. Apparently, I sat hip-to-hip with the result of that blessed union.

"No, I don't like him. Does that matter?"

"Guess not because I don't like him sometimes, either."

"Does he know you hired an investigator?" Fortunately, Charles LaChance reciprocated our feelings and never used Kevin's investigative services.

"Yeah." He squirmed, earlier poise gone. "Umm, he didn't approve." Two spots of color dotted his high cheekbones, square chin met muscled chest. "Said it wasted my money to find some two-bit whore I was better off without."

Kevin said, "David, why don't you start at the beginning? Julie's asking questions since this is basically review for me."

Finally, the chance to try out my interview techniques. I hoped I wouldn't come off as a hard-ass, and I bestowed my most sincere smile on David. "Start whenever you're ready."

His words tumbled out like a child's wooden blocks. "Sam and I met last summer working at the resort off Highway 79. I'd finished freshman year in college, thought I was hot shit, working the primo gig in the golf pro-shop." He closed his eyes. "She waited tables in the clubhouse and wasn't impressed with me in the least. I fell for her, fell hard. Crazy in love with her the first time I ever saw her." His awkward chuckle was sweet. "Sounds corny, doesn't it?"

"No, it sounds nice." I lit a cigarette. "Go on."

"We dated, neither of us expecting much since Sam was only sixteen. But she wasn't a typical sixteen."

I wondered what passed for typical these days. "How so?"

"She didn't hang around me while I worked or call me three times a day. Didn't brag to the other girls she'd hooked up with a 'frat' guy or expect me to chauffer her around. We just had fun."

When he smiled, a deep-set dimple popped out. I was utterly charmed. No wonder Samantha had played it cool. "She sounds like an interesting girl."

He nodded. "Sam was the best. She had depth, intelligence, and a great sense of humor."

"So, she wasn't much like her friends?"

David eyed my Marlboro Light with polite distaste. "She didn't have many friends except for her little sister."

"How old is her sister?"

"Meredith?" He scratched his chin, perplexed. "I dunno. I guess about fifteen."

"So, if Sam had a problem, she'd talk to . . ."

"Meredith usually, or me. Sam was pretty much a loner." He shrugged, as if that were natural. "Sometimes she'd go to a priest at her church if something really bugged her."

"What about her parents?"

He gave me: you've-got-to-be-kidding.

"Did she tell you everything?"

"I think so."

"Were you intimate?"

His chin notched higher, but the brightness in his eyes showed discomfort. "Not until the last few weeks of summer. She was pretty hardcore Catholic and wanted to wait." His cheeks flamed. "But, well, we didn't."

Ah. Guilt. At least he wasn't yet full of male swagger, but no doubt with his looks that'd happen eventually. Pity. "Did you continue your relationship after you'd gone back to college?"

"Yes, we talked on the phone and I came back to see her at least once a month. We spent all of our time together during Christmas break."

I balanced the killer whale ashtray I'd bought Kevin on my knee. "How did your parents and her parents feel about your relationship?"

"My father dismissed her; my mom was concerned that I'd 'get her in trouble.'" David picked at the corner of his thumbnail. "Her parents didn't care."

"What do you mean, 'didn't care'?"

"Look, its no big secret Shelley had a drinking problem. It embarrassed Sam. She never wanted me to come inside when I picked her up at her house, since Shelley was usually wasted. Dick wasn't a hell of a lot better. Most nights he's at Fat Bob's, that biker bar on the outskirts of town."

I let the last sentence sink in. Just another perfectly

adjusted Midwestern family. "Did she consider running away?"

"Never." David's troubled hazel eyes locked with mine. "That's why I hired Mr. Wells. She'd never just disappear."

Wisps of silence hung in the room much like the clouds of mist outside the window. What David revealed about Samantha Friel didn't fill in the gaps. It made for interesting conversation, but we were talking about death, not love. Why hold anything back when he was paying for answers? I waited, using the time to practice my hard cop stare.

"David. Julie can't help if she doesn't know everything." This from Kevin, my silent partner.

"Can I have one of those?" David pointed to my soda.

Kevin handed him a can. I watched David open it, the carbonation slowly released in little pops and hisses. He fiddled with the metal tab, twisting until it snapped off. A quick flick of the wrist — *ping*, it dropped inside the garbage can. One teeny sip followed another.

God. A fifty dollar bottle of Merlot deserved that much enjoyment, not a Pepsi product. I tamped down my impatience.

At last, he looked directly at me. "Sam found out recently Dick Friel wasn't her biological father."

My gaze flickered to Kevin, but he'd hunkered over his notebook. Remarkable; he played blind man as convincingly as deaf man today. I stubbed out the cigarette. "How did she find out?"

"Two months ago, her mother checked into that private alcohol rehab center out on Highway 44. It's a long program, something like three months. Sam was thrilled Shelley had finally acknowledged her problem and prayed this time the treatment would work."

I held up my hand. "Wait a minute. Shelley's been in rehab before?"

David stared deeply into his magic soda can. Finding no answers, he glanced back at me. "Twice. Once for drugs when Sam was five, then for alcohol three years ago."

Twice. The initial flashback I'd had last night to that long ago keg didn't create the same warm, fuzzy feeling. "Was Shelley doing okay in rehab this time?"

"Sam thought so. There's counseling sessions: one-on-one, family, marriage . . . This one counselor had a 'break-through' with Sam's mom and insisted all of Shelley's drinking problems stemmed from one suppressed incident. Naturally, this counselor convinced Shelley in order to 'heal' she needed to come to terms and 'share' it with her family."

The sarcasm in David's voice surprised me. He didn't think much of counselors. We were on the same page there. In my experience, most mental health workers filled heads with double-speak mumbo-jumbo bullshit that meant nothing. Any combination of words sounded reasonable when emotions ran high. Their professional solutions were nothing besides the patient's words rearranged and tossed back in the form of a question. I equated it to asking a panhandler for advice on managing your stock portfolio. "I take it Shelley 'shared'?"

The empty pop can crashed into the garbage as David stood. "God. I shouldn't be telling you this." He paced and I resisted my urge to trip him. Pacing is pointless, an irritating waste of energy that just plain pisses me off. Guess I still needed to work on the patience angle.

"David." We glanced at Kevin. His steely stare matched the inflection in his voice. "Tell her or I will."

David clenched his fists at his side. "Shelley was gang-raped when she was nineteen. She got pregnant and told Dick the baby was his." He turned to watch my reaction.

The soda burned in my stomach like battery acid, rising halfway up my throat before I swallowed it back down.

CHAPTER FIVE

"JESUS. SAMANTHA TOLD YOU THIS?"

"She freaked out and called me at school right after the session ended. I drove all night to get here." He sank deeper into the chair, deeper into himself. "She was a fucking mess."

I started to ask another question but David interrupted.

"Do you want to know the worst thing?"

I shrunk back, not believing there could be anything worse.

David's bitter voice peeled the air like old paint. "Dick Friel, her *father* for her whole fucking life, told her he didn't give a shit about her since she wasn't his kid. Wasn't his kid," he repeated. "What kind of man does that?"

I thought of my own father and how ruthlessly, almost gleefully, he'd abandoned his own child. Yeah, I knew exactly what kind of man Dick Friel was. But this wasn't about me, although the parallels were eerily similar.

"David?" I prompted at another bout of his silence.

He'd dug his elbows into his knees, handsome head cradled in his youthful, unlined hands. I couldn't see his face. God, I hoped he wasn't bawling. Men always complain when women cry, but it was a cakewalk compared to a sobbing boy on the cusp of manhood. "Yeah?"

"Can you tell me the rest?" He overlooked my tight smile, intent on memorizing the boldly colored, Native American artwork of Richard Dubois over my right shoulder. Hours, days, months passed. At least he wasn't pacing, but I didn't think he'd appreciate me snapping my fingers and yelling "Focus." Instead, I waited, which I rarely do well.

"It's kind of a blur," he said finally. "When I got into town, I picked her up and took her to my mom's."

"Your mom was there?"

"No. She was in Denver."

"What about your dad?"

"My parents divorced when I was two. Anyway, that afternoon, I took Sam out to the rehab center and while she talked to Shelley, I found the counselor."

"Why?"

With his back snapped straight, the carefree college stud disappeared. "I told that woman after what she pulled she'd better counsel Sam, too, for free, or else I'd get my father to slap her stupid ass with a lawsuit so fast it'd make her head spin."

Okay, so I didn't care for the extreme focus he turned on at will.

That mini-tirade put a new spin on Mr. David La-Chance. I took another swig of soda, wetting my cotton mouth. "Did this counselor agree?"

David leaned closer, his eyes bright like small, shiny tacks, his mouth a smirk that curled my innards. "Without question she agreed. You may not like my father, Ms. Collins, but his name does invoke fear in most people around here."

More disgust than fear, I wanted to point out, but kept my mouth shut. David resembled his father far more than I'd initially believed. "Samantha wanted the counseling?"

"At first she wanted to forget the whole thing and go home. She stuck it out for a few days. I think she was dealing with it, but her mom didn't want her there." His harsh bark of laughter fit this new persona. "No big surprise. Nobody wanted Sam anywhere. About two weeks later, she and Dick had a big fight and he kicked her out."

"Where'd she go?"

"Some dive up on East North Street."

That surprised me too. The north side of Rapid City has a bad reputation, deservedly so. I've read the police and Social Services reports: stabbings, sexual assaults and child abuse run rampant. The population is largely poor and Native American; a few college kids and elderly people on fixed incomes remain among the gangs and transients. Couple that demographic with the excessive number of casinos, bars, and pawnshops, and the crime rate soars. Most homicides, rapes, robberies — not to mention unsolved drownings — occur within a two-mile radius.

"Alone?" I said skeptically. "She didn't have any other family or friends to crash with for a while?"

He shook his head. "The only relative that lives here is her grandma, but she spends the winter in Arizona."

"What about out-of-town relatives?"

"I'd hoped maybe she took off to stay with her cousin in Lincoln, you know, to get herself together. By the time I talked to Meredith again, it'd been two weeks since anyone'd heard from her."

The muscles in my shoulders grew tight. The next few questions wouldn't be easy for me to ask or for him to answer. "Why is it so important for you to find out where Sam was those last two weeks?"

David's gaze turned murky. "Last time I talked to her, she seemed . . ." He faltered. "Less angry, more . . . smug. Something had changed. *She'd* changed. Like she had this great big secret. She swore the next time we got together, she'd explain everything."

Kevin glanced up sharply.

A sixteen-year-old with a secret. How novel. But most young girls' secrets weren't serious enough to get them dead.

"How long did she stay at the place on East North?"

"A few days, I guess, she didn't have much money. She had a job waiting tables on weekends up at Johnson's Siding."

Coincidence her body had been found downstream from where she'd been slinging hash? "That's ten miles out of town. How'd she get there?"

"Dick bought her a piece-of-shit car when she turned sixteen. But she barely made it to work and back." David sneered. "You'd think a mechanic would make sure her car ran."

"So, realistically, she could have earned enough money to live anywhere for a couple of weeks?"

"Doubtful. After the tourists leave, the tips drop way off. She said it was depressing."

"Was she depressed often?"

"I'd never seen her depressed before any of this happened, and believe me, she had plenty to be depressed about."

"Would she attempt suicide?"

His face paled. "No, she's Catholic."

I snapped my mouth shut. Catholics expected Protestants to accept that statement at face value, for any situation, as a testament of true faith. I never did.

"After what she'd been through? Wouldn't she at least consider it?"

"No."

"Julie, you're getting off track here," Kevin said.

"Not even to make her parents sorry? Make them suffer?" I paused. "Did Sam use drugs?"

David's guilty eyes darted away when he admitted, "We smoked pot once or twice."

"Could she have gotten mixed up with more serious stuff?"

"No."

"Did she drink?"

His jaw clenched. "For Chrissake, *no*."

I had one chance left to test my theory. "Maybe she changed in those two weeks. Maybe you didn't know her as well as you thought."

After his deliberate pauses, his vehement denial came swiftly. "I knew her better than anyone. She was upset, yes, but she'd never run away, or kill herself, that much I do know."

"Then why is she dead, David?"

"I don't know."

A placating, sympathetic comment arose, and I shoved it aside, hating the hard-nosed bitch act that fit me like a second skin. I lit another cigarette and considered him through the haze, knowing it hid the turmoil in my eyes.

"Apparently, you don't know too much."

He jumped to his feet, looming over me like a Cornhusker linebacker. "You have no right to sit there and make me feel like I did nothing. I gave her as much support as I knew how . . ." His hands squeezed open, then shut in tight fists. "It's not my goddamn fault this happened in the middle of midterms. My Dad told me if I didn't pass, he'd stop paying my tuition. I couldn't leave, so I hired *him*." He pointed a slender finger at Kevin. "A lot of good it did. Sam is dead. I don't have a fucking clue where she spent the last two weeks."

Rage and frustration, unanswered questions, all familiar to me, yet somehow I didn't feel either the empathy Kevin expected or the sympathy David deserved. I felt like I'd been ambushed.

"David, that's enough. Sit down." Kevin shoved his pen into the holder and his chair back.

Kevin didn't apologize for me. But it wasn't enough to ease my mind that I'd somehow taken a wrong turn and couldn't go back.

David's shoulders slumped, his face a mask of despair. "Don't suppose you're going to help me now?"

His petulant look had zero effect. I moved to the window behind Kevin's desk while he murmured to David and escorted him from the office. I tuned them out.

Saturday traffic flowed smoothly alongside the rain rushing into the street drains. Everything lacked color, the sky and clouds, the wet streets and sidewalks, the dirty gush of water thrown over the curb by passing cars. I exhaled, watching the gray smoke from my lungs dissipate into nothing. The whole lot seemed bleak; a pointless gray, neither black nor blue: the air in the room, the day outside, my present mood.

Few people braved the weather and I wished I hadn't either. Sensible people were snug in their houses, doing normal, rainy day things. Why was I here subjecting myself to more sorrow?

"Julie?" Kevin's voice tickled my ear. "I'm sorry."

I faced him. "If today is 'piss off your best friend day', I didn't get you a card."

His slight smile didn't reach his eyes.

"I don't like this and I don't appreciate that you've suddenly become mute. Tact isn't my strong suit, you know that."

"I know." He gently moved a hank of hair behind my ear; his thumb skated across my cheek. "But the way you asked the questions was good practice for when I convince you to come to work with me."

Great. Now we were back at another subject I'd been avoiding. But I'm not entirely sure it's just a professional association Kevin wants. I haven't found the guts to ask him for clarification, so like everything else in my life, I steer clear of the issue.

"Julie?"

"Yeah, yeah, I'm listening. But do the words 'just listen' ring any bells with you?"

Kevin hummed "Jingle Bells."

I slugged him.

"Come on, I'll admit that you aced the good-cop,

bad-cop routine," he offered as a truce.

I rolled my eyes. "And yet, somehow the point of that eludes me."

"And yet," he said as he tapped my temple, "your pointed, less-than-subtle questions worked because the information he gave you differed from what he gave me."

Kevin wasn't blaming me for my rigid bitch act? If he only knew the pretzel state of my internal organs from what I'd heard today. Or how often I wished I'd turned out soft and gentle, cooing wisdom and compassion like my mother. Fate chuckled deep in my subconscious and then my father's cold voice told me to stop whining. "How so?" I said.

"More emotional. When he hired me he provided the basic details and a retainer." Kevin scowled and rubbed the bridge of his nose. "This business about a secret is new."

"But you knew about Shelley? Why didn't you tell me?"

His eyes narrowed. "Would it have made a difference if I did?"

"Yes."

"Why?"

I broke eye contact and sat down. "It just would have."

"Julie . . ."

"Goddamn it Kevin, this is hard, okay?"

"I know. I thought you could help. I thought it might help *you*."

Normally Kevin took my moods in stride and didn't

push. "Is that why I'm here? Because 'poor Julie's' brother was found floating in the creek? You need my expert advice on what it's like *not* to have answers?"

He stared at me in silence.

I shivered in my cashmere sweater. A 2000-gauge wool coat wouldn't warm me, as the chill went deep, beyond flesh and muscle to the bone. "It's not the same situation because there'll be answers for David. Sixteen-year-old girls do *not* just disappear in a town this size. Someone knows something. Sam was young and tragic and . . ."

"White," he finished. "I never expected prejudice from the champion of racial injustice." Kevin crouched at my knees, forcing me to meet his eyes. "You're right, it is a different situation, but not because she's white and the other drowning victims were Lakota."

"What makes you so sure?"

Kevin's icy voice cut through my indignation. "Because she didn't drown. Whoever killed Sam slashed her throat. Slashed it from ear to ear. She bled to death before ending up in the creek."

Just like Ben. The words weren't spoken aloud, but they hung in the confines of the gray office nevertheless.

I shut my eyes against the ghastly image, pushing my head back until the stucco wall scraped my scalp. That one little difference in the cases changed everything. And nothing. It sickened me; it incensed me, as Kevin knew it would. I didn't want to get involved; yet I felt the pull. "When did you find out?"

"Sergeant Ritchie Schneider from the police department called with the details right when you walked in."

"Why?" Kevin's dad had been a Rapid City cop for years so I knew he was tight with the PD. And, we'd known Ritchie Schneider from our hell-raising days back in high school. Still, the attitude of the RCPD was more like Sheriff Richard's when it came to investigators in the private sector.

"He knew it was my case and figured I deserved to know what I was up against. The FBI was called as a courtesy; at this point everyone still has access to everything, but that could change."

"Why didn't you tell David?" My eyes burned beneath my lids and seemed to be glued shut. "Do you think David could've killed her? Hired you to cover his tracks?"

I heard his sigh before it crossed my face, sweet, minty, close. "I'd considered it, but he seems to be the only one who gave a damn about her. But remember, we're not trying to find out who killed her, we're only trying to figure out where she was hiding and why."

Slowly, I opened my eyes knowing Kevin would be right in my face. I wasn't disappointed.

His eyes, an intense green, locked on mine and I resisted the urge to squirm. He believes the crap about eyes being windows to the soul and reads me accurately on most days. I didn't want him delving that deeply into me right now.

"What?"

A cocky smile later, he backed off. "You'll help me, won't you?"

He knew he had me but I hedged just the same. "It probably won't make a difference."

"You'll make a difference, I feel it."

His sweetness left me flustered and confused on the outside as harsher feelings roiled inside me. "I don't know what I can do."

"You have a history with Shelley. I think she'll talk to you easier than she would me."

Ancient history. The weekend kegs and sporadic confidences from days past didn't give me the right to infringe on her grief, or her attempts at overcoming her addictions. "Kevin, I knew Shelley years ago. She probably doesn't even remember me."

"Everyone remembers you."

My knuckles rapped his chest. "Flattery won't work, slick."

"What will?"

"Money, good tequila, a weekend in Cozumel with unlimited sexual favors, you know, the usual."

He frowned and moved behind his desk. "I'm serious."

"Me too. Hard not to be with what I've heard today."

"You understand why I didn't tell you everything in the car last night?"

A wave of sleepiness washed over me. I wanted nothing

more than to pull the covers over my head and ignore the
horrors of the morning. "Yes, but it doesn't make it easier.
I don't want to intrude on Shelley's privacy."

I didn't want Kevin intruding on mine, either. This
case would drag up unpleasant incidents I'd done my best
to forget.

"Just try it. If she doesn't cooperate, I'll . . ."

He shoved his hands under his armpits, staring at the
cold, dismal day mocking us outside his window.

"What?"

"Honestly, I don't know what I'll do. A simple missing
person's case has turned into a nightmare. David paid me to
find answers. I will find them, with or without your help."

His apparent obsession confused me since he wasn't
hurting for work. Add in the fact that Samantha Friel was
already dead and my confusion tripled. But my own obses-
sions are hard to comprehend, and Kevin at least tries to
understand. As a friend, it was my turn to return the favor.
"When do you want to do this?"

"Soon. The funeral is set for Tuesday, so maybe Thursday?" At my appalled look he added, "Don't worry, you
can skip the service. I'll set up the meeting with Shelley."

A yawn escaped. "You owe me big time for this." I
grabbed my knock-off Prada purse, and ran my hand
across the back of the smooth leather chair one last time as
I moved, sloth-like, out to the reception area. "You up for
a pizza and a movie tonight?"

Kevin weighed his response before answering. Never a good sign.

"Lilly arranged this bed-and-breakfast thing for tonight. Can we do it another time?"

I dug for my keys as an excuse not to look at him, blocking out the image of him and Callous Lilly rolling around naked, sipping champagne and rolling around naked some more. "Yeah, sure, no big deal. Call me."

I bounded down the stairs before he called over the railing. "Julie?"

"What?"

"Thanks. I mean it."

His teeth sparkled in the insurance salesman smile I've always hated. I should've said something friendly, but tact really wasn't my strong suit today. "Glad one of us is getting some tonight, but for God's sake don't forget to wear a condom."

The glass rattled as the outside door banged shut, courtesy of my well-placed kick.

I would've been better off staying in bed.

CHAPTER
SIX

KEVIN CALLED TUESDAY NIGHT to remind me of the meeting time with Shelley. By his clipped tone, either he was unhappy Ray had answered the phone, or was still ticked off from my parting shot on Saturday. Either way, I didn't feel I owed him an apology.

Thursday afternoon, I met Kevin in the parking lot at the rehab center. I dashed from my car to his, shook off the cold rain, hoping his mood wasn't as chilly as the day.

"Hey. You look nice."

I'd worn a short, black rayon skirt and a form-fitting black jacket, a purchase from The Gap a few years back. He'd seen me in the outfit a million times and always complimented me. As much as I told myself that had nothing to do with why I'd chosen it today, it did. I smiled. "It's okay?"

"Perfect." He casually pulled a loose hair from my

collar and let it float to the floor mat.

I've never been a demonstrative person, never expected or wanted it from anyone, friends or lovers. But with Kevin, I've come to rely on his effortless affection; he's my personal touchstone. I refuse to think of the day when simplicity isn't enough between us any more. I sandwiched his palm between mine. "Been busy?"

"Yeah. Mostly I've been mad."

"At me?"

"At you, at this case, at the damn weather."

"At Lilly?"

He dropped his hand. "Julie, don't start."

"Sorry." I blew out a breath, frosting the window. "I really am sorry."

"I know."

He leaned over and drew a smiley face in the patch of fog, gifting me with an unsure smile. As I'm a sucker for his sweet side, I punched his arm. "Anything unusual happen at the funeral?"

"Dick Friel showed up. David was convinced he wouldn't bother."

"Anyone else interesting?" Rain drizzled down the windshield in streaks of quicksilver.

"Like someone wearing a big, flashing sign saying, 'I killed Samantha Friel'?"

Kevin's sense of humor escapes me at times. "On TV the killer always goes to the funeral," I pointed out.

"On TV the ace detective wraps up the case in ar hour." He drew my hand back to his, idly stroking the bone on the inside of my wrist. "Real life ain't TV, babe."

The actuality hit me then. This wasn't make-believe, a fictional primetime show where I played the part of Nancy Drew, stumbling around for clues. I was about to question a grieving mother on the violent death of her child. Kevin steadied my hand when I fumbled with a cigarette, hold ing the lighter to the tip as I inhaled.

"I don't know if I can do this."

"I need you to do this. It's important."

"You're coming with me?" He nodded and rolled down the passenger window a crack. "What should I ask her?"

"Get her to talk to you about Samantha, find out wha she remembers from their visits in the last month."

I exhaled out the window. Kevin hated my smoking bu never complained, so I tried to be polite. "If she won't?"

"She will." His determined mouth softened. "Come on, Jules. Remember how you felt when Ben died? How everyone avoided discussing him? Grief needs an outlet She'll help us."

As much as hiding in the trunk appealed, I said "Let's go."

The main lobby had the impersonal, sterile atmosphere I associated with hospitals. We signed the logbook at the receptionist's area and she disappeared behind a glass par tition. We waited in silence, afraid to sit on the matchy

matchy gray and mauve sofas, furniture store art hung precisely above. Kevin paced and I perched on an end table.

Muzak drifted from hidden speakers. Normally I tune it out, but forcing myself to listen calmed my nerves. I challenged Kevin: "Name the song."

He cocked his head. "Easy. 'Super Freak', Rick James."

"Wrong." Kevin and I've had "Name That Tune" wars since high school. Our musical tastes are similar and we're evenly matched, but smugness encircled me like a secret cloak, knowing I had him cold. "Five?"

"You're on. What do you think it is?"

"I know it is 'Der Kommissar'." I hummed a few bars. "Listen and pay up, bub."

He listened again, cursing me when I sang along. "Bet you don't know who sang it."

"You really want to give me all your money today?"

"You're bluffing."

"I never bluff. Okay. Double or nothing?" He nodded. I snatched the five from his fingers and held my palm out for more. "After The Fire. Pay up and repeat, 'Julie is the master'."

"Julie is a master . . ." He paused and grinned, "Bator." He wadded up another five and tossed it at me just as a stout woman resembling a warden exited the locked double doors.

"Follow me." I traipsed behind her and stuck my tongue out at Kevin. He tapped me none too gently on the butt and hissed a vile suggestion in my ear. My nerves quieted. At least he and I were back on track even when it felt as if we were about to board a runaway train.

A spacious corridor twisted past rooms with the shades drawn. The beige walls were devoid of the inspirational posters I connected with self-help programs. When we stopped at an empty room, my heart sped up.

Kevin squeezed my shoulder, seating me on the right side of a conference table. He flipped open a small notebook and settled next to me.

I thought I was fine, I thought I was ready; I thought I might actually pull this off, until Shelley entered the room.

She looked old. Stringy hair, toothpick arms and legs, sallow complexion, slightly distended beer belly. The years of drinking hadn't been particularly kind to her, but the lines on her face weren't as unsettling as her eyes. They held defeat; a woman who's seen the best part of her life ripped away. I rose, giving an impromptu hug, but she stiffened and stepped back, like I'd given her static shock.

"Shelley, I'm sorry about Samantha."

"Thanks." She moved to the head of the table and tossed a pack of Marlboros down before dropping into the padded chair.

"We weren't sure you'd meet with us."

"Well, I almost didn't. Don't understand why you're here." Shelley slapped the unopened pack on her palm unwrapped the plastic, tore out the foil and extracted one cigarette.

Kevin had his lighter out before she'd put it between her lips.

"Thanks." She blew a stream of smoke and studied me. "Don't know how I can help you. The cops have already been here a couple of times."

"I'd like to ask a few questions; they might've missed something."

"Like what?"

"I don't know. That's why we're here."

"You a reporter now, Julie?"

"No."

Her glance slid to Kevin and back. "A private dick?"

I wondered how many times he'd heard *that* witty moniker. "Part-time. Most days I work in the Bear Butte County Sheriff's Office."

"So, you're a cop."

"No," I repeated the tiresome word. "I'm a secretary."

"You getting paid for this?"

I didn't answer.

She said, "Then, why do you care?"

"Because my brother died in Bear Butte Creek three years ago."

"So?"

"He was a homicide victim. Same as Samantha. I do know the frustration of what it's like not to have answers."

"Answers?" Her sharp, cynical laugh danced on the edge of maniacal. "What answers? She's dead. End of story." Hand shaking, she plucked at the pocket of the faded flannel shirt, hanging on her frame like a discarded flour sack. "There ain't an answer in the world that'll bring her back." She glanced up and scoffed, "Or your brother."

Apparently Shelley responded better to anger than tea and sympathy. Good. *That* I could handle. If I got past her mistrust, maybe I'd get through her defenses, and this ugly business would just go away. "Sucks, doesn't it? Won't get any better either. So, why don't you tell me about her?"

A resigned sigh gusted from her chapped lips. "Like what? Her favorite color? Her friends?"

"No, tell me about the Samantha you knew."

She reached for the ashtray, dumping in the discarded wrappers. The plastic melted, the foil caught fire. She watched it burn before looking at me again. Melancholy filled her eyes, her voice tinged with pride. "Sam was great. A good kid. Responsible, sweet, never caused me a minute's worry. We got along all right, had a few normal mother and daughter fights, but nothing major."

"What about your other children?"

"She got along with them most of the time, better with Meredith. She didn't have much chance to be a kid, though. I counted on her." Shelley spoke directly to the tip of her smoke, and little bits of ash swirled down like dirty snowflakes with her every expelled breath. "Most nights

I'd pass out and she'd have to cook, do laundry, and take care of Meredith and RJ."

"Did she resent that?"

"Sometimes. Didn't complain much, and if she did it wasn't to me."

"Would she complain to Dick?"

"Maybe, if he was home, which wasn't often."

"Didn't he help out when you were . . ." I fumbled for the right word. "Incapacitated?"

Shelley coughed up a nasty bit of phlegm disguised as a laugh. I took it as a sign to quit smoking before I started hacking up chunks of lung in public.

"Don't sugarcoat it," she said. "I'm a drunk. Been a drunk most of my life. Dick got tired of it early on in our marriage. Besides, his idea of helping out was bringing home a regular paycheck."

"He never took care of the kids?"

"Never. Not his job." She leaned over and ground out her half smoked cigarette. "You don't know him so let me fill you in. Dick Friel considers himself a 'man's man.' Little League games, music recitals, and family dinners are for pussies. Real men work hard and play hard. He spends nights and weekends at Fat Bob's. Figures he's entitled to spend his free time and money however, wherever, the hell he wants."

Another lost candidate for Father of the Year. "Doesn't it bug your kids that he's not around?"

"They don't know no different." Curiously, she glanced at Kevin then back to me. "You two have kids yet?" A mean smile kicked up the corner of her thin lips. "Or are you working on your careers first?"

I matched her attitude with a nonchalant shrug. "Kevin and I aren't married."

"We're not involved," Kevin added, a bit too quickly to suit me. "Julie and I are just colleagues."

Shelley's gaze moved back and forth between us before she shrugged. "My mistake."

She wasn't the first to make that mistake. Kevin and I almost made the same mistake a long time ago. A lifetime ago, but I wasn't falling for Shelley's stall tactics. I shook out a smoke from her pack. Naturally Kevin lit it before I opened the matchbook, but I didn't proffer a smile, or my usual thanks. Wouldn't want Shelley to read anything intimate into it. "When was the last time you saw Samantha?"

For the longest time she fixed her stare on a spot on the bulletin board behind my head. "Three weeks ago, maybe four, hell, I don't know. Time runs together here. I'm only allowed visitors twice a week. She showed up on an off day and caused a scene."

"What did she want?"

"To yell at me, I guess. Pissed off that Dick kicked her out and wanted to know what I was gonna do about it."

"What did you do?"

"Nothing." She gestured around the drab room. "I'm stuck in this awful place for the full three months. I told her to apologize to Dick and maybe he'd let her back home."

"Did she?"

"No, according to him. He claims he never saw her again."

Claims? I wondered if Shelley had suspicions about her husband. "Did you see her after that?"

She gazed out the window. "No."

I didn't know Shelley well, but I was adept enough at reading body language to recognize she was hiding something. I shifted back and my nylons stuck to the fabric chair. Kevin's hand squeezed my thigh. I dropped my hand over his as I struggled with my next words. "We know that Dick wasn't Samantha's father."

"I figured as much." She faced us again. "If you're not cops then you're not doing this for free. Who hired you?"

Kevin fielded that question: "My client prefers to stay anonymous."

"Doesn't matter. I know it's David. His father is a blood-sucking leech, but he's a nice kid."

I peeked at Kevin from the corner of my eye. His face remained blank. But I knew from his increasing grip on my thigh that he wasn't unaffected by this conversation.

We waited for Shelley to comment further.

She expelled a world-weary sigh; fingers yellowed from nicotine rubbed her temple. "Hindsight's twenty-twenty, isn't it? None of this should've happened. If I could do it over again . . ."

Faced with her vagueness, I tried a softer approach. "What would you do differently?"

"I wouldn't have listened to that goddamn counselor, for one thing." Shelley's anger ricocheted off the walls. "I wouldn't have told her. Sam should've never found out. Especially that way."

She pinned me with a haunted look I'd never forget.

"Now, she's dead."

The enormity of the simple sentence echoed, bringing nothing but continued stillness on our part.

Finally, I managed, "Why did the counselor insist you tell your family?"

"Seemed logical. Maybe this go-around I could quit drinking if I owned up to the past. Part of me felt relieved, part of me wanted to forget that night, as I'd done for years." She licked the dry skin hanging from her bottom lip. "Guess I should've listened to the 'forget about it' part instead, huh?"

"What happened?"

"What do you *think* happened?"

"I don't know," I said trying to keep my temper at bay. One furious person was enough in this situation. By default, Shelley had the bigger right to anger. "That's why I asked, that's why we're here."

"Well, it sure as fuck wasn't some big, goddamn crying

scene with everyone hugging and talking about forgiveness. Dick exploded, called me names, called Sam names and then told her he should've known she wasn't his kid. Informed me the next time I heard from him would be through his attorney."

"And Sam?"

"Sam?" Her abrasive tone dropped to a small, quiet pitch of despair. "It was like I watched a part of her die right in front of me."

Shelley's anguish filled the room. The urge to run from the horror nearly overpowered me, yet I felt emotionally crippled and physically stuck to my chair as Kevin gripped my knee. I trembled; sickness seemed to seep into my every pore.

"Shelley, I'm so sorry."

She dismissed my apology with a wave of her hand.

"I know this is hard."

"Do you?" She bent closer, the line of grief in her eyes as threadlike as her patience. "Do you really?"

"Look, I'm not trying . . ."

"You don't have kids, do you?"

I blinked and said nothing, understanding she wouldn't have heard me anyway.

"Then how would you know how I feel?" She stabbed her finger my direction, adding as an afterthought, "I ain't talking about your brother's death, either."

I knew what was coming and braced myself, but was

pretty sure in those few seconds I forgot how to breathe.

"Have you ever been raped?" she asked.

My eyes didn't waver. Neither did my voice. "Yes, I have."

CHAPTER
SEVEN

SHELLEY SCOOTED BACK INTO HER CHAIR and scrambled for her cigarettes. Kevin wasn't so quick with the lighter this time. She and I exchanged a long look.

"Then you do know."

She inhaled, her mouth a misshapen smile, her eyes tiny slits. "So?"

"So, you want to tell me about it?"

"Why? You want to compare notes?"

"No." Her hostility aside, I wasn't about to get sucked into a pity contest because I'd lose. "Why didn't you have an abortion?"

"Because I'm Catholic."

"Well, I'm not. Doesn't the Pope agree rape is an acceptable reason to terminate a pregnancy?"

"Did you get pregnant after your rape?"

"No."

"But if you would have gotten knocked up?"

Nausea rose sharply against the back of my tongue, cutting the words out. "No question. I would've had an abortion."

"You think it would've been better if I hadn't had Sam at all?"

My legs trembled and I pressed them together, knocking off Kevin's hand. "You tell me."

She paused, smoking for several agonizing seconds, which bled into minutes.

"I liked you in high school," she said. "You were different from those snotty girls that showed up at Falling Rock, trying to be tough. You were the real deal. Haven't changed much. Still got that rigid bitch act down, don't you?"

She almost smiled. I almost didn't dare to breathe.

"If you'd have come in here weepy, full of fake sympathy and bullshit, I'd've gladly sent you away with a black eye." The stoic line in her spine cracked at the same time as her voice. "Jesus, most days I feel like punching somebody. This whole thing is a fucking nightmare. I'm sick to death of reliving this shit."

I was no stranger to that sentiment.

She drummed her fingers on the table, maybe stalling, or maybe gathering pieces of her nightmare.

"Fine. Here's the truth. Dick worked in Wyoming on and off the summer after we graduated. He left the end of June and returned the middle of August. I missed him."

The muscles in her jaw constricted. "Hard to believe that once, we actually liked each other. Anyway, we were practically living together, screwing like rabbits, and being Catholic, not using any birth control."

At her hesitation I urged, "Go on."

"That night is still kind of hazy. The Central States Fair had started and I'd gotten drunk in the German tent with some friends. You know the duck dance and all those drinking games they play?"

I nodded.

"My summer had been pretty boring with Dick gone. My car broke down and I'd spent most of my nights either at home with my folks or working, so I decided I deserved to cut loose."

"How did you get to the fairgrounds?"

"Remember Nancy Rogers? Married Troy James? We worked together that summer. She picked me up."

"Wasn't she going to take you home too?"

"Not after I got stinking drunk." Shelley made a face.

"God, she's still such a priss. Anyway, she whined that I was ruining her night."

"Were you?"

"Probably. Anyway, I drank too much, threw up, and stayed behind when everyone headed to the midway because I didn't think my stomach could handle the rides."

I stared at her. "Nancy just left you?"

She rolled her eyes. "Think back. Every girl ditched their

friends when a guy was involved."

"Who were the guys?"

"Troy James and that gang of jocks he ran around with."

I pictured the six or so guys that'd gotten laid on the periphery of Troy's athletic greatness: Danny Christopherson, Tim O'Reilly, Bobby Adair, Mike Lawrence, and occasionally, our friend Jimmer. The list also included Charles LaChance. "What happened after they left you?"

"I stumbled behind the Porta-potties, puked my guts out, and passed out for a while." She tapped her fingers on the table, a brittle sound of frustration. "Then someone pulled my arms behind my back, tied them together, and threw a coat over my head. I had no idea what the fuck was going on."

My palms started to sweat, my head to pound. "Did you scream?"

"I don't think so, don't remember if I did. I was wasted. Heard maybe, six or seven voices and then they tossed me in the back of a pickup."

Shelley closed her eyes. "Everything was muffled. My body kept bumping up and down, hitting metal. I felt like I was gonna throw up again, but when I tried to sit up, some rough, sticky hand pushed me back down. Somehow my shirt got ripped, my tits were pinched until the damn nipples were bruised and bloody.

"If I made a sound, I got smacked. Then everything went black. Next thing I knew, I laid sprawled in the grass, naked, hands tied, coat over my head, some guy humping me. As soon as he finished, another one started. Guess I passed out a couple of times, and when I came to, they were still pounding into me like I was some life-size blow-up doll."

I let her catch her breath while I caught mine.

"Hours," she murmured. "It went on for hours. I drifted in and out, which was probably a good thing. After I'd been left alone for a while I moved around. The sun was up, my head pounded from the booze, and my body felt like . . . God, I had bruises everywhere. I had come spots in my hair, on my boobs, around my mouth, on my ass. They left my clothes. Can you believe they left my fucking clothes? I put them back on and walked home."

My jaw dropped. "You *walked* home in that condition?"

"I guess." Her gaze lingered on the paper clean-up procedures taped to the back of the door. "Don't really remember."

"Where had they taken you?"

"That open field on the hill behind Tech."

"How far were you from home?"

"Three miles or so."

"Three miles?" I repeated inanely. "And no one saw you?"

"If they did, they didn't stop." Her hands spread flat on the table. "Everything else is pretty much a blank. Took a shower, probably popped some pills and slept for two days."

"Didn't your family get suspicious you were holed up in your room?"

"Not really." She shrugged. "My dad was a mean bastard so I usually avoided him anyway. Told my mom I had cramps or something."

Kevin let out a slow, quiet breath. Shelley didn't notice, but I did. "Shelley, why didn't you go to the police?"

"Did you?" she countered.

I shook my head.

"Then you understand. By the time Dick got back, I knew I was pregnant, knew the baby wasn't his, and if I told him the truth, he wouldn't believe it. He'd accuse me of screwing around. I had no desire to do the right thing and live up to my dad's prediction that I'd become just another unwed mother."

"You never considered abortion?"

"For about ten seconds." She clasped her hands — probably unconsciously — in a prayer-like pose. "I may be a lapsed Catholic, but I'm still Catholic enough to feel guilt. And at that young age, my ideals hadn't yet soured. I believed that maybe it'd happened for a reason. Maybe God had a higher purpose for the child."

"And now?"

"I'm not sorry I had Sam. After Dick and I got married, I convinced myself it never had happened, that she really *was* Dick's kid. I stayed sober, for the most part, when I was pregnant." She shuddered. "Worst times of my life."

"You never thought about counseling before coming out here?"

"Once, about three years ago, I went into Catholic Social Services. I hung around for a while and then I saw . . ." She faltered; her limp hair obscured her face. "I saw that it was too late to help me, so I walked out."

Kevin lit a cigarette. I've only seen him smoke twice. Once, when I was seventeen and my father beat the shit out of me; the other, after our friend Todd's funeral. Messy, disturbing business, this case, and it reminded me I'd gotten off track. Nothing Shelley related so far seemed significant to the case. But that was the kicker; I knew she hadn't told us everything. "Did the counseling out here help Samantha?"

"Just made her act worse. That damn counselor badgered her and then Sam stopped talking to everyone."

"Including you?"

"Especially me. I told her to go home. If she needed to talk it out she should try CSS. Maybe they could offer her the peace they couldn't give me."

Kevin said, "Shelley, this is very important. Did Sam try counseling there?"

"Somewhere. I don't know when, or how often she went, or who she talked to, but she did go."

"How do you know?" I asked.

"She told me she knew exactly who could help her." Another cryptic teenage remark or an actual clue? "That's all she said?"

"Yep." She tilted her head, gaze zooming briefly to the dry erase board by the filing cabinet. "Rather snottily, too. Told me she'd take care of it herself, since she was used to taking care of things without my help."

"Did this person help her?"

"Not that I ever noticed."

Kevin took over the questions. "How did she act the last time you saw her?"

"Not like my Sam. Went from being pissed off to suicidal."

Fine, greasy blond hair swept Shelley's narrow shoulders. "That pissed me off. Goes against everything I believe in, what I'd taught her. Suicide is the only unforgivable sin, not only according to Catholic tenets, but in my eyes as well. It's the most selfish act known to God."

I disagreed. Murder, unlike suicide, was never a choice. I closed my eyes and hoped Kevin had sufficient information for today. I'd heard enough.

"Did Sam tell you where she'd been staying?" Kevin asked.

"No."

"Didn't it bother you that you didn't know?"

The chair creaked as Shelley shifted her weight. "I'm isolated out here. I go for days without visitors or phone calls, and Dick and I weren't exactly talking."

"Can you think of a reason why someone would kill

your daughter?"

My eyes flew open in time to see Shelley flinch.

"No, the police asked the same question. I've had nothing but time to think about it." She concentrated on manicuring a ragged hangnail to perfection with her teeth. "The answer hasn't changed."

Kevin glanced at his watch and pulled a business card from the inside pocket of his sport coat. "We've got to go, but if we need to, can we come back?"

Shelley nodded without enthusiasm.

"If you think of anything else, call. Day or night."

I added my phone number on the back and slid it next to her cigarettes. "Same goes. You need anything, call."

We moved toward the door and Shelley stayed motionless.

"Julie?"

The quaver in her voice chilled me. "Yes?"

"No matter how she'd been conceived . . . she was still mine, and I loved her." She wiped a fallen tear and repeated, "I always loved her, even when I had a piss-poor way of showing it. No matter who killed her, I want them to pay."

I didn't respond. I turned away and reached for the warmth of Kevin's hand, knowing I couldn't console her, but at least I could comfort myself.

CHAPTER EiGHT

KEVIN SIGNED US OUT and I made a beeline for fresh air.

Standing in the slate courtyard, the hills behind the rehab building appeared darker, more ominous than when we'd entered. The rain had stopped, but puddles clogged the sidewalk; clouds the color of wet cement hung low, obscuring the view.

It'd seemed months since I'd felt the warmth of sunlight on my skin. I fantasized about current temperatures in Jamaica or Cancun or Ixtapa, any place that required a full bottle of sun block. Anything bright to keep my mind off the shadowy corner of hell I'd just witnessed.

Rain is depressing. I'd never survive in Washington or Oregon. I'd pull a Kurt Cobain inside a year. Most people say the same thing about living in rural South Dakota, but at least the weather doesn't require umbrellas twelve months out of twelve.

Cold, damp and miserable, inside and out, I fought off a shiver.

I made it to my car before the shakes started. My keys dropped to the ground, I retrieved them only to hear the jangling clank when they hit the pavement again. Kevin picked them up without a word, led me to his car and bundled me inside.

When he fired the motor, I closed my eyes, and like a coward, feigned sleep. Kevin was patient, but not stupid. I couldn't avoid his questions forever.

The fact I'd been raped had shocked him. But not as much as the fact I hadn't told him.

Truthfully, the time I was raped hardly crossed my mind any more. I'd buried it where it belonged, in the past. It hadn't changed my attitude toward sex or men; it affected the way I view situations. I don't hang out in unfamiliar bars, restaurants, or churches. I don't take for granted anyone's sage advice that so-and-so is a "good guy." I don't go on blind dates and I absolutely do not date men with beards. Or facial hair of any kind. Never. No exceptions.

"Julie?"

My eyes opened but I directed my gaze out the window. "Not now, Kev, okay?"

He mumbled as he hit the gas and pulled onto I-90.

The wheels clicked over the grooves on the interstate and the clacking rhythm pacified me as I watched the scenery change. Open fields and rolling hills stretched into steeper, rocky embankments with patches of dirt the color of powdered Tang. Houses were springing up all over; a couple of ranches, a variety of businesses had popped up along this stretch of highway between Rapid City and Sturgis in the last five years. Mostly manufactured home displays, RV and car lots, heavy equipment sales with an occasional restaurant and convenience store. Billboards were scattered every few hundred feet.

In such wide-open spaces with cheap advertising, every tourist business within three-hundred miles tries to lure vacationing families off the beaten path to Yellowstone and into their communities. Devil's Tower, Medora, North Dakota, and The Little Big Horn Battlefield competed for vacationers' dollars against the local draw of Mount Rushmore, Wind Cave, Custer State Park, Deadwood, and Crazy Horse Memorial. Before too long, the interstate would be jammed with out-of-state cars, motor homes, and tour buses. That doesn't include the hundreds of thousands of motorcycles that descend on us during the Sturgis Motorcycle Rally and Races in August. South Dakota depends on tourism to survive, but few of us look forward to the increased traffic and gasoline prices.

The tip of Bear Butte poked above the ridge to the right of my exit. Kevin slowed; the car bumped over the railroad tracks and headed up the hill. Once we were inside my house, he enveloped me in a bone-crushing hug that left me breathless.

He didn't say anything. If I thought about it too hard I might consider his instinctive behavior odd. So, I skipped the heavy contemplation and clutched him like the lifeline he is. For a minute I secretly wished to be the type of woman to give in to a dramatic crying spell. Of course, I sucked it up, tough girl that I am.

When I finally squirmed, he stepped back. "Let me ask you something. What is your gut reaction to Shelley's story?"

Thankful that he'd switched gears, I found it puzzling he'd refer to the difficult parts of Shelley's life as a story. The whole ordeal seemed surreal. Still, her almost militant re-telling had bothered me. "She was lying about something."

"What makes you say that?"

"She got into minor details, explicitly, but the major details escaped her." I patted my pockets for a tissue. "I think we should talk to Meredith before we approach Dick Friel at Fat Bob's. Or should we start with Nancy Rogers?"

"Nancy is a dead-end, especially if she didn't stay friends with Shelley. I'll call Meredith and see if she can meet with us Friday night." Eyes soft, he asked, "Are you up for this?"

"What?"

"This case." He watched me wipe my nose on the back of my hand and scowled before tossing me a box of Kleenex. "And talking about your rape."

The tensed line of his back disappeared into my

kitchen. Guess the time for comfort was over.

Kevin returned a minute later with my half-empty bottle of Don Julio tequila and two shot glasses. We were taking comfort after all, just in a different form. "Would you believe me if I said there wasn't much to talk about?"

"No."

"Really . . ."

He slammed the bottle on the coffee table and knocked back a small shot. "Do you believe if you'd bothered to tell me this earlier that I would've asked you to help on this case?"

"Yes." Our gazes locked. Surprised by his distress, I pressed on. "I'm the perfect choice. Not only was my brother murdered but I've dealt with being raped . . ."

"I didn't know that. And stop being so goddamn blasé."

"I'm not." I reached for a shot glass and poured double the amount he'd given himself. Still clutching his empty glass, he moved to the window and back.

"No? This is some serious shit, Jules, and now there are issues I have to consider before I let you continue with this fucked up case."

"*Let* me continue?" So, Kevin was upset. A barrage of swear words from Mr. Clean Mouth was my first clue and the path he was beating in my shag carpet was the second. He paces and I hate it, so normally he refrains from doing it in my presence.

But, why had he decided my help was now negligible?

Had I done the unthinkable and morphed from Julie the invincible to Julie the victim? I'd kept the incident from him not because of embarrassment, but because I couldn't stand to be pitied.

On Kevin's next pass of the table he poured another shot. His face remained unreadable when he closed his eyes and slumped into the couch. "When?" he demanded. Even though he wasn't scrutinizing me, I fidgeted. I patted my pocket for my cigarettes and remembered I'd left them in my purse. I took my time digging them out and lighting up, but the nicotine didn't offer me its usual calm.

"Fine. I'll tell you, but I'm not being blasé when I say it doesn't matter." As I inhaled, my thoughts drifted back. "It happened the August you were in basic training. Susan Dagle and I stopped at the Corner Pocket for a beer after work."

His eyes opened and he frowned. "The Corner Pocket? You always hated that place."

"Yeah, well, it wasn't my first choice. Anyway, this table of guys kept begging to buy us pitchers. Susan decided if they wanted to pay we should let them, so they joined us. One guy looked like Dusty from ZZ Top. He kept talking to me. I must've made a stunning impression," I said dryly, "because when I left, he followed me."

The smoke drifting from my cigarette brought to mind how the heat rose from the blacktop in the dark parking lot that summer night. The stench of bar food rotting in the Dumpster. And the burst of fear when a sticky palm landed on my bare shoulder and spun me around. A rough shove against the car door, the bitter taste of secondhand beer gagging me as the man thrust his thick tongue into my mouth. His over-eager hands squeezing my breasts to the point of pain. But mostly, I remembered how I hated the rasp of his beard against my face and skin.

"Julie?"

I shook my head, scattering those thoughts.

"At that point it was apparent he wasn't after my conversational skills. I didn't panic even when he kept touching me, acting like it was a mutual attraction." I crushed out the cigarette and withdrew another.

Kevin flicked the lighter and I sank back into the plush cushions.

"He was drunk and bigger and determined. I didn't put up much of a fight."

Kevin's insightful comments were slow in coming.

"Anyway, it was over pretty quick. I kept telling myself . . ." I remembered my back pressed into the stinky carpet in his van and I swallowed the thick blob of emotion threatening to suffocate me. "I kept telling myself if he believed I was there willingly, he might not hurt me."

"Did he?"

"Hurt me? Physically? Not really. Like I said, it was fast." I squeezed my eyes shut, recalling how even after he'd rolled off me his pungent smell had clung to my hair, clothes, and skin. I'd tossed that outfit in the burning barrel at home right after taking an hour-long shower. The mental barrier I erected that night usually worked.

Except sometimes I wake at night and swear the overpowering weight on my body and the sticky whispers in my ear are real. His voice haunts me. I had survived. However, I never stepped foot in that bar again. Susan was shocked when I abruptly ended our friendship too.

The digital clock beeped, and Kevin glanced at it, then at me. His eyes were dark and thoughtful.

Finally I couldn't stand it any longer. "Say something."

"Like what?" He stared at me, *through* me until I knew he recognized the torment I wouldn't cop to. "That I feel sorry for you?"

My eyes narrowed.

"See?" He pointed with his shot glass before setting it down. "You're glaring at me. You don't want my sympathy." He grabbed my hand, brought my palm to his lips, and pressed a single kiss.

I resisted closing my eyes and wishing for something from him that I couldn't have.

Kevin rubbed my hand over his jaw. "I am sorry that I brought you into this and if you'd rather back out, I'll understand."

"No." Part of me hoped there'd be therapeutic benefits in simultaneously dealing with two traumatic events in my life. Part of me wanted to chug the remainder of tequila until I passed out. I was saved from making the choice by a fierce pounding on the door.

I pulled my palm from Kevin's grasp and reluctantly answered the summons.

Ray didn't bother to mask his fury when he jerked the screen door open.

"Hi," I said brightly. "I didn't know you were coming over."

"Didn't know I needed to make an appointment to see my own girlfriend."

The way Ray insisted on referring to me as his girlfriend made me think I'd outgrown the role.

He angled his head toward the SUV parked in my usual spot. "That Wells' car?"

"Yeah, it's my car," Kevin said over my shoulder. "Why? Did you run into it?"

Ray ignored him and said to me, "What the hell is he doing here again?"

"Didn't know I had to make an appointment to see your 'girlfriend'," Kevin mimicked.

"Very fucking funny."

Might as well be raining testosterone. And me without my sharp-tipped umbrella to jab both of them in the ass. What else could I have piled on today?

"Actually, it is pretty funny because Kevin was just leaving."

Kevin frowned. "I thought we were going to get your car?"

"Where is it?" Ray asked.

"Now that Ray is here, he can drive me to get it." I added as a sweet afterthought, "Besides, don't you have plans with Lilly?"

Kevin's eyebrow lifted. I never gave a rip about his plans with Lilly. Hell, most of the time I tried to *ruin* their plans. He smiled, bent down, and kissed me squarely on the mouth.

"Nope. You wore me out today, hot stuff. I'll call you tomorrow." Sidestepping Ray, he climbed in his car and drove off.

I wiped Kevin's sloppy kiss from my lips and smiled under the cover of my hand. No doubt he'd won that round, but unfortunately he didn't get the spoils of war. Me.

"What the hell was that about?" Ray demanded.

"Nothing."

He punched the support beam on the porch. "Didn't sound like nothing."

Ray's periodic bouts of anger don't bother me; I suspect it's all for show. I can handle it, even when that side of him reminds me of my father. Was it some subconscious thing that I was attracted to men who resembled my dad? I shivered. I'd had enough mental traumas today to even consider the idea. I wanted to erase the day's events by retrieving my Sentra, eating a decent meal, and indulging in a sweat-soaked round of sex or two.

Not necessarily in that order.

"Let's just forget about it, okay?"

Ray shook his head, and shoved me aside with a practiced pout. "I don't like the way he looks at you."

"Who?"

"That asshole Wells."

"How does he look at me?" I breathed against his rigid jaw, inhaling sweat, anger, and dust. "Like this?" I slid my hands up his denim shirt, kissing him until his heartbeat increased under my palm. Then I whispered a suggestion in his ear that would not only wipe the look off his face, but would most likely cross his eyes.

No big stunner that Ray followed me inside without any additional stupid questions.

At that point sex as a cure for emotional ails seemed less dangerous and addictive than tequila.

CHAPTER NINE

MISSY CAME IN AHEAD OF SHIFT CHANGE on Friday so I could leave early. Although we'd forged a truce of sorts in the last week, I doubted she'd ask me to co-host her next Mary Kay party. The sheriff stayed tight-lipped and terse in my presence too, even after I scrubbed his office. Al, well . . . Al was just sweet, harmless Al, a bumbling, red-faced buffoon. Sometimes I wondered what it'd take to get him riled.

I'd kept Ray in the dark about my Friday night plans with Kevin. He'd get pissed off and pouty, whine that another Friday slipped past and I didn't hang around to watch him play pool or offer to chalk his stick.

The things I put up with for a decent orgasm.

On the drive to Kevin's office, I popped REO Speedwagon's *High Infidelity* into the CD player. Music chronicles most events in my life. These tunes reconnected me with the vortex of grief after my mother's death. AC/DC thrashing guitars bring to mind wild kegs in the Hills and my lost virginity. The B-52's, The Cure, and Oingo Boingo were reminders of the offbeat path I'd chosen in college. Ditto with the hair bands, Dokken, Winger, and Tesla in my dusty LP collection. When Ben died, nothing besides REM offered me comfort.

Meredith Friel was close to the same age I'd been when my mother died. Did she use music to drown out reality? Or did she ignore it? Would she even open up to us? Or would she presume in her youth that we, as adults, couldn't possibly understand her angst?

God, I hated just how much I did understand.

I parked in the back lot and huffed up the stairs. Damn. I'd been smoking way too much lately. Usually, I kept in shape by long hikes in the Hills and target practice shooting with my bow, but the only activity I'd participated in recently — which counted as an aerobic workout — was of the sexual variety. A regimented exercise program is not my style. Donning Lycra tights and prancing around in public? Forget it. The only time I run is if someone is chasing me. Still, panting like an overweight basset hound at age thirty-four is completely uncool. I waited in the hallway until my breathing evened out. Wouldn't want Kevin to see me wheezing.

The reception door was ajar and I stepped inside. Kevin's suite of offices is enormous — not the tiny

windowless, airless, colorless cubicles which are the bane
of new construction. Kevin had let me decide the decorating scheme, and frankly, I'd outdone myself.

No neutral colors; walls painted the hue of toasted
pecans to showcase Native American artwork, deep-cushioned Berber carpet in a cinammony red; chocolate-colored
leather furniture; beaded, metal and stone sculptures scattered on wrought iron pedestals. The space oozed warmth
and civility. I felt more at home here than I did at either the
sheriff's office or my father and stepmother's place.

As usual, the phone receiver had become one with
Kevin's ear. I tiptoed to his ubiquitous stash of Diet Pepsi.
When his murmurs gave way to a low, rumbling chuckle,
I froze. Only two things in my experience evoked that
response from men: money or sex. I sipped my pilfered
soda, snuggled into my favorite new chair, and waited.
After he'd hung up, I asked sweetly, "Good news from
your stockbroker?"

"No." Kevin scribbled on his Palm Pilot. "That was
Lilly."

Shit. It figured. "Everything is set up with Meredith?"

"Yes. Anytime after seven."

I lifted a brow. "A fifteen-year-old on a schedule?"

He shrugged. "Evidently Dick is gone to the bar by
then."

"She's okay talking with us?"

"Seems that way. Although she was pretty aloof. Why?"

"Just curious. Does she know we're going to Fat Bob's tonight?"

"I don't know that we are."

"Come on." I slurped around the rim of the can, just to see Kevin frown at my poor manners. My purpose for riling him was the old bait and switch; in his distraction, maybe he wouldn't see how profoundly his relationship with Lilly bothered me. Things were getting serious between them and I had no idea where it left me. I'd rather provoke his anger than his pity. "We planned this. We have to talk to Dick sometime."

"I know. But unless there's a stabbing or shooting, even the cops steer clear of Fat Bob's. Maybe it'd be best . . ."

Kevin's concerned glance changed the fine hairs on my nape into hackles and they rose accordingly. "Does this have anything to do with our discussion from yesterday?"

"Nope." *Chink chink* echoed as he tapped his pen against the Black Hills Bagels coffee mug next to his ten-key. "I don't know if Friday night in a biker bar is the best time or place to question Dick Friel."

His point was valid, but born out of a sense of protection? Guess I needed to remind him I wasn't on the endangered species list. "We have to. Dick Friel is my number one suspect."

"Seriously? Then waltzing into Fat Bob's is definitely a bad idea."

"But on the other hand, he might be more inclined to

talk freely on his own turf."

"Turf," he repeated, and rolled his eyes. "Been watching *West Side Story* again?"

I stuck my tongue out at him.

"Jules, have you ever been in that bar?"

"No. Have you?"

"Once, for about five minutes."

"So, what's it like?"

He sighed, his chair wheels squeaked on a backward roll. "Half as big as Dusty's, twice as smoky, and the clientele consists mostly of bikers, ex-cons, soon-to-be cons, and the skankiest women outside of *Easy Rider* magazine."

"Sounds like fun. Should I bring my bow?"

"Hold that thought, Xena. If we decide to go, I think we should bring Jimmer and leave your dominatrix outfit at home."

"Isn't Jimmer off playing terrorist in some jungle?"

"He's back. We had lunch on Wednesday."

I tried to wrap my brain around the idea of Kevin, and our 6'6", three-hundred and seventy-five pound friend, doing lunch. I assumed Jimmer ate his meat raw. After he killed it. With his bare hands. I suppose everyone's entitled to the occasional civilized meal.

"How long will this thing with Meredith last?"

"Hard to say."

"Ballpark, Kev. You know Jimmer doesn't like to be kept waiting."

He shuddered. "Don't remind me."

"So, you want me to call him?"

Kevin stretched out of his chair. "Sure. We'll hit Fat Bob's tonight, but *only* if Jimmer can make it."

"Cool." I tried rolling my T-shirt sleeve over my pack of cigarettes. Didn't quite achieve the James Dean look, nor was I showcasing a tattoo. Damn. And I'd wanted so badly to fit in. "Can I be your biker bitch?"

"You've got the bitch part down, but we're short on the bike part, babe."

He unknotted the funky tie I'd given him for Christmas — red, covered with purple flying pigs — and lifted it over his head, mussing his hair. "Tell him to meet us there at nine. I'll change and we can grab a bite before we head out."

The door to his spare office shut firmly behind him.

I punched in Jimmer's number, and waited for him to pick up. The loud mechanical whine of his ancient answering machine scorched my ear. Double damn. Kevin had said we could only go to Fat Bob's if we had backup and without speaking to Jimmer in person . . . I couldn't count on Jimmer retrieving his messages. But Kevin would cancel our outing, and frankly, I was looking forward to grilling Dick Friel. After the beep, I explained the situation, told Jimmer where we'd be, and hung up.

Then I made the call to my own answering machine. Five calls from Ray. In thirty minutes. Each one increasingly agitated. I didn't even want to think about that situation.

Kevin was still dressing when he re-entered the room. He strolls around me partially clothed, apparently believing I'm unaffected by the sight of his toned body. Not true. *So* not true as I glimpsed his rock hard pecs and lean stomach. I kept my salivary glands in check as I watched him tuck his T-shirt into the half-buttoned waistband of his 501 jeans and strap on the black nylon shoulder holster. "Did you get a hold of Jimmer?"

"Yeah." It wasn't really a lie, since he hadn't asked if I'd actually *spoken* to him. Kevin finished buttoning before he unlocked the bottom drawer of the filing cabinet and pulled out his weapon, an H&K P7. After he checked the clip, he locked it in place, testing the weight in his palm before he jammed the gun in the holster. "What?"

I almost asked if he wanted me to leave so he could fondle it in private. Then again, it might be fun to watch. "Nothing." I said.

"You're staring."

"How big is that thing?"

His depraved grin sent my blood racing. "Why, darling, I never thought you noticed."

Holy hell. I blushed. Good thing Jimmer hadn't been around to hear that one; I'd never hear the end of it.

"The caliber on this one's 40mm." Kevin patted the holster with the affection men saved for inanimate objects. "Big enough to knock anyone on their butt."

I drained the soda, sucked the last hit off my cigarette. "Now you are starting to sound like Jimmer."

Two sharp raps echoed over the open door; we spun unison toward the persistent sound. A short man, monkish coiffure, filled the threshold between the reception area and Kevin's office.

Eww. Charles LaChance. In the flesh. My own flesh beaded and crawled all the way up to my scalp. I glanced at Kevin, but he seemed unruffled.

"Charles," Kevin said. "I wasn't expecting you. Come in. Caught me at a bad time, however. Julie and I were just on our way out."

But Kevin's words were lost on Charles, busy as he was leering at my body from lips to boobs to hips. I stared back. Besides his rapidly receding hairline, he hadn't changed much from the last time we'd crossed paths: A civil case in which he'd won his client — a former Bear Butte County employee — an undeserved, lifetime supply of cash. Unfortunately his share of money hadn't changed him; I knew the skin under his expensive suit was one-hundred percent snake. I slid my hands under my thighs, a move that wasn't lost on him. No way was I shaking hands with a reptile.

LaChance's grin split from hairy ear to hairy ear. "The beautiful Julie Collins. You haven't changed a bit."

Even I occasionally succumbed to false flattery, but not in this case. "Cut the bullshit, Chuck. What do you want?"

Kevin laughed out loud.

Charles set his briefcase on the antique library table on the wall opposite Kevin's desk.

"Charming as ever, I see." His pupil-less eyes focused on Kevin. "Do you always let your friends speak to your customers that way? No wonder your business is," his pitying gaze swept the office, "sadly lacking."

Kevin smiled benignly, far above our petty behavior. "I assume there is a reason you're here?"

The locks on his briefcase clicked open. "Yes. I'd like to hire you."

I snorted and crushed out my cigarette.

"For what?" Kevin asked.

Charles angled his head at me. "I'd rather discuss it in private."

I stood. "I'll be waiting downstairs. I'd say it was nice seeing you again, *Chuck*," I emphasized the nickname, knowing it annoyed him, "but hell is full of liars and cheats and I've no interest in spending eternity with you. However, it was nice meeting your son. Glad to see bad genes can be overcome."

LaChance's soft, feminine hand on my arm as I brushed past sent waves of disgust rolling across my skin. "How do you know David? You in on this business of bilking him out of his inheritance?"

"You'd know all about that since you perfected that trick, righto, Chuckie-poo?"

"Julie," Kevin warned.

"What? You and I both know he isn't here to hire you. And you'd never work for him anyway." Against my better judgment, I leaned in, witnessing up close the black void of his beady eyes. "Am I right? You're here to buy the rest of David's contract?"

He laughed with gusto. "Still smart as a whip too." His bout of hilarity was short-lived as he withdrew a checkbook ledger. "Drop this ridiculous wild goose-chase."

"Why?"

"Because Samantha's been found. There is no reason for Kevin to continue investigating."

Probably not smart to say the first thing that popped into my head, but — big surprise — I did it anyway. "Why? Afraid of what we might find out?"

He flashed his creepy smile again. "What are you insinuating?"

I shrugged. "Wonder why you're so hot to have the case dropped. Rumor has it you didn't like your son dating Samantha."

"Dating is an antiquated phrase isn't it? He was fucking her. For some reason, the boy has confused sex with love."

I clenched my left fist to my side, then my right. Assaulting a lawyer. Appealing, but a complication I didn't need. In my mind I slugged him. Hard. One little punch and he was laid out cold on the Berber carpet.

"Look," he said in his best no-nonsense attorney

tone. "The apple doesn't fall far from the tree. Samantha would've turned out just like her mother. Drunk, loose, trapping David into marriage with a lie . . ."

"But instead Samantha was murdered." A mere coincidence? Or convenience?

"Which is exactly why *how* she spent the last two weeks is irrelevant. I've heard the Feds are involved . . ." He studied his manicured fingernails before smirking at Kevin. "I don't see the need to waste any more of my son's money or your time. She's dead. David needs to get over it."

"David is my client," Kevin told him. "When *he* decides to 'get over it', then I'll stop pursuing the case."

After tossing the unused checkbook back in the briefcase, Charles faced me. "How does Shelley feel about this? The two of you dredging up her painful past?"

"Why do you care? She's a drunken whore, right?"

Charles held up his hand. "I never said that specifically. I know her life hasn't been easy. Or fair. And she deserves compensation for her suffering, but it's not right to expect . . ."

The ugly truth dawned. "You sick bastard. You've talked to Shelley, haven't you? You're tempting her with some kind of lawsuit. This 'drop the case' bullshit isn't about your son's welfare. It's about yours. What are you afraid we'll uncover?"

"Maybe you aren't so smart after all," Charles sneered. "You have no idea who you're dealing with."

"You?" I laughed, scraping a disgusted glance down his torso. "Save your breath. You don't scare me."

His balding pate became a blotchy red mass, but his tone remained composed. "I should. You're wrong when you assume I've got no clout in this community. I'm not the same punk you remember from years ago. Don't push me, Ms. Collins. I guarantee you won't enjoy the results."

I curled my fingers into my palms. "You threatening me?"

"Not threatening, just offering a friendly *warning*. You don't have a clue about what's really going on."

Kevin's gaze narrowed. "And you do?"

"Apparently I know more than either of you."

"Right." I rolled my eyes. "You don't know jack and you're here on a fishing expedition."

"I know that Dick Friel wasn't Samantha's father and Shelley claims she was raped."

That stopped me cold. "Claims?"

Charles fussed with his vulgar, Black Hills Gold tie tack. "I'm not disputing she was raped. I'm just saying Shelley hasn't been honest with anyone about her attack."

"How on earth would you know that?"

A superior smile lit up LaChance's face, from fish lips to reptilian eyes. "Because I was at the fair that night, along with a plethora of now prominent men in this town. And despite her 'I was drunk and don't remember' denial, I believe Shelley knew *exactly* who attacked her."

The sentence hung in the dead air like a slab of rotten meat. No one moved.

"That's bullshit." I said finally. "Why would she hide that information? What possible reason would she have for lying?"

"Maybe you'd better ask her." Charles grabbed his briefcase and swaggered toward the door. "You won't consider dropping this matter?"

Kevin shook his head.

"Your call. I just hope for both your sakes, it is the right one."

Charles turned toward me as if an afterthought. I didn't buy his act, but was curious to hear what low-down scheme he'd hatched on the spot.

"You know, Julie, if you ever want to pursue *your* legal options with your brother's unsolved case, call me. I've got contacts in the BIA and FBI. I'm sure if we hired a competent investigator, we'd figure out some way to get compensation for your pain and suffering."

Before I had a chance to respond, he'd slithered away.

CHAPTER
TEN

KEVIN AND I SAT IN THE McDonald's parking lot gobbling super-sized Value Meals. "You think Charles LaChance is blowing smoke?" I asked.

"No. He knows something."

"Or *thinks* he knows something. I wouldn't put it past that sneaky bastard to try and lure us off track."
Kevin crumpled the fry box into a misshapen red ball. "What track? We've got nothing new."

"Stop it. See? He's poison. What do you always tell me?"

"Besides that you have lousy taste in men?"

I cuffed him lightly under his stubborn chin and said, "Start at the beginning. Think back to when this was just a missing person's case."

I lit a cigarette, watching him cram burger wrappers and spent ketchup packets into the paper bag.

"I figured Sam would turn up before I found her.

When she didn't, I called her boss, her cousin in Lincoln. Since she was a minor, the school angle was a bust. David didn't want me approaching Dick or Shelley. So I followed Meredith. Felt like a pedophile, trailing after a fifteen-year old girl."

A mock shudder rolled through him.

"Anyway, David didn't know where Sam had stayed up in North Rapid so I canvassed motels. Every one. Three days of hitting every shift of every dive and still nothing. Not one person saw Samantha Friel in over two weeks."

"You offered them . . ."

"Money, booze, a get-out-of-jail free-card, you name it, I thought of it. But every clerk I talked to swore they hadn't seen her."

"What's that tell you?"

"Either minimum wage doesn't inspire employees to give a rip about what goes on around them," his fingers curled on the steering wheel, "or Samantha lied."

I nodded. "She had to stay someplace. So, where was she?"

"Hell if I know." He aimed his brooding stare toward Toby's Casino across the parking lot. "I've gone over this until I can't think. Why would Sam lie to David if he was the only one who cared about her?"

"Maybe she was scared," I offered.

"Of him?"

"No."

"Of what, then? Of the big secret David alluded to? First I'd heard of it. And from what little I've gathered, Sam was more pissed off than scared."

"Someone killed her, so apparently she had reason to be scared."

Kevin mulled that over. "This sucks. I wish . . ."

"What?" I brushed my fingers over his, hoping for once, he'd let me give him reassurance.

"I wish I would've taken this more seriously from the start." His sigh went beyond weary. "It was supposed to have been a simple case. Find girl, return her to arms of loving boyfriend, collect fee. Easy cheesy, right?"

"Stop beating on yourself."

"Maybe Charles is right. What can I find out that the locals can't? And if I do find something, who the hell is going to benefit?" He moved to look at me, knocking away my hand like one would a pesky fly. "Would it make a difference to you? If you ever figure out what Ben was doing at Bear Butte instead of that casino in Arizona? Will it ever make any goddamn sense? Will it ever lessen your grief?"

With my show of compassion rebuffed, I didn't reply.

He sighed again, exasperated with my silence. "Let's go talk to Meredith Friel."

The irony that the Friel house resembled the houses in my shoddy neighborhood wasn't lost on me. Kevin and I walked up the cracked sidewalk and rang the doorbell.

My first thought upon seeing Meredith Friel was that

she didn't resemble Samantha at all. She seemed closer to twelve than fifteen, petite, with waist-length, flaxen hair, brown eyes accentuated with heavy black makeup. After shaking our hands and taking Kevin's business card, she invited us inside.

However ramshackle the outside of the house appeared, the inside was immaculate, except for the dingy walls and the heavy odor of cigarettes. Had Dick hired a cleaning service? Or had Samantha's responsibilities fallen on Meredith's slim shoulders? I declined her very grown-up offer of coffee and waited for Kevin to begin.

"Thanks for agreeing to talk to us."

Meredith lowered her head. "Anything I can do to help."

"I understand you were pretty close to Sam. When was the last time you saw her?" He didn't add *alive*, it was implied.

"Three weeks ago. Umm," she said as she folded one toothpick thigh over the other, "she came back here. Guess she needed some money."

"She say for what?"

"Food and gas. I waited until Dick fell asleep and lifted sixty bucks from his wallet."

Meredith called her father *Dick*? Interesting.

"Did Sam ask you to do that?"

"No. But if she had, I would have, no question." Despite the quivering chin, her eyes snapped defiance. "I would've done anything she asked."

"When she came back . . . how did she seem?" Kevin asked.

"What do you mean, 'how did she seem'?" Meredith repeated.

Kevin loosely draped his forearms across his legs and shrugged. "I mean her emotional state. Was she sad? Depressed? Angry?"

"She was completely destroyed. Said her entire existence was a joke. Wouldn't talk to anyone about it."

"Not even you?"

"No."

"How about the counselor assigned to Sam at the rehab center?"

Meredith leaned back into the threadbare Lazy Boy recliner, her rosebud mouth a perfect teenage moue of revulsion. "You're joking, right? Sam hated that woman."

Kevin saw his opening and took it. "Your mother knew Sam didn't like the counselor. But she believed Sam might've gotten counseling outside of the rehab center."

"*Shelley* told you that?" Meredith mocked.

Hmm. Shelley and Dick. Not Mom and Dad. Was this first name basis a recent development?

He nodded. "Actually, she suggested Sam should try Catholic Social Services for counseling. You know anything about that?"

"Doesn't matter because I know Sam didn't go to CSS."

"Why wouldn't she go to CSS? Especially if she was short on cash? It's free, isn't it?"

"Yeah." Wax-pale fingers stopped smoothing the crease in her washed out jeans, flitting upwards to twist the silver chain circling her neck. "But if it was Shelley's suggestion, Sam would've purposely avoided it." Meredith's blank look turned thoughtful. "Although Sam did mention once I should try going to church with her because her prayers had been answered."

Kevin lifted a brow. "She went to church? Alone?"

His surprise matched mine. A sixteen-year-old *willing* to go to church?

"Probably. She and Grandma Rose normally went together, but Gran's been out of town for the last few months, so I'm sure Sam went by herself."

Meredith gazed past the slate blue Priscilla curtains shrouding us from the outside world.

"Sam had a faith in God I didn't understand. So, naturally, Gran gave Sam the family rosary after her first confession." A ghostly smile loosened the corners of her mouth. "Sam totally freaked if it wasn't in her purse. Said it made her feel protected." Her glazed look turned shrewd. "Did the police find the rosary? Pink pearl beads with a big, white cross?"

"I haven't seen the police report, but I'll check."

"Thank you."

Kevin let Meredith gather her thoughts and I longed

for a cigarette. For a shot of tequila. For a rabid dog to bite my leg off so I didn't have to sit politely and listen to the screaming silence of grief.

"Back to the counseling idea," Kevin prompted. "You think Sam might've talked to one of her parish priests?"

"No. The priests at our church are as old as dirt. I can't imagine they would spew anything besides the 'honor thy father and mother' line of rhetoric bullshit." She wrapped her arms around her slight upper body, a self-hug. "God, how stupid is that? My mother lied to her for her whole life, and then my father kicked her out. Sam was supposed to honor that behavior? Get real."

"Were you here when Dick kicked her out?"

When Meredith averted her eyes again, I recognized the maneuver. She wasn't hiding something; she was trying to get control of the pain. Whatever she was about to say wasn't pretty.

"He literally picked her up and tossed her out the front door. Told her never to come back."

"Meredith, I know this is difficult, but do you think your father could've . . ."

Killed her?" she said without an ounce of shock. "First, he'd have to remove his fat ass from the barstool. But I've never seen him in such a rage." The turquoise ring twisted round and round on her thumb. "He wanted to hurt her really bad, I could tell. But usually he saves the harshest beatings for Shelley."

She glanced up sharply, apparently startled she'd spoken that tidbit out loud.

I watched Kevin digest Meredith's proclamation, but he plugged away with more questions, no matter how much the answers bothered him. "After she left here, where did she go?"

"David told me someplace up on East North Street."

"But she didn't tell *you* where she'd been staying?"

"No." Her gaze slid to the cuckoo clock in the dining room, memorized the crooked, ruffled lampshade on the black lacquer end table, and studied the metal coat tree by the front door before coming to rest on her ring again.

"You're sure? Anything would help us at this point."

"And nothing is going to bring her back." She cocked her head; the necklace spilled over her shoulder. "Why are you here asking these questions? I know David hired you. Ask him."

"What do you think of David?"

"Why does that matter?" The gist of Kevin's question slapped color in her ashen cheeks. "You don't think *he* killed her?"

Kevin raised his hands.

"No way." Fine hair moved back and forth, pale seaweed, as she shook her head. "David loved her. David and I were the *only* ones that loved her. He wouldn't hurt her." Kevin expertly worked Meredith over with silence.

"I'd never hurt her either, if that's your next stupid

question," she snarled.

"But aren't you hurting her now by not being honest with us?"

Kevin's gentle chiding never had good results with me either. I watched the wheels come off of Meredith Friel.

"Don't you think if I knew *anything* I'd tell the cops? They've been here." Meredith jumped to her feet, folding her arms over her scant chest. "I want someone, *anyone* to care enough to find the son-of-a-bitch that killed her. I want to watch him die for what he did to her. And I want my parents to live in hell for the rest of their lives because it's their fault that Samantha is dead."

In the ensuing silence, I wondered if she noticed my heart slide from my body and land on the floor at her tiny, fairy feet.

"Meredith . . ." Kevin began again gently.

She whirled on him, blond hair swinging a perfect arc. "Don't tell me you understand, because you don't. No one can possibly know how I feel. I hate him. I hate them. I hate everyone. I hate that the only person I ever gave a shit about is gone forever." Head buried in hands, her rapid-fire gunshot sobs ricocheted off the dead walls.

Her outburst shrank the room. The air shriveled, and left my lungs. I was suffocating, drowning in sorrow.

When she lifted her tear-filled gaze to mine, I couldn't speak. I couldn't swallow either. In that instant, with my guard down, Meredith recognized that I *did* understand her pain.

I wanted to tell her that living in a constant state of fury only postponed the inevitable breakdown. It would happen to her. If she weren't strong enough to deal with the emotional backlash, it would destroy her, as it nearly had me.

I couldn't let that happen. As much as Kevin knows his job, he knows little about the gut-wrenching grief that leaves you breathless. Meredith needed someone who knew it, who'd survived it, most days anyway. Grief 101, I knew it well. I'd come back. Another day. Regardless of the consequences to my mental well being.

"I don't know anything else. I've got to pick up my little brother in a few minutes, so could you please leave?" Kevin reached to squeeze her shoulder; she deftly dodged his touch without moving her feet.

"Anytime you want to talk," I said lamely, completely out of touch.

She turned and fled into the kitchen.

We let ourselves out.

My sense of futility lingered. Inside Kevin's car, I drifted into the deep pit where I stored the agony of living through Ben's death. Also in that murky hole, I stumbled across the sharp pain of losing my mother. Somehow, I clawed my way back to the surface, but found myself still in the dark, staring at the orange glow of Kevin's dashboard. Night had fallen, pitch black and moonless.

But Kevin hadn't been driving aimlessly while I'd been brooding; we slowed to pull into Fat Bob's parking lot.

The metal building looked innocuous at night; temporary banners boasted good times, cold beer and hot video games. Pick-ups, older sedans, SUV's, and bikes, Harleys mostly, circled the perimeter, but the neon motorcycle perched on the roof drew my attention.

Kevin slammed his hands on the steering wheel. "Shit."

"What? Forget your ID?"

"Ha. Ha." He scowled. "Can we just forget this? It doesn't feel right."

"Why?"

"We haven't exactly had an auspicious beginning to the night, Jules. First, Charles LaChance drops in, and then Meredith Friel freaks out. I'm thinking . . ."

"I know what you're thinking, but forget it."

"What monumental revelations do you think we're going to glean from Dick Friel tonight?" Spooky, how his white teeth shone yellow against the orange lights. "A tearful confession?"

"He is guilty as hell." I scooted sideways, pressing my back into the cool glass, kicking my Caterpillar boots up on the armrest dividing the bucket seats. "Okay, Ace Ventura, who's on your short list?"

"We're not looking for the killer. We're only supposed to figure out where Sam spent the last two weeks."

I rolled my eyes. "If you tell yourself that enough,

Kev, maybe you'll believe it. Come on. If we find out where Sam was and why, we both know we'll have a better shot at figuring out who killed her and why. So give it up. Using your best educated guess, who do you think killed Samantha Friel?"

"Charles LaChance."

"Seriously?"

His lips parted on a short, frustrated puff of air. "I don't know. Nothing has changed. We still don't have squat."

"Wrong." I faced forward again, flipping open the lighted visor to apply a fresh coat of lipstick. "Charles LaChance may be a prick, but I don't think he was lying. Or he'd stoop to murder. What we need to find out, is exactly who *else* was at the fair that night."

In the mirror, I smoothed my top lip with the bottom. "Maybe I'll talk to Nancy Rogers since you think she's a dead-end. She's gotta remember something."

Kevin gave me his "Barney Fife" look. "You expect people to remember details from one night more than seventeen years ago?"

Then it clicked. Details. If Shelley had been passed out, how could she have discerned any voices? Not to mention six or seven *separate* voices? When riding in the back of a pick-up? With a coat thrown over her head? She couldn't have, especially if she'd been in that drunken, blurry state she'd claimed. So, why had she lied?

But what if she had recognized *a* voice? Or two? The

voice of my rapist haunts me still. Was that weasel-dick Charles LaChance right when he'd claimed Shelley had known her attackers? Who else had Shelley "shared" with? Was the information important enough to kill?

"Jules?"

His voice startled me and the lipstick tube veered off course. "What?" I dabbed at the red smear on my chin. "Thought I lost you for a minute there."

"Sorry, not so good at multi-tasking when I'm deep in thought." I wiped away a mascara smudge from under my left eye. "You and I both know that Shelley was keeping something from us."

"What about Meredith?"

My hand stilled. "You can't possibly believe Meredith is capable of killing her sister?"

"No, not that." He rubbed the stubble on his jaw and raked a hand through his hair; his grooming ritual complete, lucky dog. "But her angry blast of shit didn't hide my gut feeling that she knows something, but doesn't trust us."

"Would you? If you were fifteen and your world had crumbled? By the way," I pointed the lipstick tube at him, "she didn't seem so aloof to me."

"You bring out the best in people, baby."

I puckered and pressed my lips together. "Any more smudges?"

"Yeah." He stared at my mouth. "Right here."

His thumb delicately rubbed the sensitive skin under my bottom lip, firing every neuron. His breath, warm and sweet, flowed over my cheek. Something indefinable lurked in his gaze. Something I did not want to deal with tonight.

"Thanks," I murmured.

"Anytime," he said. "Maybe Meredith isn't aloof, but even you have to admit that she's unstable."

"She's grieving, Kev. Of course she's unstable. I still think our best bet is good ole' Dickhead."

Kevin didn't smile at my attempt at humor. Instead, he cupped my face in his palms, turning my head back toward him.

"What if we're both wrong? What if Samantha was a random victim? What if we never discover where she spent the missing two weeks?"

I didn't respond because Kevin wasn't expecting a specific answer. It helps him to work things out, out loud. I wanted to offer whatever assistance I could, but I'd been rebuffed once, so I subtly removed my chin from the tempting warmth of his hand.

Money, cigarettes, and my ID tucked into various pockets: I was ready to roll. "Well, then, it's up to us, Scully, to uncover the truth." I grinned, hoping to lighten the mood.

He finally smiled back. "Fine, Mulder, we'll do it your way. Still, I don't see Jimmer's vehicle. With our luck . . ."

"Our luck is bound to change, right? What else could

possibly go wrong tonight?" I patted his gun for reassurance.

Kevin's groan reverberated through the dark night air as we exited the car. "You know I hate it when you say that."

CHAPTER ELEVEN

THE MIXTURE OF CIGARETTE AND pot smoke blasted me in the face when we stepped into Fat Bob's.

While a bouncer checked our IDs, I checked out his tattoos. I'd flirted with the tattoo idea the year after I graduated from high school, seeing the markings as rebellious, a bold statement of originality. The concept lost its appeal when I realized a tattoo wasn't unique if everybody had one. Here, everybody had one.

The bouncer making change had a black and red snake curling around his wrist, traveling up his bulging bicep. Every time he flexed, the body of the snake flowed like water. Cool trick. The snake's head looked to be in the middle of the bouncer's massive chest, hidden under a ripped and faded black Harley Davidson T-shirt. Even though I hated snakes, I stepped closer, hoping for a peek at the rest of the workmanship.

An overgrown sow dressed in pink bulled her way beside him.

"What're you lookin' at?" she snorted, slanted eyes hidden in piggish folds.

"Just admiring the snake," I said to the male bouncer. "Any chance I can see the whole thing?"

He shook his head and Miss Piggy gargled, "Fat fucking chance. Roger don't show that to no one, least of all to perky blondes."

Perky? I'd been called many names, but "perky" was a first. I purposely stared at the two inches of black roots which eventually morphed into her frizzy orange hair. "Since *you* are a bottle blonde, I'm assuming you haven't witnessed the wonders of his snake either?"

"Get inside or I'll throw you out before you get drunk and give me an excuse."

I was about to give her a decidedly non-perky suggestion when Kevin nudged my shoulder.

"Come on, let's find a seat."

Her blubbery thighs rubbed against mine as I passed. "I'll be watching you, smart mouth."

The third bouncer turned our direction, swinging a butt-length braid around from a single strip of hair on the back of his head. Reminded me of a Shaolin Warrior from one of those 1970's kung fu movies. His tattoos weren't of the pictorial variety, but symbols. Recalling my failure of hieroglyphics in junior high, I imagined that if I questioned him on the meaning of the black squiggles, he'd probably throw me out on my ass as an answer.

Once we stepped into the main part of the bar, the music didn't stop; no one gaped at us like we'd intruded on a private party. We weren't challenged to a gun or fistfight. Again, the real life of a PI wasn't like on TV. But miraculously, the bouncers hadn't patted Kevin down, so he still had his piece in case trouble came our way.

"Where to?" I yelled in Kevin's ear over the bleating sounds of The Allman Brothers singing "Ramblin' Man."

"I see an open booth in the back."

I latched onto his belt loops, using the opportunity to press against his excellent butt. A girl had to take her thrills where she could get them.

We skirted the throng of sweaty bodies surrounding the pool tables. Just as we reached the booth, it filled with two very large, very hairy men, who immediately fell into deep in conversation or, I suspected, a drug deal.

They'd probably take notice if Kevin flashed his gun. But that move was more Jimmer's style and since he wasn't here and I didn't want to remind Kevin of that fact, I kept my "Dirty Harry" fantasies to myself.

"Now what?"

Kevin scanned the area above my head. "Perfect. Two spots just opened up at the bar."

We made a mad dash for the barstools only to be thwarted again, this time by a pair of bleached blondes in studded, leather halter-tops. Two sets of cleavage rivaling Missy's had brought bartenders scurrying from every direction.

But Kevin held their attention. Using his most devastating grin, he leaned over and spoke directly into blonde No.1's breasts before gesturing over his shoulder. Skeptical glances gave way to dazzling smiles as they tossed teased hair and puffed out already puffy chests. Ample butts slid from the barstools, an extra wiggle of generous hips, a high-pitched giggle and they were gone.

"So, slick. What pearls of wisdom did you impart?" I asked.

He seated me first, signaling for two drafts. "Those men in the back booth swore up and down they were models for *Juggs* magazine and they wanted to buy them a Slow Screw."

"*Juggs*? You read *Juggs*?"

"Nah. Jimmer does. He'll be disappointed he missed them."

Didn't know if Kevin was speaking of the women or their jugs. The frosty beer hit the spot and I lit up to make the decadent taste complete. "Do you see Dick?"

"Yep. At three o'clock."

Two barstools over, a chunky, redheaded man with a gray-flecked, red beard sat in a secluded corner, gazing myopically into his half-empty mug while the men around him hooted. Pity welled in me for a second before I snapped it down. "He looks like shit."

"Don't sound so happy."

"Can't help it."

I stared at Dick, hoping he'd feel the weight of my glare and turn around. Nope. I'd ask Callous Lilly, queen of dirty looks, for some pointers. "What's the plan, my man?" I said to Kevin.

He shrugged and spun his mug on scarred bar top. "Good cop/bad cop?"

"Nah. Too predictable. I wanna catch him off guard."

"You could ask him to shoot pool."

"Or . . . you could just shoot him. That'd get his attention."

"Probably, but I'm not as sure as you are that he's guilty."

I choked on a lungful of smoke. "How can that be? You heard Meredith. And Shelley."

"We're not looking for Samantha's killer. We're here to find out if Dick knew where she went after he kicked her out. That's all." He studied me over the foamy rim of his beer. "My impression is that he didn't care about Sam one way or another. Killing her is the ultimate attention grabber."

"So what if Dick never paid any attention to her? He was still pissed off that Shelley had lied to him. If he liked to beat on her before, imagine what he would've done to her if she hadn't been safe in rehab jail. And think about the fact Samantha wasn't."

Kevin lifted a brow and waited.

"Come on. Nothing is more dangerous than a man who's taken a shot to his ego. What better way to get back at Shelley than to kill Sam? Get a couple of his biker pals to snatch her, slash her throat, and dump the body. No sweat." I glanced around at the men in the bar. Damn, if they didn't all look the same, bearded and shifty-eyed. Probably all smelled like sour beer and drove hopped-up conversion vans.

"You're reaching," he said, bending down to examine my eyes. "You know what I think?"

I forced myself not to retreat. "What?"

"I think you *want* the killer to be Dick Friel. I think the parallels between Dick washing his hands of Sam, and your father doing the same with Ben, are clouding your judgment."

"Then why did you ask for my help?"

"Because you do bring a different, almost bizarre perspective to things, babe." He set his hand on my forearm, thumb tracing the fine hairs until my skin began to tingle in an obvious attempt to soften his next words. "You've tried and convicted Dick without even talking to him."

His hand dropped like a rock when I raised my arm and drained my beer.

After one last drag of my cigarette, I spun the barstool away from Kevin and slid to the sticky floor. "Fuck you, Freud. I'll remedy the I-haven't-talked-to-Dick situation right now."

He sighed, but didn't stop me.

Dick glanced up as I set my elbows on the bar right next to him. I smiled, full on, *Playmate of the Year* style. "Hey, Dick, remember me?"

His gaze oozed over my body. A shiver of revulsion worked loose from the soles of my feet to the top of my head. "Can't say as I do."

"Julie Collins?" I prompted with my usual charm. "I graduated three years behind you?"

"Sorry."

"Falling Rock, Four Bridges, we partied together probably a dozen times." I gave a little pout. "You seriously don't remember me?"

"Nope." He reached for the shot glass the bartender had placed in front of him and sucked it down.

Since the bartender had hung around, I signaled for one of the same.

"I ain't buying that," Dick said, and the men sitting next to him snickered.

"Not even for old time's sake?"

Dick muttered something under his breath that sounded suspiciously like an insult. Aww. And I'd so wanted to do this the nice way. "I'm sorry, Dick, what did you say?"

He angled his head from my earshot, and added a bit of wit to his fellow bar rats, causing another bark of male laughter.

Which pissed me off. If his utterance was so god-damned funny, he should share it. Hell, I could take a joke, even at my own expense. "Actually," I said, "I guess I was friendlier with your wife. How is Shelley, by the way?"

That got his attention. "Still the same drunken slut she always was," he said. "And newsflash: She ain't my old lady anymore."

The bartender placed the shot in front of me and I knocked it back, handing him a five. Yuck. Jaegermeister. Some people had no taste. "The same way Sam wasn't your daughter anymore, Dick?"

The air finally gave pause in the way I'd envisioned since the moment I'd walked in.

"What do you know about that?"

I ordered another shot and ignored Dick, realizing I was completely blocked from the view of the rest of the bar and Kevin. My heart kicked into high gear even when I knew it wouldn't help to panic.

"Who the fuck are you?"

"I told you."

"What do you want?"

"A friendly drink." I smiled coyly. "To rehash the good times, you know, the usual."

"Bullshit. What do you really want?"

"Answers." This time I didn't bother to hide my repugnance. "Just looking to uncover the truth about how Samantha ended up with her throat sliced right after you found out she wasn't your daughter."

Bull's-eye. His face darkened.

"I'll give you an answer." He adjusted his stance and I got a whiff of his angry, licorice-scented breath. "The truth is Shelley is a fucking loser. Always has been. I should've gone with my gut reaction and skipped town when she pulled that bullshit pregnancy story."

"Yeah? Liked her enough that you managed to knock her up twice more."

He laughed. "Sure, I fucked her, wasn't like she was ever unwilling." His smile grew crafty. "But who's to say them other kids are even mine?"

I let his words sink in. "Yeah, who's to say? Big guy like you probably has a little . . . Dick, is this conversation making you uncomfortable?"

His mouth tightened as the group of men around him whooped and hollered. "Think you're clever, don't ya?"

"Nah. I think *you're* clever. Good plan when you kicked out a sixteen-year-old girl. So, where'd she go?"

"Don't know and don't care. Listen you . . ."

"No. You listen." I came nose-to-nose with him. "Were you embarrassed when you found out that Shelley had been raped? Or are you one of those asshole types that think she deserved it? What about Sam? Did she deserve what happened to her too?"

The bartender set down two shots and I drank them both without losing eye contact with Dick. Without caring that one of those shots *had* been Dick's.

"You don't know shit," Dick harrumphed. "You ain't a cop, and those bitches from Social Services wouldn't step foot in here. So, I'm wondering who the hell you are and what you want." His eyes went flat. "Did that fuck-up Shelley hire another lawyer?"

I shrugged.

"No matter, cause I ain't giving her a red cent. Not for her or them goddamn kids. Tell her that."

"You're forgetting blood tests can prove paternity." I dropped a ten on top of the empty shot glasses. "Then the courts will force you to pay child support."

"Is the fucked up court system gonna give me credit for the years I supported a kid that ain't even mine?" He slammed the beer mug on the bar. "Where were the goddamn blood tests then?"

"Good question. But were you pissed off that you'd fed and clothed Samantha, when it wasn't your royal blood running through her veins? Did you take action yourself? Decide enough was enough and you'd be getting revenge on Shelley by getting rid of her daughter?"

His beard brushed his flannel shirt when he shook his head back and forth. "Jesus. You are a fucking psycho. Yeah, she's dead, but I sure as hell didn't kill her."

"Prove it. Answer some questions. Then I'll go."

His lip curled before it disappeared under his walrus mustache. "Nope. Don't think I will." He pointed to my change on the bar edge. "You're finished and I ain't got nothing else to say. I think you'll go *now*."

I studied my nails. My hands weren't shaking but my insides felt like they were in a margarita blender.

"What? Are you deaf? Get the hell out of my bar."

Making a slow pass over what I could see of the room, I said pointedly, "*Your* bar? Does that mean Shelley's entitled to half?"

"Piss with me, bitch, and you'll get more than you bargained for."

"Free country, *Dick*. I can stay here and drink as long as I want." I smiled and angled my chin defiantly, catching movement from the corner of my eye too late.

A determined voice drifted over my shoulder. "Sorry. It don't work that way. If Dick don't want you here, you're gone."

Great. Tattooed snake man. "Why? I'm just having a friendly conversation with my old friend, Dickhead."

"Start moving."

I smiled again, wishing for pounds of cleavage to flash. The bouncer crowded closer, but his gaze didn't dip below my mouth. Or maybe I was beyond the help big boobs could've provided me. Ever the girl with the rotten luck.

"You've got about ten seconds to walk out on your own or I'll escort you out, understand?"

"*No hablo englesh.*" My pathetic Lucy Ricardo imitation fell flat as he began to count backwards from ten. At one, he tried grabbing my arm. I twisted away, synapses in my brain frantically trying to formulate a plan since Kevin was the one holding the firepower.

"Look," the bouncer said. "You're pissing me off."

"Feeling is mutual. So, why don't you just back away?"

"Cuff the bitch and drag her ass out," Dick snapped. "She probably enjoys it rough, anyway."

I didn't dare glance away from the bouncer to respond to Dick's suggestion. "Touch me again and I'll break your nose."

The bouncer advanced on me.

I stood my ground.

"For Chrissake, Jake," Dick complained to the bartender, "tell Helen to take care of this since Roger here is such a pussy."

"Why don't you take care of me yourself?" I taunted Dick. "Seems your style, picking on women."

"Come on," Kevin said from somewhere behind the bouncer. "Let it go."

The bouncer gestured to Kevin with his head. "You'd be smart to listen to your boyfriend."

"Boyfriend?" My brows lifted; a parody of surprise. "I've never seen him before in my life."

"I carded you two when you came in together, remember? So don't give me that line of bullshit. Time to leave."

"Fuck you," I said amiably. "I'll leave when I'm ready."

He reached for me with both hands and I ducked.

Spinning, I faced him again, pleased with the shock on his face. Before I could demonstrate breaking his nose with my elbow, a ham hock wrapped around my neck. My arms were wrenched behind my back. Searing pain shot in a line down my shoulders, spine, ending at my sacrum. The fetid smell of sour mash assaulted my nostrils.

A gravelly female voice said, "Give me a reason, Barbie. I've wanted to kick your bony ass since the minute you walked in."

Shit. Miss Piggy. Her stranglehold was cutting off my air supply. I went completely still when Dick finally moved off his barstool and towered over me.

His silver chain of keys jangled against his heavy thigh. He rocked back on his cowboy boots, surveying me as if I were a serf to his lord. Fear coiled in my stomach, crawled up my throat, and settled in deep, paralyzing my vocal cords. But I wouldn't allow my gaze to move from his reddened, impassive face.

"Let me tell you something. You don't come in here," he said, gesturing around his domain, "and think 'cause you have some fucked up history with my ex-wife you got the right to ask questions. You don't. You give that cunt, Shelley, a message," he paused for effect. "And since you asked so nicely, I *will* take care of you myself."

Me and my big mouth. I didn't believe he'd actually hit me with a roomful of witnesses. Scare me maybe, but not use physical force.

His fist plowed into my stomach, leaving me stunned. The breath exited my lungs in a rush. The natural urge to double over and clutch my ribs was prevented by Helen's iron grip on my throat, stopping any anguished sound that might've burst forth.

With the bouncers surrounding us and blocked by Dick's girth, no one saw Dick hit me a second time. Or a third. Or maybe they did and didn't care. The blows hurt. I wanted to take that chance to retreat, but no sound emerged.

Apparently enraged at my silence, Dick hit me again. Harder, clipping the edge of my ribs. As the blood pounded in my ears and my vision swam, a scuffle erupted behind me. Kevin. Coming to my rescue? Too little, too late.

A final double punch and Dick ambled back, cocking his head to study his handiwork; me in pain, afraid, and unable to breathe.

"Get them both out of here," Dick commanded as he resettled his bulk on his barstool. He turned his yellow back on me, my fate decided, as if the conversation was over.

But it wasn't. Not by a long shot.

CHAPTER TWELVE

WHILE HELEN SQUEEZED ME AGAINST her spongy body and dragged me away from Dick, I noticed Roger, the tattooed snake-man, had grabbed Kevin. God. What a rotten pair of crime-fighters we made. I should've kept the damn gun; then again, I might've shot Dick and I'd be headed for jail right now. Not the one in my friendly, quiet county, either. Jeers and catcalls burned my ears on the way out the back door.

My body jarred into Helen's when she rammed her large ass into the release bar on the steel side door. Her motions loosened the grip around my neck. I inhaled a lungful of crisp night air before she abruptly let go and tossed me to the ground.

I hit knees and hands. My left palm scraped against the graveled parking lot, imbedding dirt and rocks beneath my skin. Clouds of dust kicked up and blocked my already wavering vision. The stinging sensation galvanized me into action and I spun, crab-walking as fast as I could away from the sound of Helen's advancing footsteps. Out here the bar sounds were muted. Pain would come later, after the adrenaline rush wore off.

"Where you goin'?" Dust rose with every heavy footfall.

I didn't answer, just held my breath and kept crawling.

"Got nothing to say? Funny that big mouth of yours suddenly ran out of smart ass remarks. Like it closed up or something. Too bad. I was looking forward to a shot at shutting it."

A greasy laugh slipped forth, and my insides rolled with a combination of fear, Dick's sucker punches, and too many shots.

"You ain't so tough or clever when you're crawling on the ground like a dog, are ya?" she sneered.

My shoulder hit the metal side of another out-building and I scrambled to my feet. The sharp pain traveled up my spinal cord and short-circuited the quit-while-you're-ahead section of my brain.

"I've been officially removed from the bar. Now you're providing me with an escort to my car?" I shook my head with forced dejection, sliding two feet to the right. "Sweet of you, Helen, but really, I can manage."

"How you've managed not to get that pie-hole kicked in before now is a fucking miracle." She shuffled closer. "We ain't done yet."

When she spit out the side of her mouth onto the ground — a bad-guy move from a spaghetti western — the urge to laugh nearly undid me. "You really get your jollies out of this intimidation crap, don't you? What do you want? Money?"

I made a big show of patting my front and back jeans pockets while I moved sideways.

"Sorry. Fresh out of cash."

Helen's rage was apparent, even in the near dark. "Fuck you and your money. I want to see you cry."

Taking another large step to the right, I cleared the side of the building. In the open lot I had better odds of not getting cornered and beaten to a bloody pulp. Still, my mouth ran unchecked from pure fear. Been one helluva long time since I'd actively participated in, or picked a bar fight. "If I get another up close and personal look at your face, then I'll guarantee you I'll cry."

I wasn't positive, but I thought I heard a snicker somewhere to my left.

"Shut up," she yelled as she charged me.

For a fat chick, Helen was surprisingly agile. I'd have bet fifty bucks she'd aim for my center and try to knock me to the ground. If she parked her large carcass on me, I'd be a Swedish pancake.

But her punchbowl-sized head smacked into my chin; I saw a profusion of stars, not the ones twinkling above my head. I flew back, wind-milling my arms to retain my balance. Still upright, I immediately shifted into a left-side fighting stance, my left hand blocking my face, my right hand waist level, ready for battle.

She swung.

I blocked.

She swung again. Harder. I blocked again, but followed through by cuffing her jaw hard with my right.

She stumbled, partially from the force of my strike, but mostly in shock that I'd actually landed a blow. Chalk one up for martial arts Barbie. Changing tactics, once again she hunkered down and rushed me.

But this time I was ready. As soon as she got close enough, I dropped to the ground and rolled, sweeping her off her feet. An ungraceful trip and she face-planted in the dirt. Her howls were muffled as she dragged herself on her elbows, simultaneously crawling away and protecting her ugly face in her hands.

I jumped up and the motion shot a bolt of pain to my ribs. Blood trickled down from the corner of my mouth where her head had split my lip open.

She rubbed her hand under the meat that used to be her nose.

Helen flinched when I leaned close — but not too close — to see her bloodied face. "Who's crying now?"

My arms were jerked behind me for a second time.

With my adrenaline running high, I didn't wait to react. The tread of my boots raked down the attacker's shin, my fingers clawed into the closest skin I could find; a groin. I squeezed the testicles hard, giving the whole package a decisive twist.

No big surprise I was released instantly. Keeping my hand high to block blows, I turned, executing a swift kick at the kneecap, then used my fists to slam into his ears, as if I were playing the cymbals.

Roger, the tattooed snake-man, writhed to the ground.

Still in a defensive position, I glanced around, searching for Kevin. Gravel crunched. Kung fu man stepped from the shadows, gesturing to Kevin with Kevin's gun. Out of the corner of my eye, I saw Helen struggle to her knees. Roger was out for a while. But still we were outnumbered and outgunned. Outgunned by our own gun. Sounded like the smarmy title of some country western tune.

Kung fu man pointed the gun at Kevin. "No more of that kind of shit. Nice technique, though, what was that? Sabatka slap?"

I bowed. I couldn't help it. Hurt like a bitch, though.

"Looks like we've got a situation," he continued. "I can let you go, or have the cops arrest you for disturbing the peace."

"I vote for letting us go," I said immediately.

"Wise choice. But if I do let you both walk without calling the cops, there is a condition."

Breathing hard, I managed, "What's the condition?"

He answered with a small laugh and I waited for the

punch line.

"Helen gets a free shot at you, blondie."

Looked like I *was* the punch line. "Why?"

"Because it'd be unfair to sic Roger on you, no matter how tough you think you are."

Roger, still prone, moaned once.

"So you're gonna give Helen free rein?"

He shrugged. "My penance. It shouldn't have gotten to this point."

"Not my problem."

"Not true. You made it your problem by antagonizing Dick. She was doing her job." He angled his head to the dust-covered lump of flesh sitting on the ground. "Besides, you're the type of woman she hates. She'll whine for-fuck-ing-ever that I didn't back her up. I don't need to be re-minded she got her ass kicked by a skinny white girl. Word gets out? No one will be afraid of her."

I glared at him and wiped the liquid, blood probably, trickling from my chin. "I win and she gets to hit *me*? That's a lousy fucking condition."

He shrugged again. "Your choice."

"What's the alternative?"

"I wait until Roger's balls aren't blue, and then the three of us kick the shit out of the two of you, call the cops and," he said as he spun Kevin's gun on his finger, "I get to keep this sweet piece."

My laugh, born of fear, bordered on frantic. "You

won't call the cops."

"Try me."

"Julie," Kevin said calmly, "he's bluffing. Don't do it."

I stalled to catch my breath and swore I'd give up smoking after this pack. "Did Dick put you up to this? Why can't that lazy son-of-a-bitch fight his own battles?"

Had that actually come out of my mouth? Shit. As if my throbbing ribs and aching abdomen weren't proof enough that Dick had done his fair share of battling tonight.

"He doesn't have to. That's my job." His upper body shifted fluidly, while his feet stayed grounded. "What's it gonna be?"

I opened my mouth and snapped it shut.

"Jesus. You're not seriously considering this, are you?" Kevin asked.

I didn't answer him, busy as I was trying to remember if my health insurance covered plastic surgery. Or major dental work.

"One lousy shot, Harvey?" Helen whined as she lumbered to her feet. "That's not fair . . ."

"Shut up," Harvey snarled. "If you weren't such a lard ass, this wouldn't be a problem." He directed his glower to me. "So?"

"I'll give her a shot, but I have a condition too. If her blow doesn't knock me down, then I get another shot at her."

"Oh, for Christ's sake," Kevin muttered.

"We'll see," Harvey said, nodding to Helen.

Full of false bravado, I flung my arms wide. "Take your best shot, Oh Helen of Ploy, with the face that launched a thousand quips."

Missing my pun, Helen cracked her knuckles.

I rolled my eyes. Had I really been disappointed by the lack of cheesy clichés? I braced myself as Helen approached.

She circled me, heavy breath expelling stale booze; sweat plastered her hair to her forehead.

The sound of a shell being chambered in a shotgun broke the unnatural silence.

All six-foot six of Jimmer Cheadle stepped from the shadows. A Remington 870 pump shotgun pointed at the bouncer. "Step away from her. Give him back the gun, Harvey."

A startled hush further muted the night sounds.

Then Harvey's high-pitched giggle sent chills up the back of my neck. "Jimmer. Long time no see. These guys' friends of yours?"

"Yeah." Jimmer didn't lower the gun. "What the hell did they do that warranted your personal attention?"

Harvey's preening at Jimmer's backhanded compliment made me want to barf. Okay, so maybe the stomach punches were finally catching up with me and the adrenaline was wearing off.

"They," he said pointing at me, "that one in particular,

messed with a customer. Tony's favorite customer actually."

"Who?"

"Dick Friel."

"Dick Friel?" Jimmer said, shaking his head in disbelief.

I met Kevin's gaze and he shrugged. One never questioned Jimmer on his connections, but no doubt he got around.

"Yep," Harvey said. "And you know how Tony feels about Dick. Nothing I could do, man, it's just my job, nothing personal."

Jimmer nodded. "Well, I'm sure Julie didn't know Dick's status around here or else she wouldn't have been *stupid* enough to try something like this, right, Julie?"

I held my hands up, palms out, a gesture of innocence. "I swear I just started a friendly conversation and it got out of hand."

"Right," Harvey intoned dryly. His gaze never wandered from Jimmer when he spoke to Helen and Roger. "Head back inside. Jake and Lee probably need help." Helen started to protest but Harvey growled, "That wasn't a request."

They moved faster than I thought possible considering they'd both been limping. Seemed Harvey was much scarier than me.

"Return the piece," Jimmer repeated.

No one-handed toss for Harvey. He politely handed it back to Kevin — barrel first.

While Kevin re-holstered his gun, Jimmer lowered the shotgun and came to stand beside me. "You okay?"

"I guess. Been thrown out of better places than this."

His mouth twitched. "I hear ya. Not your usual hang-out. Mind telling me what the hell are you two doing here?"

"Working a case."

His black bushy eyebrows rose clear up his forehead. "Involving Dick Friel?"

"No. Samantha Friel."

Harvey's head snapped gracefully at the mention of her name. "You were here asking Dick questions about Sam? What? Are you fucking nuts?"

"Why?"

He exchanged a look with Jimmer that wasn't lost on me. "Ask him."

I turned to do so but Harvey's too-soft voice grabbed my attention.

"Another piece of advice, blondie. Don't ever set foot in this bar again. 'Cause next time, I won't be so cooperative."

"You tell Tony I was here," Jimmer said.

Harvey nodded.

Before I blinked, Harvey had disappeared. A stealthy Ninja trick I couldn't help but admire.

Then Kevin was by my side, tipping my face back to gauge the damage. "You're bleeding."

"Not much. It mostly stopped now."

"That's comforting."

I closed my eyes when he jerked me into his arms and muttered against the top of my head.

He pulled back when I whimpered. "What?" he said.

"My ribs."

Yanking up my shirt, his warm fingers skimmed down the center of my stomach over my ribcage until my flesh beaded. "Here?" He sucked in a harsh breath. "Babe, you're gonna have some nasty bruises."

"What the hell is going on?" Jimmer pushed closer.

"Dick punched me," I said as Kevin lifted my shirt higher. "Twice," I lied, shifting my jaw side-to-side. Not broken, but sore.

"Wrong. It was more like five or six times."

Back arched, I kept a firm grip on a batch of girly sobs that threatened to erupt as Kevin poked and prodded me. I tried a lighter approach, "So, what do you think of the new bra? It's one of those push-up kinds."

"Shut up," Kevin said against my stomach, still testing my ribs for breaks. "I can't fucking believe he hit you." Jimmer hauled Kevin to an upright position before he spun him around. "Dick Friel punched her? How the fuck did you let that happen?"

Kevin twisted out of Jimmer's grip and pushed him back a step. "Don't you think I've been asking myself that same question?"

My T-shirt slid down to my hips. "Not his fault,

Jimmer. Harvey and Roger kept him back while Helen held me. It wasn't so bad," I fibbed again.

Kevin growled at my flip response but knew arguing wouldn't change anything. "Yes, it is my fault," he said. "For letting her badger me." His tone turned flat. "By the way, where the hell were *you* when Julie became Dick's punching bag?"

"I hauled ass here as soon as I got Julie's message."

"I'm *fine,*" I repeated. Playing the blame game was pointless now. I'd suspected what Dick Friel was capable of. Not their fault I hadn't heeded the warning signs.

"Yeah, well you're luckier than shit," Jimmer said.

"Because Dick only got a few licks in?" I joked.

"No. That Harvey didn't get involved. He's one mean mother."

"Yeah?" I said picking the bits of gravel from my palm, sucking in my breath at the razor-sharp sting.

"You really don't know, do you?"

That comment tore my attention away from my torn skin. "Know what?"

"That he's the enforcer for Hombres."

"The local biker gang that ran the Hell's Angels out of Sturgis a few years back?"

Jimmer winced. "Never call them a gang. They're a club."

"So? What's his connection to them?"

"Who do you think owns this bar?"

My mouth dropped open. "No shit?"

"No shit." Jimmer pulled the slide back on the shotgun and the shells ejected out the side. He shoved them inside his flak jacket. "Let's get out of here."

He got no argument from Kevin or me.

With one tree trunk-sized arm slung over my shoulder, and the gun perched on the other, he looked the part of a true slinger. "So, where'd you learn those moves? Some pretty fancy fighting skills there, little missy."

I hate it when Jimmer calls me "little missy." He knows it, but does it anyway. That's just the way Jimmer is. It was oddly comforting. Almost as comforting as when Kevin gently slipped his hand into mine.

"Oh, that? It's nothing," I said. "Little Ju-Jitsu, little *Buffy the Vampire Slayer.*"

"You learned those moves from watching TV?"

"Yep. You might try watching something besides the 'Playboy' channel some time."

Jimmer shook his head. "Forget it. I'd rather get my ass kicked."

CHAPTER
THIRTEEN

AT KEVIN'S CONDO, JIMMER SAID, "Why didn't you guys tell me you were working a case involving Dick Friel?"

"We aren't." I popped four Excedrin and chased it down with the last of my soda. "Besides you've been gone."

"Only on vacation," Jimmer said as he set a Coors suitcase on the table, ripped it open and distributed beer: one for Kevin, one for me, three for himself.

Kevin shook his head. "*No one* vacations in Nicaragua."

"Thank God." Jimmer guzzled a beer and reached for another.

I tried grabbing my can but the frozen bag of peas Kevin held against my mouth pressed harder into my swollen lip.

"Ouch! Goddammit, that hurts." I batted his hand away. "Its fine, it's not your fault, so leave it alone."

Kevin squatted down and gingerly brushed his lips over mine before he pulled back. "Quit being such a baby and let me take care of it."

"No. It's fine."

"Christ. This is getting old. Why don't you two just fuck each other's brains out and get it over with?" Jimmer punctuated his irritation with a loud belch.

Kevin and I both froze.

Discretion wasn't Jimmer's style. He claimed friends didn't need that bullshit. After the freak kite electrocution, which killed his younger brother Todd, we, as Todd's friends, inherited Jimmer as our surrogate brother. Hence, he felt entitled to speak his mind. Freely. And unfortunately for us, frequently.

Kevin cracked open his beer, taking a long swallow. His normally soothing voice was encased in steel. "Let it go, Jimmer."

"Well, it's the truth, even if you're both too chicken-shit to act on it." Jimmer leaned his chair back against the wall and waited for further fireworks to erupt.

"Can we get back to Dick Friel?" I said, trying for peace instead of my usual habit of saying the first thing that popped in to my mind.

"That guy is bad news. It was ludicrous to even think he'd talk to you. Especially when he's surrounded by Tony's goons."

Ludicrous? Evidently Jimmer, the boxing nut, had been watching Mike Tyson interviews again. "Why?"

"Why do you think a fat, stupid, piece of shit like him

is so well-protected at Fat Bob's?"

I sneaked a glance and Kevin and he shrugged.

Jimmer answered his own question. "Connections. Rumor has it if you need any bike, and need it fast, Dick is the go-to man as long as you're not too picky about serial numbers and have the cash."

"So he's trafficking stolen bikes? For Tony Martinez?"

"Possibly. I ain't about to ask. Dick is small time. Bikes and the occasional insurance repair scam. Course, Dick does all the maintenance on the Hombres bikes so he's ass deep in the organization. So, whatever Tony Martinez needs, Dick provides without question."

"Could Dick have gotten involved in something else?"

"Such as?"

"Drugs?"

Jimmer easily crushed the beer can in one hand. "I don't know. Screw that. I don't wanna know. Tony Martinez is another scary dude. You'd better stay far away from him too."

"But, could Dick have somehow found something out he wasn't supposed to and inadvertently pissed Tony off . . ."

"You're going the wrong direction," Kevin said.

"How so?" I demanded. "Maybe *Tony* owed Dick, hence all the protection."

"Apparently keeping Dick happy ranks highly on Tony's list of priorities if you can't even talk to him in Tony's bar. Consider this: Dick freaked about Sam and

Shelley, and before he did something stupid that threatened the setup he had with Tony, maybe Tony decided to do him a favor and deal with it."

I gave him my skeptical look. "Without Dick's knowledge?"

"Maybe Dick suspects something and that's why he went after you when you asked him questions. Especially in Tony's bar."

To Jimmer I said, "Does Tony have the kind of connections to make Samantha go away permanently?"

Jimmer nodded.

"But that doesn't make sense. Why?"

"You tell me," Kevin said. "You're the one that thinks Dick Friel is guilty."

"Don't you?"

"Not without a better motive. Too risky for both of them for something as inconsequential as paternity. It appears you and I are the only ones that weren't aware of the connection between Tony and Dick. And if Tony did make Samantha disappear, he's probably the first person the local boys would look at."

He stretched his legs out to get comfy before he imparted his theory.

"On the other hand, if Dick had something on Tony and blackmailed him, and Tony used Samantha as an example of what happened when someone crossed him, do you really think Dick would be hanging in Tony's bar with

Tony's bouncers watching and protecting his every move? Doesn't make sense."

His logic sunk my hopes. "No, I guess you're right."

Kevin said to Jimmer, "Could you check around, *discreetly,* and see if Dick owed anyone money?"

"Sure," Jimmer said.

Jimmer's pawnshop was a veritable candy store of information. He made it his business to know the financial status of all minor and major players in the four-state area. Apparently, Dick and Tony were players. Since I hadn't known that, I was obviously relegated into the non-player category.

"Maybe we should check and see if there was a life insurance policy on Sam," I mused aloud, then snapped my fingers. "With a double indemnity clause and find out who stands to benefit."

"You really do watch too much TV," Kevin said.

I lit a cigarette, wincing when the filter pulled the scraped skin on my lip. Damn thing hurt but I smoked anyhow. "Do you think we should talk to Martinez?"

"Hell, no," Jimmer bellowed. "For Chrissake, Julie, haven't you been listening?"

I faced Kevin and his silent nod of agreement. "After all this new information, you still believe Dick had nothing to do with Sam's disappearance?"

His eyes clouded and he frowned at his beer. "I don't know."

The front door banged. Callous Lilly's syrupy voice wafted up the stairs. "Kevin? Honey? Where are you?"

"Up here."

Hoo-fucking-ray. And I thought my night couldn't get any worse.

"Be nice," Kevin warned.

I dragged deeply on the cigarette, blowing in and out to let the blue haze fill the enclosed area instead of my lungs.

Petty? Yeah. I dared her to say something, after all, it was *Kevin's* house, not hers. Besides, I was here first.

When Lilly stepped into the kitchen, her pert nose wrinkled. Her breath hitched — a delicate little cough. Crossing to Kevin, she waved away the smoke while her bright eyes zeroed in on the empty cans on the table. Her hand slimed Kevin's shoulder. "Looks like you're celebrating."

Jimmer, ever the gentleman, grabbed a beer and held it out to her.

Her glossy brown bob stayed board stiff as she declined with a slight shake of her fat head. A slim, peach linen-covered hip Velcro-ed to Kevin's chair.

I blew a perfect smoke ring in her direction, but darn it, she wasn't impressed.

"I didn't realize you had plans," she said softly. "I feel like I'm intruding. Maybe I'd better go."

Kevin circled an arm around her. "Don't be silly. Stay."

She flashed him an indulgent smile before he pulled

her onto his knee. Her muted, delighted squeal grated on my soul like fingernails on a chalkboard.

God, I hated her.

I hated that she'd clouded Kevin's judgment with her simpering ways. I hated that he was so stupidly male and had fallen for her entirely faked demeanor. A demeanor that smacked too creepily of sappy, sweet Miss Melanie Hamilton Wilkes for my taste.

Where did I fit in my bizarre comparison to *Gone with the Wind*? Was I supposed to act the part of Scarlett? Vying with her for the attention of Ashley?

Fuck that. I didn't want to be Scarlett. I wanted to be Rhett. Rhett didn't take shit and I'd had my share tonight.

I stood, zipped up Kevin's leather jacket to cover the bloodstains on my T-shirt, and kept my limping to a minimum. "It's late. Jimmer? Will you take me to my car?"

"Sure." He grabbed the remaining beer, saluted Kevin, and was out the door.

"Oh, Julie, I didn't mean to run you off," Lilly said.

Like hell you didn't. I smiled at her even though my face nearly cracked from the effort.

"You aren't. Got an early morning." I patted Kevin's shoulder, the one that wasn't encircled by her talon. "See ya."

For once I left without making a smart remark. After all, tomorrow was another day.

When I pulled onto my street an hour later, cars lined both sides of the road. Looked like Leanne was having a party. Again. Hopefully Kiyah had a quiet corner to hide in. I briefly considered joining her when I noticed Ray's pickup parked in my driveway.

The thought of dealing with him had me throwing my car in reverse, whipping a U-turn, and backtracking to the sheriff's office. Sad, when an empty jail cell and listening to drunks throw up cheap booze was more appealing than my own king-sized bed.

The sheriff came in the next morning at five thirty and woke me. I changed clothes, cleaned up, clocked in, and started my workday.

My work duties kept me busy enough not to think about my aching body. Our small county doesn't have the budget for separate departments or job titles. I'm responsible for everything from reordering toilet paper to fixing the copier. The secretarial tasks are mundane, but on occasion I get to do more than file and answer phones.

I'd considered at one time taking the required courses to become a full-fledged deputy. Carrying a gun, driving a patrol car, and handcuffing bad guys, yeah, I'd romanticized it just a tad. I'd even given myself a radio handle, "JC" for those urgent conversations with dispatch when my full name was too long. The reality? The pay scale is lousy and the training schedule rigorous. Sitting behind a desk with access to a clean bathroom and a soda machine doesn't seem so bad.

For now I'm content living out my bad-girl-packing-attitude fantasies with Kevin part-time. I don't love this job, but it sure beats working retail.

From weekend traffic tickets to domestic abuse calls, I know this county's secrets well. The files do make interesting reading. Some days I'll scour every case, other days I'll file them with barely a second glance. My stack had shrunk down to the second-to-the-last folder, when the name jumped out. Leanne Dobrowski.

Damn. Leanne and her daughter Kiyah are my neighbors. We live in a low-income housing development built specifically for people with modest means. Modest meaning: There aren't doctors, lawyers, or even insurance salesman gracing our block parties.

Our development is comprised of one-hundred single-family houses centered around a playground/picnic area complete with a regulation horseshoe pit. The houses are either 1970's split-foyer or ranch style. I live in the smaller, split-foyer model. A lot of house for a single woman, but condo and apartments are scarce in our community. After the six months I lived in a trailer court, I grew to dislike anything shaped like a shoebox. Hard to believe my house is considered a step up.

In reality, I'd only traded tin for tin. These houses

were slapped together quickly with cheap building materials, saving the state and the taxpayers precious dollars. It doesn't help that few of the homeowners take pride in their houses. Trucks on blocks and broken plastic yard toys are acceptable forms of landscaping. Besides the Indian reservations, low-income housing is the Midwestern equivalent of a big city ghetto.

I opened Leanne's file. Disturbing the peace. Figured. Evidently she'd had a more interesting Wednesday night than usual. Deputy John responded to the call placed by the boyfriend's neighbors. Seemed Leanne and Bobby were arguing on his porch at three in the morning. Drunk, naked and hysterical, she'd failed to make her point with Bobby and was pissed off at Deputy John's intrusion. She piped down only under the threat of an additional charge of drunk and disorderly. Her court date was set for two weeks from Thursday.

I wondered where she'd stashed Kiyah that night. Had she been in that trailer listening to her mother's drunken rantings? Or had Leanne left her alone again? I pored over the report but John hadn't made mention of a child. How could she possibly justify leaving a six-year old kid home alone?

Leanne Dobrowski epitomized white trash. Sober, she wasn't half-bad, but add alcohol and men, and Kiyah ceased to exist. Leanne excused her behavior because of the stresses of single parenthood. She claimed she deserved to cut loose on occasion. But the occasional nights of partying turned into entire drunken weekends. People wandered in and out of the house at all hours, lately not restricted to Saturdays and Sundays. I've got nothing against the choices an adult makes except when it adversely affects a child.

It affects Kiyah. For two years we've been pals, and the sweetness I cherish in her is rapidly disappearing. Her innocence has been replaced by skepticism, her childlike joy held in reserve. Am I drawn to her because of some latent mothering gene? Or because she's part Lakota, like my brother Ben? Some things are better left unanalyzed. I love her and she simply accepts it.

On weekends she sneaks over for cookies. We color pictures and watch silly videos. She fills the tub with bubbles and emerges pink and clean. Sometimes it's her only bath for the week. Leanne doesn't bother with details like clean clothes, or nutritious meals. I do, even while knowing that someday Kiyah will break my heart.

At eight o'clock the Sheriff approached my desk. Without preamble he asked, "Who gave you the fat lip?"

Unconsciously, my tongue darted over the swollen skin. "Nobody you know. Why?"

"Well, that coupled with the fact you slept here last night makes me wonder." The chair nearly groaned when his solid muscle frame dropped down into the plastic seat. "I know we don't always see eye to eye, but you wouldn't let that fella you're seeing use you as a warm up, would ya?"

"No." I hid my surprise at his concern. "Actually, it happened at the bar last night."

"A bar fight at Dusty's?" He frowned at the stack of papers on my desk. "I didn't hear anything about it."

"That's because I was at Fat Bob's."

One black eyebrow winged up. "Fat Bob's? The biker bar? What the hell were you doing in that rat hole?"

I fiddled with my slim Bic pen wishing it were the world's longest cigarette. Waving it around, a la Bette Davis might make it easier to evade. God. Maybe I *was* watching too many hours of "American Movie Classics."

"Look. You're going to find out sooner or later."

His pupils narrowed to fine points. "Find out what?"

"That Kevin had been hired to find that girl."

"The one they found floating in the creek last week?"

"Yeah. He asked for my help and I agreed to lend a hand."

"Before or after they found her?"

"After."

He considered my answer. "Does Rapid City PD know about Kevin's connections to the case?"

"I assume so. Don't they know about most everything?"

"Yeah. Why did Kevin ask you?"

Sheriff Richards didn't approve of my moonlighting gig. Although there were conflicts of interests between the private and the public sectors, no law said I couldn't do both. Still, I'd never lied to him about anything involving my work with Kevin, nor did I use my access to privileged information to benefit Kevin's business. But, if the Sheriff found out about my involvement from anyone besides me, I'd be seriously screwed. I'd been warned before and his threats were never idle.

"Because Kevin and I went to school with the girl's mother."

"This case isn't somehow tied to your brother's?"

"No. But you know I can't get into the details." I smiled amiably. "Client privilege and all that crap."

He dry-washed the thick black whiskers on his chin. "Did Kevin consider this might not be the easiest situation for you to deal with?"

My mouth automatically opened to protest, but was stopped by the combination of his strange hesitation and enormous palm in front of my face.

"Ben's case eats at you, Julie. I see it everyday. Doesn't this make it worse, to bring back all your unanswered questions?"

Ben's case did gnaw at me until my insides were raw. "Yes," I admitted, "but Ben's murder is always there, the questions never go away. Samantha Friel left people behind that have those same questions. They deserve to know the truth. If we find it, maybe then they'll find peace."

"Will their peace offer you any?"

I stared at the uncharacteristic kindness softening his normally harsh features. The lump in my throat was difficult to swallow without the benefit of salty tears, but somehow I managed. "I don't know."

"Think about it. And remember what I said to you from the beginning. Don't go messing in something that'll make a mess for this office. You're a good worker, but no one is irreplaceable." He stood, turned on his heel, and disappeared into his office.

It'd taken him longer to get to the point than I'd imagined, but it was crystal clear nonetheless.

After my shift ended, I stopped at the Kum-n-Go for a six-pack. God, I love small communities. No one thought it odd when I flipped through magazines, checked the expiration date on the chip dip in the dairy case, and chatted with Melinda, the weekend clerk, about the escapades of her twelve cats.

Yeah, I was stalling. Part of me didn't want to go home and find out if Ray darkened my doorstep. As flippant and cool as I imagined myself, it was never easy ending an intimate relationship. And it was way past time to make the break with Ray.

Ray's truck wasn't parked in my driveway, unless he'd gone incognito and was currently cruising around in a rusted out Chrysler K car sporting Pennington County plates. My gaze narrowed to the two small figures sitting on my steps. Meredith Friel. And Kiyah. Although I didn't believe little bitty Meredith was capable of killing her sister, I didn't know her. Hence, I didn't trust her, especially not with Kiyah.

Kiyah giggled. Strange, that Kiyah didn't seem to have a problem trusting Meredith, and Kiyah was pretty tight-fisted with her trust.

Brown bag clutched in one hand, I headed up the steps.

Meredith spoke first. "I hope you don't mind. When you said I could contact you anytime . . ." She glanced away with that sheepish, embarrassed look teenaged girls do so well.

"No. That's fine. I see you've met my pal, Kiyah." I smiled at Kiyah, ruffled the greasy hair that hadn't been close to a bottle of shampoo in several days. "Hey, Yippee Ki-yi-ay, whatcha doin'?"

Kiyah stood, eagerly banding her thin arms around my middle. She backed off so quickly I wondered if I imagined her spontaneous hug. "Momma sent me outside to play. But I came over to wait for you."

Pleased as I was that Kiyah would rather be with me, I knew it wasn't normal. And I wanted normal for her: riding bikes with neighborhood kids, a best friend, and weekends packed with birthday and slumber parties.

But mostly I wanted someone to give a shit whether or not she was lonely. Or hanging with a thirty-four year old woman with problems of her own. Someday all these questions would have answers, but not today. I smiled again and extracted a can. "You wanna go grab a couple of sodas for you and Meredith?"

Kiyah's chin dropped to her chest and she shuffled her feet. Her dirty, bare feet. The sour taste in my mouth was not entirely attributed to the yeasty tang of beer.

"I'm not thirsty, but can I watch *Dexter's Lab?*"

"Sure."

She showed her toothless grin and raced inside.

Meredith faced me. "You don't lock your doors?"

"Nothing here worth stealing. Besides, everyone knows I work for the sheriff."

"You work for the sheriff?" Her skin went milk pale. "But . . . but I thought you worked for Mr. Wells?"

"Only when he asks or I'm short on cash. Public servants are notoriously underpaid. Why?"

"No reason."

I withdrew my cigarettes and lighter and fired one up.

Meredith pulled a pack of Virginia Slims from her backpack-sized purse. "Thank God," she said after exhaling with gusto. "I was afraid you were one of those crusading nonsmokers."

Apparently my snort of disgust was an adequate enough answer, and for a while we smoked in peace.

"Don't suppose I could have one of those?" She pointed to my open Coors.

"Afraid not."

She sighed. "You wonder why I'm here, don't you?"

"The thought had crossed my mind."

Her intense gaze landed on my split lip and the

kaleidoscope explosion of black, blue, purple, and green under my chin. "Did Dick do that?"

I kept cool, wondering how she knew about my run-in with her father. I considered lifting my shirt and showcasing the trio of bruises he'd gifted my ribs, but decided she'd probably bolt. Thinking your father is a monster is entirely different than having the hard, cold facts laid bare before you.

I shrugged.

"Dick called Tony this morning. I overheard your name and Fat Bob's and, well, I don't have to be a detective to figure it out." She peered at me curiously. "Are you all right?"

"Yeah. Doesn't matter."

"Sure it does. That means you found out something."

Her earnest faith made me wish I had information that would bring a sparkle to her serious brown eyes. "Meredith, why *are* you here?"

Switching her gaze to the tip of her cigarette, she looked like a younger version of Shelley. "I don't know," she said. "Feeling guilty probably."

"Why?"

"Because of that." She glanced at my mouth. "Knowing Dick I'm sure there's more you're not showing me. Or telling me."

It was hard letting her struggle, but I did it anyway.

"But I understand, because I wasn't completely honest

with you guys last night," she said after a time.

I popped the top on another can. "I figured."

She genuinely seemed surprised. "You did?"

"Yeah, but what I can't figure out is why. We're the good guys, Meredith."

"I know. But I wasn't sure I could trust you."

"Me specifically?"

"No." She inhaled and blew smoke out the side of her mouth. "Mr. Wells."

I didn't comment. Trust is two-way. "You should understand I won't keep any information from him. So, if you're not sure you should tell me whatever it is you've driven twenty miles to get off your chest, then don't."

She gaped for a split second but composure settled over her features, giving the appearance of age beyond her years. "I didn't trust him because David hired him."

"Refresh my memory," I said casually, savoring the cold brew. "Didn't you tell us last night that you didn't think David killed Samantha?"

"I don't believe he killed her, but that doesn't mean I don't think he wasn't somehow indirectly involved in her death."

My pulse leapt, but I kept my face noncommittal as I steadily smoked and drank. "I don't understand."

"I know." Meredith flattened the cigarette butt under the boot heel of her black Skechers. "I lied. Not only to you guys, but to the Rapid City cops, Dick, and Shelley. Everyone."

"Why?"

"Sam asked me to."

The dry air filled with the uneasy promise of things I wasn't sure I wanted to hear. "Was this a little white lie?"

"No. It's a whopper of a lie." She faced me and dropped the bomb. "I know *exactly* where Sam spent those last two weeks."

CHAPTER FOURTEEN

MY MOUTH DID ONE OF THOSE cartoonish drops to the floor. I was pretty sure my eyes bugged out. "*What* did you say?"

Meredith's smug smile was the first true sign of her age. "You heard me. I know where Sam was hiding."

"Where?"

"At my Grandma Rose's house."

Thank God she didn't drag out her answer to build the drama. I exhaled in a whoosh, unaware I'd trapped air in my lungs. "Why didn't you tell anyone?"

"Like I said, Sam told me not to. Grandma spends winters in Arizona. Sam had a key and crashed there."

"Didn't your Grandma realize someone had been staying there when she came back for Sam's funeral?"

Meredith's feathery hair brushed her thighs in a sad shake of her head. "She didn't come back for the funeral. She'd just had some kind of hip replacement surgery and couldn't travel."

Little details bored a hole in my brain. "Sam never checked into a motel up on East North, did she?"

"No." She had the grace to look guilty. "She told David that so he wouldn't know where she was."

"Why? If they were . . ."

"Whatever they once were, something changed and Sam didn't trust him. Happened right after David's father came to see her, and right before Dick kicked her out." Seemed old Chuck had been skulking around. But why?

"When was Charles LaChance at your house?"

"Before you ask what they talked about, I'll tell you I don't know. I really don't. They stayed outside."

By the haunted expression on her face I knew she wasn't withholding anything else this time around. "Can you guess?"

"I assumed he wanted her to break up with David because David had spilled the details about Shelley's rape. He didn't want them getting serious. Or, for Sam to get knocked up." An angry sneer tilted the corner of her mouth. "Anyway, I looked out the window when the yelling started. David's dad got right in her face and then he left."

"What happened after he left?"

"Sam came inside. She was seriously pissed off. Wouldn't even talk to me. Except to say Shelley had better tell the whole truth this time. Then, she didn't come home that night." Meredith curled into a ball, the picture of dejection.

A car passed, sending blue smoke fumes drifting across the steps. A bird twittered. A child laughed somewhere close, yet I felt no connection to normal sounds. Meredith and I were in our own little world, and it wasn't pretty.

"Is that why she and Dick had a fight?"

"Yeah. Normally he didn't give a rip about anything she did, but after Shelley's little confession, he treated Sam worse than dog shit. Watched her like a hawk whenever he was around."

She used the toe of her boot to dig the weeds out of the cracks on the sidewalk.

"He called Sam a whore. Said if she wanted to fuck around like her mother she could live someplace else. He even suggested she should go pro. Then, at least she could support herself."

I lit a cigarette and handed the pack to Meredith, not trusting myself to speak. I almost handed her a beer. God knew she deserved it after the hell she'd lived through. Ever the upstanding adult, I refrained.

"Course, Sam didn't help matters, saying she'd prefer living under a bridge screwing strange men to spending another minute with a loser like him." Meredith gnawed on her lip as she unconsciously curled her fist. "Her parting shot was the reason he tossed her out."

"What did she say?"

"She'd rather have the entire world know she was conceived in rape than have anyone ever believe Dick Friel was her father. He threw her out and forbid RJ and me from ever talking to her again."

Pins and needles poked my butt and I shifted back on the steps. Meredith flinched. I knew Shelley wasn't the only one in the Friel household subjected to Dick's wrath. "When did you hear from her?"

"Only twice more. Once to say she was hiding out at Grandma's."

"Have you been to your Grandma's since . . ."

"Of course." She scowled. "That's the first place I looked."

I imagined a grieving fifteen-year old tossing the place in hopes for clues to her sister's disappearance. So much for preservation of the scene. Once the cops found out that Meredith had withheld information on a murder case, she'd be in huge trouble. I couldn't let that happen. Kevin and I needed to see where Sam had been holed up and figure out why, without interference. Then we'd turn over the information to the police, putting an end to this unholy mess.

"Meredith, Kevin and I need to take a look at your Grandma's house. Can you get us in there tomorrow?"

"Tomorrow's Sunday?" She looked thoughtful. "Sure, if we can do it in the morning. About nine thirty? I'll tell Dick I'm going to church. That's the last place he'd ever look for me."

I ripped off a piece of the paper bag and dug in my purse for a pen. "Write down the address and we'll meet you." I watched as she scribbled. "Earlier, you said Sam contacted you twice. What did she want?"

"She needed money and told me to put it in Grandma's mailbox. Said once she had everything figured out, she'd call me." She wasn't quick enough to blink the tears away. "I never heard from her again."

I wanted to offer comfort, I really did, but words failed me. My arms should've encircled her. Instead, they felt encased in concrete, hanging uselessly by my side. Jesus. I was pathetic.

"It never gets any better, does it?" she said in a small, impossibly young voice that reminded me of Kiyah.

"No. Some days are better than others." I remembered my chat with the sheriff. "It never goes away completely. You never forget."

"Are you gonna tell me how *you* know about all this grief shit, or do I hafta ask?"

I smiled at her. Meredith Friel was going to be okay. Never the same, but okay nonetheless. I gave her the short version of my life and Ben's death. She didn't ask too many questions, just nodded in all the right places.

Our quiet discussion was interrupted by Leanne, from next door, standing on her steps and yelling, "Kiyah! Get your ass in here *now*. We gotta go." The screen door would've slammed shut behind her if it hadn't been busted in two.

I collected the empty beer cans before I stood. "Guess that means Kiyah should head home before Mommy Dearest leaves her to her own devices."

Meredith blinked. "Alone? Isn't she like, six?"

"Yep." Curious about her reaction, I asked, "Didn't Shelley and Dick ever leave you alone when you were a kid?"

Her gaze flicked to Leanne's ramshackle house, the untended yard, the junker car in the driveway. "No. I was never alone. I always had Sam. Always."

"You were lucky."

"I know. Sometimes I think she'll come barreling through the door and yell at me for messing with her stuff. God, I'd give anything just to have her scream at me. I miss her so much." She wiped her hand under her nose. "Stupid, huh?"

"No." I couldn't eke out another word without falling apart for what we'd both lost.

She stood and turned back to me after she'd reached the street. "You'll still work on the case? Even after what happened last night with Dick?" Her brown eyes held the first glimmer of hope I'd seen. "I *will* see you tomorrow?"

I nodded and watched her drive away. Kiyah scooted home immediately, not bothering to say goodbye.

The walls inside my house didn't morph into anything

interesting for the hour or so I stared at them. Beige walls. Blank mostly, unlike the white noise spinning in my brain. The thoughts would eventually turn gray. Then black. I felt myself retreating into the dark place I avoided. Once submerged sometimes it took days, or even weeks to resurface. I didn't have that luxury now.

I called Kevin. No answer. I left a message and didn't dwell on what activities he and Callous Lilly were indulging in that excluded answering the phone. Jimmer was always up for something. Partying. A movie marathon. Once, we'd even gotten lit and tried cow tipping only to find it was a myth.

I dialed his number and waited. He wasn't home either. Seemed I was completely alone. My own sorry company wasn't appealing. I almost called Missy. I debated on calling Ray. When I seriously considered phoning my dad, I locked the front door, grabbed the bottle of Don Julio, and went straight to bed.

But my dreams offered me no rest and were far from sweet.

Tiara clad, my mother sits atop a homecoming float, smiling coyly, her golden curls shimmer as she waves her gloved hand beauty pageant style. She looks exactly as she did at seventeen. The blurred edges of the dream hide the fact I didn't know my mother at her age seventeen, or at my own.

Her name is chanted in secret whispers: *Samantha, Samantha*.

I pause with confusion. Why is everyone calling her Samantha?

While the marching band drones on and collectively stumbles over miles of black cables, my mother/Samantha, tosses small squares of Bazooka Bubblegum and wax paper-wrapped taffy. The blacktop is littered with candy, but no other children rush forth to claim the treats. I look around slowly. I am not merely in the crowd; I am the crowd, the only one, the lone bystander. But she still doesn't notice me.

My shouts for her attention battle with the wailing trumpets. Diverted by a flock of blackbirds, she gazes above my head and points as she waves, not at me, but the black mist I feel creeping over my shoulder. I don't want to look, fearing if I do, she'll disappear forever. Helplessly, I turn my face into the damp, wet softness, and close my eyes, expecting the comforting scent of my mother's Jean Nate' perfume.

But I gag against the hated odor of overripe apples mixed with the sour stench of decaying leaves. Those autumn smells remind me of the season she died.

Then, I do remember, in a sick, slow motion. She *is* dead.

I force the horror away and my eyes open to find the parade stopped. A crowd surrounds me. The happy sounds buzz and hum, comforting, yet disconcerting. Frantically, I now look for Samantha, but she no longer rides atop the float. She is hiding.

This is a game. I'm angry because I don't want to play and she is winning. I am obsessed with finding her; I am obsessed with filling my pockets with sweets. I drop to my knees and crawl through the maze of legs, greedily shoving pieces in the pockets of my yellow windbreaker. One butterscotch disk is kicked out of my reach, and I scramble faster, closer to the float.

The crowd vanishes. Again, I see why no other child bothered with this last piece of precious candy. Not only is it broken, but next to it an ankle pokes out from underneath the float — a bloody, nylon covered ankle still wearing a low-heeled silver pump. A shoe worn by a beauty queen.

I scream. I scream until I'm hoarse. I move forward to touch the shoe, and the foot curls up under the float, like the witch's shoe in *The Wizard of OZ*. Frightened, I turn away and stumble, and am righted by steady hands. I fling myself into the unfamiliar arms, grip the neck tightly, pleading if I had one more chance, I'd never let go, not for any reason, not for anything, not for anyone.

A sticky beard burns my face. I struggle, but am trapped against a body covered with hair. A hot breath whispers across my repulsed flesh, "It's too late. You are always too late."

I jerk back to try to catch a glimpse of the stranger's face. But my brother Ben is standing there, wooden as a drugstore Indian.

Then, I am plunged into icy cold water and everything goes dark.

I wake soaked in my own sweat, fear, and tears.

Kevin's call woke me at seven. I'd finally fallen asleep about four, but that restful REM cycle eluded me. I showered, sucked down a half a pot of coffee, and drove into town.

My skin prickled, but my rearview mirror remained empty. I had the oddest feeling someone was following me. Ridiculous. I chalked it up to residual effects from the nightmare.

At the small café near his condo, Kevin had already staked out a corner booth in the nonsmoking section. I gazed at him critically as I walked over. He probably was unaware of how spiffy he looked in khaki pants and an olive green sweater. I wasn't. But was it for my benefit or Lilly's?

I slid across from him and smiled. Without my smoke hazed around him, I was acutely aware of how clean he smelled. Still wearing a smile, I debated on running my finger across the back of his hand, bringing it to my lips for a nibbling kiss. I snapped upright. What the hell was wrong with me? I spend one terrified night alone and I'm hungering for Kevin like he's breakfast?

"You look like hell," he said. "Rough night?"

His lack of flattery put everything back in perspective. "No. I went to bed early. Why?"

"No reason." He folded his newspaper and leaned in. "So tell me."

I relayed my conversation with Meredith. Kevin didn't say much, just kept his gaze steadily on me. "You might make a full-fledged PI yet, young apprentice," he said, in his bad Yoda imitation when I'd finished.

"Great. As if my goals in life aren't pathetic enough." I slurped the last drop of coffee. "Let's go. We're taking your car."

Grandma Rose's house was another one of those 1970 split-level types, tucked at the end of a secluded cul-de-sac. No wonder no one had noticed Samantha hanging around. Meredith had parked her car in front of the garage and poked her head out the minute we set foot on the steps.

"I can't stay long," she said, her eyes refusing to make contact with Kevin's. "Dick is acting his usual asshole self. Expects me to show him a Sunday church bulletin so I've gotta stop and get one on my way home."

I lifted a brow. "Is everything okay?"

"Yeah." She smoothed the lines of her black skirt and opened the door.

Kevin bent down and removed his loafers; I slipped out of my moccasins.

The tiny house was stuffy but clean. Too clean, I thought as I checked out around the living room for items belonging to a teen-age girl, amidst the floral brocade sofas and coffee table covered with every Hummel figurine imaginable.

"It looked like this when I came in. I didn't mess with anything," Meredith said.

"Good thinking," Kevin said.

I stood in front of a china hutch filled with Fostoria crystal. Sadness and anger gave me a one-two punch in the gut. My mother had owned some of these same pieces. They were the wedding gifts and birthday presents which had chronicled the special moments of her life. Too bad my father's new wife thought them tacky and donated the whole lot to Goodwill.

Kevin searched while Meredith and I watched.

"I take it Sam wasn't messy?" he asked, sifting through stacked papers on the oak buffet with the eraser of a pencil.

"God, no. Sam was a neat freak. Kept her side of the room clean and organized. I hated it, 'cause I'm a pig." Meredith trailed her fingers over the yellow rose pattern on the back of the couch. "Do you know if they found her rosary?"

He shook his head. "Was Sam the type to keep a diary?"

I nearly fell over. Now why hadn't *I* thought of that? Most teen-aged girls had an outlet for their angst whether it was music, writing, church, or something less wholesome. Guess Jedi Master Kev was right; I was still in the PI apprentice stage.

"No," Meredith said. "But she did have one of those silly day planners with kittens on the cover. Wrote everything in it, homework assignments, phone numbers, church choir practice times. Wouldn't give it up even after I gave her a rash of crap about being anal."

My gaze locked with Kevin's. We couldn't possibly be that lucky. "Do you think it's here?"

"She forgot it at our house when Dick threw her out. The police took it."

Damn. Kevin shrugged and moved into the kitchen. I followed, wondering if Sam had found another place to jot things down.

Course, I was disappointed by the state of the kitchen. No dirty dishes littered the orange Formica countertops. The garbage can hadn't been ransacked for clues, leaving smelly rubble on the faded linoleum floor. The refrigerator was empty.

Kevin wrapped a tea towel around the avocado slim line phone. "Disconnected," he said. He turned to Meredith. "Show me where she was sleeping."

They left the kitchen and I wandered to the table,

careful not to touch anything. The cops didn't need extra prints — especially mine — to muck things up. I gazed out the window to the backyard. Looked like this was another dead-end. What had I expected? A hastily written note detailing who Samantha had thought wanted to kill her and why?

A repetitive chirping interrupted my frustrated musings. I listened, following the source of the squawk to a cuckoo clock. The bird popped out five more times, signaling nine o'clock. I glanced at my watch and frowned. It was ten. Apparently the clock hadn't been set ahead after the spring daylight savings time change. My gaze dropped to the calendar hanging on the side of the fridge next to the clock. A glossy picture with bouquets of tulips announced the month. April. Scribbles filled the square blocks of several days.

My frown deepened. It didn't make sense. If someone had changed the calendar to the right month, why not the clock too? Especially considering their close proximity? I squinted at the loopy handwriting. Pretty girlish for a grandmother.

Who hadn't been in here in months.

Bing. Light bulb. As usual, Sam had been chronicling the events of her last days. But not in the kitty day planner.

I yelled for Kevin.

CHAPTER
FIFTEEN

LIFE IS FILLED with compromises.

I wanted to steal the calendar. Kevin didn't. So we didn't.

Instead, we copied the information into one of the notebooks Meredith uncovered in Samantha's bedroom. Kevin decided that Meredith, in the guise of being helpful, should point out her Grandmother's vacant house in another day or two. Kevin said purposely keeping the cops out of the loop was career suicide, but we needed a head start. And the information on the calendar was our first lead.

At the café we fit the dates into a timetable.

"Shelley was right. Sam did try counseling elsewhere. Looks like she waited a couple of days."

"Meredith was right too," I pointed out. "Sam didn't take Shelley's suggestion since she tried a different

Catholic church."

Kevin snapped his sleeve back and frowned at his Seiko. "Meredith also said something about the priests in their parish being old, right?"

"Yeah. So?"

"Think this Father Tim is 'young and hip' to the scene? Is that why Sam switched? Found someone to confide in that might understand?"

"Beats me," I said. "Father Tim. Think that's his real name?"

"Why wouldn't it be?"

"Seems too easy just to call up the diocese office and ask at which heavenly branch Father Tim usually works."

He didn't even crack a smile.

We decided to try every Catholic church in town. Since it was still early on the Lord's Day, I hoped we'd get lucky and not have to drag this out for more than one Sunday.

"Even if we do find him, he probably won't tell us anything."

"Why not?"

Kevin gave me his patented, you-are-an-idiot look. "Ever heard of priest confidentiality?"

Duh. I'd suffered through an episode or two of *Father Dowling Mysteries.*

"You think this is a dead-end?"

"I hope not. But I'm beginning to think this *case* is at a dead-end. We found where Sam spent the last two weeks.

By all rights, David should decide if we should continue."

"Well, I think it's worth a try."

Coffee sloshed over the rim of the cup as he checked the illuminated face of his watch again. Then he shuffled the two pathetic sheets of paper — a pretense of studying our meager notes.

I pulled the notes from his hands. "Okay, what's up?" Kevin glanced at me sharply. "What?"

"You've looked at your watch twice in the last five minutes. You late for an appointment?"

"Sort of. Lilly and I have brunch reservations at Sylvan Lake Lodge." Fiddling with his sleeve, he rechecked the time. "In an hour."

I waited, giving him ample time to consider his idiotic statement. When he didn't become contrite, I said, "We finally get a break and you're gonna run off and 'do brunch'?" I supposed it was marginally better than him running off to do *Lilly*. Still, it wasn't jealousy; I had no desire to search for Father Tim alone. I'd had enough of my own company last night. "Jesus, Kevin. When did you let Lilly tie a string around your dick?"

He stared at me, his expression somewhere between incredulous and cruel. "Do you always have to be so crude?"

Sufficiently put in my place, my cheeks flamed, but my cheap shot didn't make the facts untrue.

"Sorry if it offended your delicate sensibilities. But blowing this off to get your fair share of quiche Lorraine and apple brown Betty is ridiculous. You asked for my help on this case, I didn't volunteer." Might as well play the final queen bitch card, seeing as he'd already cast me in that role. The last swig of my latte' didn't sweeten my words. "And, I've yet to see a paycheck."

The padded chair banged into the wall when he stood. As he strode away from me, he unclipped his cell phone. I followed a minute later. Screw his privacy. I needed a cigarette and wasn't about to wait with bated breath for him to dismiss me. I'd been summarily dismissed enough in the last week. Had he called Lilly at his house? Or hers? His hostile look prevented an inquiry.

"You ready?" he asked in that brusque tone which always makes my hackles rise.

"Seriously? You just cancelled your date with her?"

"Yep." His long, angry strides ate the distance to his car.

I chased him, relieved I wasn't stumbling in high heels. "So, is Lilly gonna have a cow? Make you pay for this later?"

"Not likely, since I blamed it on you." He climbed in and slammed the door.

Great. I slid in, flipped on the CD player, not caring what music spewed out as long as it masked the thorny silence.

Our first stop was St. Augustine's. People dressed in Sunday finery milled about the parking lot; two priests stood outside the rectory, glad-handing parishioners. We watched without comment for several minutes. I turned when Kevin whistled softly. "What?"

He pointed to the priests. "See that one, brown curly hair, young, he's got his back to us now? Watch when he turns around."

I got eye strain studying the man, even when he faced us. Nothing about him made me gasp and say, "Oh, my God! It's him!" He did seem sort of familiar, but I gave up. "Okay. Am I supposed to recognize him?"

"Yeah. Remember Tim O'Reilly?"

Vaguely. We hadn't exactly hung out with that crowd. My thoughts clicked to sophomore year in high school and my one wild night of partying with the senior class studs at some cheerleader's house; Troy James, football star and his group of hangers-on including big-mouthed jackass, Danny Christopherson, brooding Bobby Adair, know-it-all Mike Lawrence, and token funny man, Tim O'Reilly.

Tim had kept everybody in stitches as we'd played quarters. Even in my drunken oblivion I remembered he'd had a wicked sense of humor, one of those lovable life-of-the-party guys all teenage girls love to hang around with but wouldn't be caught dead dating. Is that why he'd turned to the priesthood? No better offers?

"No way," I said.

"Way," Kevin countered. "Looks like we've found our Father Tim. Let's get to him before another old lady bends his ear."

We skirted the piles of construction material blocked off by yellow tape. I took a fleeting look at the huge skeletal structure of concrete, two-by-fours and roof trusses. It appeared the coffers in this church were full if they were putting on an addition that rivaled the Sistine Chapel. Father Tim opened the elaborately hand-carved wooden door and disappeared inside the black hole.

Kevin hustled after him. I tried to keep up, but being a smoker and not all that thrilled at finding myself in church, I lagged behind. By the time I caught up, Kevin was grinning and pumping Tim's hand. The tail end of the conversation drifted to me down the dark hallway.

"I know. Joining the priesthood shocked a lot of people, but it just seemed right. I was lucky enough to get assigned back in Rapid City three years ago." He spun toward me when Kevin glanced over his shoulder.

No handshaking for me. Tim enveloped me in a suffocating hug. He stepped back and memorized every pore, burgeoning wrinkle, and weighed the luggage under my eyes.

"Julie, Julie. I'm sure you hear this all the time, but you haven't changed a bit since high school. Still drinking beer, listening to loud music, and chasing boys?"

"Until the day I die," I said with a real grin, taking in his unlined face and choirboy smile. Upon closer examination, he hadn't changed much either.

"So what are you two doing here? Thinking about

joining?" He rubbed his hands together in mock glee. "Been a long time since I've done a conversion."

"No. Actually, we've got some questions." Kevin gestured to the long stone hallway surrounding us. "Can we go someplace private?"

"Sure, my office is right down there. Watch the construction. They've moved inside this week to repair the choir loft."

Once inside the tomb-like room, Tim tugged at his vestment. "If you don't mind, I'd like to change." He pointed to the chairs facing his desk. "Make yourselves comfortable."

When he exited the room through a small door, I wondered where it went. To a secret passageway that led directly to God? I stuffed the sarcasm and studied his office.

The dark room was manly, but impressive. A rough-hewn timber desk dominated the space; every horizontal inch was piled high with papers, hymnals, and ledgers. Behind the pine monstrosity hung several paintings, religious in nature, and strands of rosaries. But the breathtaking stained glass window above it all had sucked me into a state of near euphoria.

Hard to believe that a person with an aversion to organized religion had a Jones for the works of art created in the name of God, but I did. This spectacular window offered vibrant hues of blue and purple which bled into red and orange as dawn broke over the lush golden hill of Mt. Calvary, illuminating the three empty crosses. The simplicity shook me, as did the artist's unspoken promise that some things lasted an eternity. If one believed. I didn't, and luckily, Kevin's voice broke through my reverie before I dropped to my knees, crossed myself and handed over my wallet.

"You okay?"

I nodded, flopping into the navy wing back chair next to him as Father Tim re-entered the room.

"Much better," he sighed, still wearing a collar but not formal service robes. "Now, what can I do for you? I'm assuming this isn't a social visit?"

"No." Kevin smiled. "But, I don't know if you can help us. I'm sure you've heard about Samantha Friel?"

Father Tim nodded sagely. "An awful, awful thing."

"I was hired to find her." He handed Tim a business card. "To make a long story short, we've come across information that you'd been counseling her. What can you tell us about that?"

Cut to the chase why don't you, Kev?

A startled look momentarily crossed Father Tim's docile face. His gaze dropped to the card, as he lovingly placed it on a prayer book. He steepled his hands, tapping the index fingers on his chin, pursing his lips, giving the appearance of deep thought.

Had he practiced that gesticulation? Was it rule number one in the man-of-the-cloth handbook? Every member of the clergy I'd run across had perfected that placating gesture.

After a few moments he smiled benignly. "I'll admit surprise you knew she'd sought counseling. My impression was she didn't want anyone to know."

"Did she tell you why she wanted to keep her sessions under wraps?"

"She was deeply ashamed." He frowned; a mix of pity and confusion. "I'm afraid I wasn't much help to her."

"How many times did you counsel her?"

"Twice."

I opened my mouth to protest, but Kevin nudged my toe with his and I kept quiet, letting the scene play out.

"Only twice?" Kevin asked mildly.

"Unfortunately, yes. The second visit surprised me because the first one didn't go well."

"Why?"

"Nervousness, shame, I don't really know. She pretty much talked in circles and wouldn't actually get to the point."

"And the second time?"

"Basically the same story." He shifted back into his chair, digging his finger under the white strip. "I wished I could've helped her, especially after I heard . . ."

Kevin nodded as if in agreement, but said, "And yet you didn't call the police. Why?"

My partner Kevin. Mr. Smooth.

The good Father removed his hands from his throat and drummed them on his desk. "I'm sure it seems strange, but I had good reason. First, she didn't tell me anything relevant. Second, whatever she would've told me, I'm honor bound to keep in confidence. Ethically and legally."

His grin showed far too many pointy teeth to be considered benevolent.

The door burst open and a rough voice intoned, "Goddammit, Tim, I'm sick of . . ." An overall-clothed man wielding a hammer stopped dead in his tracks upon seeing us. "Shit. Didn't know you had people in here."

Father Tim stood and glared at the man. "You'll have to forgive Bobby. Working on construction sites gives him a colorful vocabulary, and sometimes he even forgets he's in a church."

I tilted my head. Now, *him* I recognized immediately. He'd been the only guy in high school that had boasted a full beard. I withheld a shudder. "Bobby? Bobby Adair?"

Bobby straightened and gave me a fierce once-over, then repeated the process on Kevin before his questioning gaze landed on Tim.

Father Tim's bark of laughter filled the room, but it fell shy of jolly. "Rapid City is a small town, isn't it? Bobby, you remember Julie Collins? And Kevin Wells? They graduated a couple of years after us. Bobby is the indispensable foreman on our construction project."

Bobby muttered and sent his scabby hand toward

Kevin. "Still playing round ball?"

"Nah." Kevin shook back with gusto. "Pretty much quit after high school. You?"

"Played a little in the service, work the sweets offa Tim occasionally, but nothing serious."

"Not true," Father Tim interjected. "We work out down at the Cornerstone Rescue Mission at least once a week. You know, to encourage those guys to consider physical activity as a replacement for alcohol and drugs."

"Hasn't worked so far," Bobby sneered. "Like a bunch of drunken Indians are any kind of challenge."

His words were like a cold dash of unholy water. I went absolutely rigid.

Father Tim sent him another infuriated look.

Kevin, sensing my rage, swiftly changed the subject. "Miss playing ball, but I've taken up hunting since I moved back. Got a friend that deals in guns."

Bobby's ears perked up. "Who's your friend?"

"Jimmer Cheadle."

He nodded approval. "I've known Jimmer for years, great guy. Bought my last rifle from him."

"Yeah? What did you get?"

"H-S Precision Series 2000 take-down with a Swarovski scope."

Kevin whistled. "Sweet." He turned to Father Tim. "You hunt much?"

"Bobby occasionally drags me along." He shot me a

sidelong glance. "I'd much rather use my time to seek out those that are too afraid to ask for help."

I smiled tightly. "With your different philosophies, I'm surprised to see you guys are still hanging out."

"We don't nearly as much as we used to," Bobby grumbled. Father Tim's face darkened to the color of Mogen David wine before he added a forced smile.

As they exchanged the usual male sport-hunting-my-dick-is-bigger-than-yours bullshit, I considered Bobby, not without malice. Since graduation, he'd kept up his beefy athletic build; most men his age — aging jocks especially — had gone soft in the middle. I'd never understood why he — gifted with a bigger share of athletic fortitude — had always hung on the periphery of Troy James' greatness. Bobby was attractive, almost handsome, even back then. The only reason I'd determined that he hadn't been a babe magnet was his personality resembled a bowl of oatmeal. By his terse answers to Kevin's questions, I gathered nothing had changed on that front.

"Kevin and Julie are working on the Friel case," Father Tim said.

Bobby crossed his arms over his barrel-sized chest. "Got any leads?"

"Besides Dick Friel?" I quipped.

Kevin shot me his, you-have-a-big-mouth look.

"You guys are cops?"

"No," Kevin said.

Kevin didn't elaborate, which was odd. We stood crammed together in a pocket of awkward silence for several heartbeats.

"Well," Father Tim finally said with a strained chuckle, clapping a hand on Bobby's broad shoulder.

Bobby grunted, sidestepping Father Tim and his affable gesture.

"I best get on with whatever new building problem Bobby is itching to berate me about. Sorry I couldn't have been more helpful."

"If you do think of anything else, call me," Kevin said.

"Will do. It was nice seeing you both again. You really should consider coming to Mass." A milky hand swept down the front of his black shirt. "I'm fairly well known for my humorous sermons."

This time his serene smile was directed at me.

Bobby wasn't smiling at all.

Kevin gripped my elbow, leading me to the door, before I could offer my own insincere comments to the conversation.

Strange, that Kevin had usurped my usual broody persona. He waited until we'd pulled into the café parking lot before exploding. "What a load of shit."

"Which part?"

"The whole thing. Father Tim saw her more than once." He pointed to our notes and the five days Samantha had scheduled counseling sessions with Father Tim.

"Just because she wrote it down, doesn't mean she went."

"True. But did you notice he didn't call Sam by name? Not once? Nor did he ask how her parents were doing. Seems strange for a priest used to offering condolences. Doubly strange since he knows both Dick and Shelley."

Kevin faced me, resting his back against the driver's door.

"Another thing. Why did he specifically use the word 'shame' when talking about the way Sam acted? If he didn't know why she needed counseling, why wouldn't he say she was distraught? We're supposed to believe he blithely turned her away because she wouldn't open up? Wrong. Guys like him live for getting to the root of the problem." The side of his temple popped in as he ground his teeth. He stared through me. I was beginning to hate that look.

"Father Tim knew what haunted Sam, knew why Sam was ashamed because Sam told him. In one of those counseling sessions he found out about Shelley. He fucking knew and he did nothing to help Sam. Why? For Christ sake, this guy hangs out at the mission. He's probably heard it all, and seen it all. He's spooked by one harmless sixteen-year-old girl? It doesn't make sense."

"What are we supposed to do now?" I challenged. "An hour ago you were ready to drop the case."

"Not now." Kevin shifted back toward the steering wheel, scrawled something across the bottom of the notebook before checking his watch. "We found Father Tim, that's a start. But in the meantime, Lilly and I can still make a late brunch." The engine turned over. He scrubbed my heel print from the console. "I'll call you tomorrow and let you know what time to pick up your check."

Stumbling from his all but moving car, I pretended his dismissal hadn't stung.

Hah. Tell that to the beehive-sized welt he'd imbedded not only on my ass, but also on my soul.

Damn. Alone again and it was barely noon. Two days in a row was two days too many. What was I supposed to do now?

I did the one thing guaranteed to take the sting out.

I headed to Dusty's.

CHAPTER SIXTEEN

DUSTY'S IS A NO-FRILLS BAR; it's a neighborhood hangout, despite that it stands more than five miles out of town. No atmosphere or pretentious ambience, just a dark place where adults meet to share a drink, play a game of pool, swap lies, and pretend we're still in our carefree youth. Not that we're particularly fond of youth in our bar. College kids stay away; that whole age group isn't impressed with the all-country music choices on the jukebox, the lack of cool movie memorabilia or assorted sports equipment adorning the drab cement walls. Dusty's attracts workers, ranchers, housewives; anyone over the age of thirty tired of non-smoking franchise restaurants and trendy brew pubs.

I walked past the pool tables and dartboards in the front room. Slipping into the patched Naugahyde booth, I glanced around, over the scattered high tables with barstools.

Pat, the bartender, lined my usual drink order on a tray, lifted the partition, and moved past the mirrored bar. I nodded to Mr. Lambert, Dusty's oldest regular, sitting at the end of the shellacked countertop. I kicked off my shoes and burrowed my toes into the space between the cushion and the frame, resting my head back, staring at the ceiling.

The unique ambience that was Dusty's calmed me somewhat.

In an effort to spruce up the cave-like atmosphere, the last painter had dumped multi-colored glitter into the paint. Instead of the illusion of looking into a vast universe, it emphasized the fact that black paint is never the right choice. Now, the ceiling reflects as little as the gray concrete floor.

My beer slid across the table and I smiled at Pat. He grinned back, tobacco-stained teeth a nice contrast to his colorless complexion. A man like Pat, who lives his life in a bar, rarely gets a chance to see daylight, yet he looks remarkably scurvy free. Must be the orange juice in the screwdrivers.

I knew spending Sunday afternoon in the bar wasn't the most productive use of my time. Kevin and I should be tying up the last loose ends for David LaChance, interviewing Shelley a second time. Instead I found myself challenging old Mr. Lambert to a game of pool. Then darts. I beat him both times and didn't care that he was eighty and nearly blind. I'd won and that was good enough for me.

The afternoon passed slowly, not necessarily in a pleasant blur. Mr. Lambert regaled me with stories from what he called his "productive years."

Getting old in a society where people treated their pets better than their elders sucked. No wife, no kids, no friends, being alone sucked. Spending large amounts of time and his retirement funds in a bar sucked. Basically, Mr. Lambert's life sucked. He'd welcome any change.

Even death? I wondered, but didn't have the guts to ask. Or, to hang around him and contemplate that my life was currently headed in that direction. In fifty years would I be the stoop-shouldered blue-haired lady, sitting in the same corner booth, sipping off-brand tequila, sucking breath from an oxygen cylinder, and railing against the cruel world?

I shuddered and knocked back my beer.

Without forty sports channels on twenty big screen TVs, Dusty's is pretty quiet on Sundays. It was the perfect place to brood. Ray hadn't shown up — thank God for small favors. I doubted anyone knew where I was; I doubted anyone cared. But that niggling sensation started at the back of my neck again; too much time had passed for it to be the lingering effects of my nightmare.

When a swarthy Latin man slipped into the seat across from me offering an impious smile, my first reaction was "Thank you, Jesus."

"Julie Collins?" he asked in a low voice that promised delivery of hours of hot, raw sex. He rested his elbows on the table.

I nodded, mesmerized by the brilliance of his white teeth, the strong line of his freshly shaven jaw, his command of every speck of dust in the room.

"He didn't lie." His gaze swept over me, not without extreme interest. "You are everything I've heard. And a blonde to boot."

"Blame my Nordic ancestors."

"I'm thanking them."

He leaned closer. God. A little puddle of drool formed on the center of my tongue. He was just as stunning up close.

"You are a difficult woman to track down."

"Well, you found me," I cooed, lowering my lashes as I demurely traced a finger around the rim of my beer bottle. "Who are you?"

"Tony Martinez."

So much for my prayers being answered. I upended the beer as an excuse to disgorge the tiny lump of dread wedged between my heart and throat. My gaze darted over his black leather vest, standard uniform for the biker crowd, to his bare muscular arms covered in colorful swirls of tattoos. No surprise there, but the vibrant patches sewn onto his vest were eye-catching. And harder than hell to come by.

I faintly remembered a conversation about how

motorcycle club members earned patches. Merits were bestowed for prowess with a gun or knife, longevity and loyalty, daredevil stunts on a bike, and for besting a member of a rival club, either by hospitalization or death. The one that stuck with me most graphically, however, was the "red" badge or some such name, given to a man for going down on a woman during her menstrual cycle. The feat had to be performed in full view of the membership. Although the uniforms and earned patches brought to my mind the Boy Scouts, I doubted they strove for these types of badges.

My eyes narrowed to the circular patch proclaiming him "El Presidente'." Yep. No doubt. Tony Martinez had come looking for me. Why?

"So, how did you find me?"

"Secretary at the sheriff's office said it was your day off. No one answered at your place so I called Jimmer. Said you hung out here." Slowly his gaze took in every nuance that is Dusty's, as he sized up the competition.

"You just showed up?"

"Nah." He angled his head toward the bar. "Called Pat first. He and I go way back. Told me you were here. Alone."

Pat's tip from me dwindled to nothing. I glanced up as the man in question unloaded drinks from his tray. Four bottles of Coors, a full bottle of Don Julio, seal intact, two shot glasses, and a plate of limes.

I sent Pat a questioning stare but he was too busy kowtowing to Tony to notice.

"On the house," he said before scurrying back behind the bar.

Now, I was seriously freaked. Nothing was ever on the house at Dusty's, especially not a hundred dollar bottle of tequila. Tony grabbed a beer, saluted me, and drank. I did the same, not knowing the proper protocol in dealing with the president of a motorcycle club. Had Emily Post written etiquette rules for this social situation? I tilted back in the booth until my spine was fully straight. "So, why are you here?"

He laughed, a rich sound sparking a familiarity of silk sheets. "Harvey said you'd get right to the point."

I scoured the bar for kung fu man without it seeming like that was what I was doing. It didn't work and Tony laughed again.

"Don't worry. He's not here. Helen either."

"If you're expecting an apology for what happened Friday night, you're wasting your time. It was self defense, plain and simple."

His already dark eyes blackened further and he bestowed on me another killer grin. "Funny, that's the same thing I tell my lawyer."

I lit a cigarette. "What do you want? Since you're not here for my apology, are you offering me yours?"

He twisted the top off the tequila bottle, breaking

the seal and poured two shots, placing one in front of me. "Why would I apologize?"

"For the way I was treated in your fine establishment?"

Tony barely nodded a "no." He knocked back the tequila. And waited.

I raised the glass. The sweet sting crawled down my throat and curled in my belly. My cigarette smoldered. I waited. I played the game too.

Only not as well as Tony Martinez. We studied each other until I squirmed. "So? I doubt you're here to re-evaluate my worthiness as a patron."

"You really are a smart ass." His low chuckle sounded menacing, but strangely sexy too. "I find that intriguing, but I'll get right to it. Harvey said you were asking Dick questions about Samantha."

I nodded.

"Why?"

"That's what we were paid to do."

"Find out anything?"

"Besides what Dick's right cross feels like?"

He shrugged, Mr. Cool, settling back against the fake leather like it was a tufted, gilded throne. "It could've been worse."

"How so?"

"If it'd been Harvey that hit you, we'd be having this conversation in the hospital."

I plucked my cigarette from the ashtray and inhaled.

Exhaled. "Are you here warning me off about asking Dick more questions?"

"No. I'm here mostly out of curiosity."

"About me?"

He shook his head. "Why you're digging into things that oughta be left alone. Samantha is dead. Nothing Dick can do to change it."

"Yeah, but did he cause it?" Tony blanched for a second. It was brief, but I saw it. And he knew it. Not so cool after all. Point for me.

"What does Shelley hope to gain from this?"

In the ashtray, I rolled the cherry around the spent ashes, stalling. Tony didn't know any more about this situation than I did. How did I play it? Tell him Shelley hadn't hired us? Or see how far his knowledge extended to Dick's part in the screwed up mess? I smiled coyly. "You know I can't get into the details. Besides, Dick didn't tell me a thing except that he doesn't believe Meredith and RJ are his kids either."

Tony leaned in close enough that I got a whiff of his cologne. Nice.

"Do you believe him?" he asked.

"Doesn't matter if I believe him."

He raised his left brow lazily and drawled, "But you're willing to believe, on Shelley's say-so, that he had something to do with Samantha's death?"

I lifted a shoulder and reached for the bottle of tequila.

When his rough palm closed around mine, every nerve ending in my body went on high alert. Our gazes collided. His didn't falter; mine threatened to under the intensity with which he held my attention and my hand.

"Let me tell you something," he said. "I've known Dick for years. Sure, he cheats customers, lies about his income, taxes, and anything that suits his purpose. He fucks around on Shelley, gets his jollies out of beating on people smaller than he is, and drinks too much. But he's not a killer."

"How do you know?"

He paused and released my hand. "He doesn't have the balls."

"Maybe he . . ."

"Listen. The only reason Dick isn't beat to shit on a weekly basis is because he's under my protection."

"Why is he under your protection?" For a moment I didn't think he'd answer, but he spread his hands wide and shrugged.

"Simple business decision. I need his expertise. He's a mechanical genius and the only one I've found that doesn't give a damn about moving up in my organization. He does what I tell him without question and I make sure no one messes with him."

"Sounds suspiciously like you're defending him."

"I'm not. He's a fucking weasel. He'd screw his own mother for a buck. Everybody in town knows it."

I cocked my head. "And yet you're friends?"

"Business associates. That's it. Whatever he is or does in his off time doesn't concern me."

"Doesn't it concern you when shit happens in his off time in your bar?"

Something dangerous flickered in his eyes. "Momentary lapse in his judgment. Trust me, it's been handled."

That statement and Tony's hard expression pretty much guaranteed I wasn't getting an apology for his pal Dick's behavior, yet I was confused. "How can you trust *him* knowing what he is? What he does? You're telling me he's never double-crossed you?"

His teeth gleamed white in the dark bar. "He's alive, isn't he?"

"Unfortunately. Might as well be dead as much good as he does for Meredith and RJ." I tipped the last swig of the beer into my mouth.

"Is that what you're trying to do? Prove he's unfit?"

I didn't answer.

"Dick's never been the family-type man." He nudged another Coors in my direction. "But then again, Shelley isn't up for Mother-of-the-Year."

He'd get no argument from me. I smoked and pulled the soggy yellow label from the beer bottle in lieu of drinking from it. Faith and Tim warbled a sappy duet from the jukebox; the electronic voice of the dart machine signaled the winner. And I waited.

"No doubt she'll get full custody of those kids even after being in treatment. What do you think of her lawyer?" he said in a tone that couldn't be misconstrued as conversational.

I hesitated, seeming intent on removing the label in one piece because I didn't want Tony to know I wasn't privy to Shelley's legal choices. I did have my suspicions on who she'd hired.

The door burst open, arcing light across our table. I tried not to jump when Tony's low voice drifted to me, breaking the silence.

"He came into the bar three weeks ago."

"Who?"

"Her lawyer, Charles LaChance."

That got my attention. "For what? To talk to Dick about the divorce?"

"No. For a meeting."

I hid my surprise that anyone besides drug dealers willingly conducted business meetings in Fat Bob's bar. Didn't share that observation with the owner, however.

"Who did he meet?"

Tony distractedly swung his empty beer bottle back and forth above the table. Although he looked right at me, he didn't see me. Hell, I recognized that look, but I was used to seeing it on Kevin. Tony was weighing whether he was going to share information.

Finally, he sighed. "Fuck it. I'm sure it's nothing."

"What? Tell me and let me decide."

The bottle stopped moving. "Not if Shelley will use it against Dick."

"She won't."

"How do you know?"

I almost admitted that I wasn't working for Shelley. Instead I gave him my best "Scouts honor" pose and said, "Trust me. It'll stay between us."

"It had better," he said slowly, "'cause if I hear you repeated this, Harvey will stop by for a chat and he ain't nearly as subtle as I am. Be a shame to mess up your pretty face." He exchanged the empty beer bottle for a full one. "LaChance met with my attorney."

"Your attorney?" At least that explained the meeting place. "Why?"

"Because his specialty is child support."

"Child support?" I frowned at the rip at the bottom of the label. "Really?"

"What?" Tony mocked. "You were expecting me to cop to having a criminal defense lawyer on retainer?"

I raised my eyes to his and nodded.

He laughed. "You don't go for the bullshit answer. I like that. Let's just say I've got a greedy ex-wife who thinks child support means bleeding me dry. Christ, if I thought I could get away with offing her, I'd gladly pay the exorbitant criminal defense fees."

"Need I remind you I work for the sheriff's office?

I'm obligated to report anything I hear involving criminal intent."

"Bullshit. You're a *secretary*. Not the same as a lawyer, or even a cop. If you had any power, my bouncers would've landed ass first in jail Friday night, right?"

He had me. And he knew it. Point for him. Guess we were even.

His forearms bulged on the table. "You wanna hear this or not?"

I nodded, trying not to stare at the bloody dagger tattooed up his wrist. Nice work, though. I wondered if the local tattoo artist gave him and his employees a discounted group rate.

"Anyway," he continued in a low baritone that caused an odd flicker in my stomach. "I recommended my attorney to Dick. Figured Shelley had sicced that low-life LaChance on him early, in hopes they wouldn't have to take the custody and support issue to court."

I wasn't drunk, but I wasn't following him. "Back up. You said this happened weeks ago. Before they found Samantha?"

"Yeah. Turns out I was wrong, but it was ballsy move of LaChance to have the meet in Dick's hangout and let him sweat."

"You were wrong? About what?"

"The reason LaChance was sliming up my bar." Frowning, he traced the metal grooves of my lighter. "Bob told me . . ."

I grabbed my lighter; his caress of an inanimate object was making me nervous and jealous. "Who is Bob?"

"Bob Lindt. My attorney."

I whistled. Bob Lindt was an impressive attorney. I didn't bring up that his specialty was family law that bordered on criminal defense. Somehow, I assumed Tony already knew.

"Anyway, Bob was puzzled. Said that LaChance hadn't been interested in the Friel kids or the support issue."

"Not at all?"

"Didn't even bring it up."

"Then, what did they discuss?"

"Mostly, LaChance grilled him about his success rates on the cases he worked involving back child support."

"Back child support?"

"Yeah. Stuff like proving paternity, suing for years worth of missed support. Evidently, if the claim can be made and proven with blood tests, the man in question has to make full restitution, even if he was unaware of the pregnancy." Tony leaned back. "So, I'm curious. Who cares about all that shit? Unless Dick is right and none of those kids are his."

Everything inside me spun. Tony's voice and the bar sounds whirled into a vacuum of nothingness inside my head. Shelley. She'd lied, but hers wasn't a little white one like Meredith's; it was a fucking whopper. She'd known her attackers. With the statute of limitations on rape, that angle was worthless. But back child support? Reached far into the realm of disbelief. Who was devious enough to come up with that idea?

Charles LaChance.

Where did he enter the picture? Or when? In our meeting, Shelley hadn't hidden her feelings about him. Why? Because he'd guessed the truth? Or, because he was slow in finding a solution? Tony's voice roused me.

"And as far as I know, Dick hasn't heard a word from La-Chance." He closed the distance between us. "What has Shelley said?"

"Not a helluva lot. I hadn't a clue that she'd hired him."

"Sounds like you need to pay Shelley a visit."

Lifting the bottle, he filled the shot glasses again.

I'd had plenty, but figured declining Tony's hospitality wasn't in my best interest, especially after what he'd just told me. I drank quickly and sunk my teeth into a lime. When I met Tony's heated gaze, I wished I'd come fully armed.

"What?" I dropped the spent fruit into the ashtray.

"Just wondering how you'd look on the back of my bike." His voice turned silky, "Or, in my bed."

"I thought we were discussing the Friels'?"

"Discussion over. On to a more interesting topic. You." He knocked back a shot. "And me."

I poured another slug, readying myself for this conversation. "Too bad you're not thinking about how I'd look hanging out in your bar."

"Sorry."

His wavy hair brushed his shoulders, making me wonder how it would feel to have those dark locks drifting over my body. Would the heat from his body increase the potency of his cologne?

"Fat Bob's is off limits. Harvey banned you and there's nothing I can do. Gotta have rules, or chaos rules."

Martinez wound a tendril of my hair around his palm, separating the golden strands over the calloused pad of his thumb. "But, you are welcome any time at Bare Assets."

"Bare Assets?" I resisted jerking my head back and leaving Tony with a hank of my hair as a souvenir. "As in the strip club downtown? You own that?"

"It's good to diversify." His gaze lingered on my mouth before he raised those coal black eyes to mine.

A punch of pure lust overloaded my system, which was immediately followed by fear. Hell fire and damn my libido. Tony Martinez was a complication I never needed in my life, especially now, no matter how physically appealing. I shook out a cigarette. He struck a match before I touched the lighter.

"Thanks," I managed through a puff of smoke.

"You didn't answer me."

"Didn't realize it was a question."

"Mmm." He folded his rough-skinned hands. "You're

hedging. So, you avoiding the issue? Or just me?"

"Both."

"Why?" He gaze zeroed in on my bare ring finger. "You involved?"

"No." I paused, thinking of Ray. "That's not it."

"Then, what?"

"You scare the shit out of me."

He smiled.

Guess it didn't bother him that prospective paramours were panicky, so I bent my head close to his. "Look, I think you might have gotten the wrong idea about me. From Harvey or Helen or Jimmer or whoever. If you're expecting some tough chick with a heart of gold, picking fights and getting kicked out of bars in the quest for justice, you've got me pegged wrong. I'm not tough, just screwed up enough to definitely not be yours, or anybody else's type."

"No. You've got it wrong."

"How so?" Ash scattered over the table as I waved my cigarette. "You don't know me, so let me fill you in on all the nasty details." I dragged deeply and blew the smoke right in his face.

He didn't even blink.

"I'm a shitty person. No one likes me, including my family. I've got few friends because of my big mouth. I smoke too much, drink too much, and cuss like a fucking sailor. I barely eke out a living at my dead-end job, and the only woman I know with lousier taste in men is my dead mother."

Tony didn't move, neither did his gaze. I, on the other hand, had the urge to wriggle out of the booth and run like hell.

"Nice try," he said with a sexy smirk, "but I don't buy it. Don't kid yourself, either. Few men would have the balls to tangle with Dick and Helen and Roger and Harvey all in one night. You did. Why? I'm guessing it *is* some perverse sense of justice for Samantha Friel that has nothing to do with the fact you're a *secretary* with the sheriff's department. And, I'm also betting you won't quit until you find whatever it is you're searching for, regardless of the personal consequences. Most people wouldn't bother. That alone makes you different."

"Yeah, as in *bad* different."

"Doubtful. But bad is very good for me. Actually, I prefer it." He grinned in that cocky, dangerous manner that so few men pull off. "Jimmer warned me about you."

"Yeah? What did he say?"

"I'd either end up killing you," he said, touching my face with reverence, "or sleeping with you." Gently he brushed his fingertips over my bruised jaw, down my chest, grazing his knuckles back and forth over the exposed skin of my cleavage before he elegantly slipped from the booth. "You guess which option appeals to me."

Shit.

"Consider what I've said, blondie. Focus your attention beyond Dick Friel."

"But . . ."

"No buts. I'll be in touch. Soon."

And he was gone.

CHAPTER SEVENTEEN

SOBERED UP BY BAD COFFEE and Tony's words, I replayed our conversation, reluctantly skipping the offer of becoming his biker mama. Since Dick Friel was my only suspect, I didn't buy into Tony's testimonial. Notes I'd scrawled on bar napkins didn't make sense. The only conclusion I reached was that we needed to meet with Shelley as soon as possible.

The next morning, Kevin still hadn't returned my calls. I made an executive decision to tackle the Shelley situation on my own. Since non-family visiting hours at the rehab center were Monday mornings and Thursday afternoons, I called in sick. I didn't see an alternative. Waiting four more days to question Shelley wouldn't help anyone.

Once I entered the rehab center, I knew the drill. Sign in, hang out, and wait. When I was ushered into a small, bland conference room, the blue air didn't hide Shelley's black mood.

"I don't know what you're doing here. I'm to the point I don't care. Just ask your goddamn questions and leave."

"Good." I jerked the padded chair away from the table, turned it around to straddle it. "Let's cut the bullshit right now. Why did you lie?"

"What do you mean 'why did I lie'? About what?"

"About everything, it seems. Did you really think we wouldn't find out that you'd hired Charles LaChance?"

The pinched lines around her mouth deepened. "How'd you find out?"

I shrugged. "They don't call us private dicks for nothing." My teeth flashed in a non-grin. "So, why? You said you couldn't stand him."

"I didn't hire him. I didn't sign a contract or anything. He was looking into some things . . ."

"Things like finding out if Samantha's biological father would be forced to pay back child support?"

The blood drained from her face. "Who told you that?"

"Doesn't matter. I want to know why that snake was working for you *before* Sam turned up dead."

Flustered, she automatically reached for her cigarettes, forgetting that she'd left one burning in the ashtray.

I pulled the pack from her grasp at the last second, figuring I'd get her undivided attention. "Which leads me directly to lie number two. Why did you tell us you'd been raped?"

She directed her glower out the window. "I was raped."

In the silence an angry, fat fly beat his body against the glass, repeatedly trying to get out. I knew the feeling.

My head began to buzz and my thin patience snapped. "Come on, Shelley. I haven't got all day."

More silence.

"It didn't happen like you said, did it?"

Finally, she muttered, "Think you're so goddamned smart. How did you know?"

"Does it matter?"

"Guess not." The gaze that flicked me top to bottom bordered on revulsion. "But I thought *you* would understand."

I didn't rise to the bait. "Again. Why did you lie?" My conscience called me every foul name in the book, but I demanded, "Tell me." When she lifted her head my direction, I steeled myself against the tears dripping from her weedy chin.

"I was raped," she repeated. "That wasn't a lie. But, not by a group of guys. By one."

By the way she was dragging this out I knew that wasn't all. And, I hadn't heard the worst.

"While another one watched," she added.

The coffee in my stomach curdled. "You knew who he was, didn't you?"

"Not at first." She swiped the tears, a surprisingly delicate mannerism. "The coat and pick-up part happened like I'd told you. I passed out for a little while. But then I came to."

"What do you remember?"

"Besides being scared shitless, thinking I was going to die?" She squeezed her eyes shut.

I knew she'd fallen back into the grotesque memory, but I could do nothing but watch, wait, and hope for this horror to end quickly for both of us.

"At some point while I'd blacked out they'd tied my hands above my head, blindfolded me, and shoved a gag covered with my own vomit in my mouth. I woke up when I felt rocks digging into my bare back. I remember hoping maybe I'd slept through the worst part, maybe they'd already left." She cupped her palms over her shoulders to stop the tremors. "Then, I heard it."

"What?"

"Grunts. Didn't know what it was at first. Then, I recognized the sounds of sex. Not the kind I was used to. When it was over . . . and they came closer, I pretended I was still passed out. But they started to argue, saying disgusting things to each other . . . and I guessed what was next."

"Who are they?"

She ignored my question. "He raped me. While the other guy watched and made sick remarks."

Don't ask, don't ask, don't ask, my brain chanted, but the words filling my mouth tasted like gravel and I had no choice but to spit them out. "What did they say?"

"The one humping me wanted to prove he wasn't a fag. Told the other guy if he could get it up for an ugly dog like me, then whatever happened between them didn't mean shit. He was no cocksucker. After he finished with me, he taunted him. Telling the other guy how good fucking a woman was compared to . . " Her red-rimmed eyes finally opened. "Well, you can guess what he said. When he got another hard on, he raped me again. Two more times, actually."

I lit one of Shelley's cigarettes and passed the pack back over. We smoked in the most hellish silence I've ever experienced. I'd sucked so much nicotine into my lungs I felt woozy. Sick. But the tough questions still needed to be asked and I needed to toughen up to get through them, even though I'd rather crawl under the table and cry.

"Did these guys leave you then?"

Her short, harsh laugh twisted my innards. "I wish. No, evidently the act of taking me against my will turned the other guy on."

Blood rushed to my face. I managed to say, "And they . . ."

"Fucked like dogs. It was immoral, the things I heard them doing to each other." She dragged the cigarette down to the filter in one inhale. "Afterward, they propped me against a tree, took off the gag, and forced me to drink Jack Daniels until I passed out again." She shuddered. "Never could stomach the stuff after that. Hell, I couldn't suck down a shot of Jack if my life depended on it. Anyway, when I woke in the morning, they were gone, my hands were untied, and my pants were on the ground."

"But, you knew who they were?"

She spoke to her ragged fingernails, "Yeah."

"Why didn't you turn them in?"

"Because they had it all worked out. Warned me if I told anyone, they'd claim that I begged them to take me home and wanted to do them both." Her chin trembled. "God, everybody already thought I was a whore. How many people saw me drunk that night? No one would've believed me anyway."

Rage brightened the room around me to vivid red. Surely, if she knew them, and had gone to the police immediately, her accusations and the physical evidence would've sent him to jail. Who was she protecting?

"And you believed them?"

"At that point I didn't know what to believe," she said quietly.

I got up and poured us each a glass of water. Shelley left hers untouched and picked the cuticle on her thumb until it bled. Then, she moved on to the next hand. At this rate her fingers would be nothing but bloody stumps. I flung her a Kleenex.

"Did you tell the counselor this? That you knew your attackers?"

"No."

"Samantha?"

Her eyes went wide.

"Charles LaChance?"

Silence.

"Jesus, Shelley. You didn't give LaChance that information? Especially when you told me you hadn't signed a contract with him?" I deliberately softened my tone. "You do realize then that nothing you said to him was privileged information?"

She started to cry again, this time without fragility. Huge, wet tears ran in rivulets through the grief etched in her gaunt face. "He came here after Sam told David about the rape. Reminded me he was at the fair that night. He started naming names, hinting around if I knew who did it, I should make the guy pay. Either with his reputation or with cash. He said he could help me. But I didn't tell him. I swear to God I didn't."

Then, it clicked. "Why did he show up at your house? Did he tell Sam that you knew who'd raped you?"

Through a watery blink, she refocused. "Charles LaChance was at my house? When?"

"I guess the day Sam came out here and caused a scene. She didn't tell you?"

"No."

She started picking the cuticle again. It annoyed me, but at least she wasn't pacing. "Why wouldn't she . . ."

"What else do you want?" Shelley snarled. "When Sam showed up she was furious, but mostly she was hysterical. Couldn't understand a fucking word she said. Finally, I just couldn't stand *her*. I told the counselors to keep her away from me."

"So, the next time you saw her?"

"That was the last time I saw her."

My mind's eye saw poor Samantha causing a scene and wanting her mommy. Only Mommy didn't want her. My skin crawled. David had been right. No one gave a shit about Samantha Friel.

I did.

Seemed my burden was to find justice for the dead. But Eve Dallas I wasn't, and without Shelley telling me the whole truth, this case would remain as dead in the water as Samantha.

I opened my mouth to speak but Shelley beat me to the punch.

"Don't think I'll just up and tell you who raped me. I won't tell anyone else. Not now, not ever." Her fist beat into the table, until the water pitcher bounced to the maroon carpet with a muffled splash.

"Fuck you for coming here and fuck me for telling you more than I should have. It's too late. I should've kept my mouth shut. Don't come back again." She swept from the room with her head held high.

Dismissed again. I was getting mighty sick of it.

I went home and called Kevin. He promised to swing by after clearing his Monday pile of paperwork. I didn't even want to think about the stuff piled on my desk. Missy wouldn't do a damn thing. Guilt filled the black chasm inside me, making my stomach churn. I slipped into my pajamas and crawled back in bed. No one had to know the sickness I suffered from was the mental variety.

The heavy pounding on the door roused me from dreams worse than reality. I tossed back the flannel sheets and shuffled sleepily to open the door, expecting Kevin. Ray stood on the steps. Anger shimmered around him like a hive of pissed off bees.

"Where is he?" he said, knocking me and the flowered welcome mat aside as he bulled his way into my house, metal jogging against metal in his canvas tool belt.

"Where is who?"

He spun around, giving me a disdainful once over. "Don't fuck with me, Julie. I'm not in the mood."

"What the hell is your problem? Why aren't you at work?"

"I'd ask you the same question, 'cept I know the answer. You called in sick today. Where is he?"

He stalked toward my bedroom but I grabbed his sleeve. "For the last goddamn time, Ray, who?"

"The guy you were with at Dusty's yesterday."

Crap. Figure the odds that someone had seen me drinking with Tony Martinez. Double the odds that someone like Pat had informed Ray. No easy way out of this sucker. I waved my hand, deciding nonchalance was my best bet. "It was nothing. Just a guy with some information about the case Kevin and I are working on."

"Bullshit. I heard you were all over him."

"You heard wrong. Besides, even if I was, what business is it of yours?"

Ray grabbed my shoulders and shook me until my teeth clacked. "Everything about you is my business. You're *my* girlfriend. You think it's funny to fuck around on me? You think I'd just put up with it?"

The fuzzy feeling left my brain. "Get out."

"I don't think so. I wanna know why you've been avoiding me." His vise-like grip tightened. "Who's this guy you've been seeing on the sly? You think I'm stupid?"

"I'm warning you, Ray," I said, against the rage building inside me. "Let go of me right fucking now and get the hell out of my house."

His jagged fingernails dug into the exposed skin of my back. "Or what? You gonna call the sheriff? Maybe your pansy-ass friend Kevin will come after me," he sneered, as his spittle dotted my face. "Does this new guy like the way you move in bed enough that he'll take me on? Or, is he another pussy hanging around for a sample of yours?"

The last thing I'd call Tony Martinez was a pussy. Retreat was impossible against Ray's increasingly painful hold, so I tried logic. "We're done. Take the hint and get out."

"We're done when I say we're done."

I dropped my shoulders, lifting my arms between Ray's and circling my hands up, pressing my elbows into his forearms. He released me, his hands fell away, and I stepped back.

But not fast enough. His right fist hammered into my jawbone. I staggered, trying to get into a defensive position. Before I could, another powerful blow connected with my already queasy stomach, glancing off my bruised ribs. He backhanded me, his class ring caught on my cheekbone. Rage had darkened his features into a mask of hatred I didn't recognize on him, but had seen on my father.

He reached into his tool belt and grabbed a hammer.

Blood trickled down my stinging cheek. I hadn't yet caught my breath from his sucker punch. As he advanced on me, I couldn't believe I hadn't taken his threats seriously. How had I ever considered him harmless? In that moment I knew he'd kill me.

The screen door banged open, feet scuffled, and the next thing I knew, Ray was sprawled on the orange shag carpet, flat on his back, staring up the barrel of Kevin's gun.

"Come on, asshole. Give me a goddamned reason." Kevin shoved the gun higher, making Ray's nose resemble a pig's snout. "You get off on hitting her? Do you, you sick fuck?"

Ray shook his head wildly and Kevin's gun slipped, gouging a chunk from his cheek. He winced, but Kevin didn't move back.

I heard a crack and looked to where Kevin's knee had ground into Ray's ribs. Kevin pressed harder and Ray sucked in a painful breath. The hammer dropped from Ray's curled fist.

"He's got a sheetrock knife on his tool belt," I said, feeling as if someone else had spoken the words through my mouth.

Kevin also removed a mini-saw before turning to study me. "For Chrissake, Julie, get in the kitchen. You're bleeding."

I shook my head slowly, running my tongue around my teeth. Didn't feel like any were loose. "Not until he's gone."

"Then call the sheriff."

"No."

"Why not?"

Like this wasn't mortifying enough. "Just get him out of here."

Ray lumbered to his feet, blood oozing down his battered, handsome face. He couldn't wipe it away with his gaze trained on Kevin's gun.

When they reached the door, I said, "Stay the fuck away

from me, Ray. I mean it. Next time I'll press charges."

"Come near her again and I'll kill you," Kevin said as he heaved Ray off the porch, throwing his tools after him. "That's a fucking promise."

The door shut with decisive click. I slumped into the couch.

Kevin didn't go after Ray, although I knew he wanted to. He deposited the gun on the coffee table and returned from the kitchen with damp towels and ice before I could object. He dabbed at the blood without comment. I closed my eyes, desperately wanting to give in to a river of tears. Kevin would understand, but tough chicks never cried, especially over a man. I sucked it up.

"Good thing you can take it on the chin," Kevin said evenly, although his breaths came in short, angry bursts like a bull in rut, "or else we'd be in the emergency room."

"I'm fine."

"I can see that." His fingers gently stroked the bump rising on the other side of my jaw, traveled up and smoothed the hair from my forehead. A sense of utter calm filled the dark hole where my courage had been sucked out.

"Hell, Julie, I've never had this happen twice in one year. And it's happened to you twice in one *week*."

The smell of the antiseptic cream stung my nostrils before the nasty stuff burned my flesh.

"Hold still, tough girl, this might sting."

I gritted my teeth, but didn't pull away. Getting

smacked around was almost easier than dealing with the medication.

Kevin placed a cylinder of lemonade in my hand and raised it to my jaw. I opened my eyes. His concentrated gaze seared me, stinging and soothing as powerfully as the first-aid treatment.

Before he could reset the distance between us, I caressed the side of his stony face. "Thank you." My hand dropped when he closed his own eyes and sighed.

"No problem." He stood, giving me his back and raking an unsteady hand through his hair. "You want a brandy or something before you tell me what happened with Shelley today?"

Brandy? Next, he'd be offering me smelling salts.

"No." I immediately launched into the morning's events, and backtracked to my discussion with Tony Martinez. Kevin didn't chastise me for questioning Shelley alone. Or chumming it up with a biker of dubious reputation. Or, for blowing off my real job. When he hadn't said anything after a few minutes, I prompted, "Kevin?"

"Sorry. Just thinking about heading up to where they found Samantha. Got directions from Sergeant Schneider, but don't think we'll find anything." His frown deepened the worry lines set between his eyes. "Although the fresh air might do you some good. Think you're up for it?"

"Sure." I darted to my feet and did a little soft shoe. "See? Good as new."

"I'm beginning to think you're part Borg."

"Only the best parts, baby."

He re-holstered his gun, letting the nylon case dangle at his side. "Don't know why I encourage you. But if you're sure you're all right, get your hiking boots on. We're goin' a-huntin'."

"For what?"

"Clues. But you'd better change out of your pajamas in case we run into Big Foot." Kevin paused and smiled, ruffling my hair. "Course, with your track record, you'd probably end up dating him."

CHAPTER EIGHTEEN

KEVIN'S TONGUE STAYED IDLE ON THE drive up Rimrock. The scenic road was another reminder of why I've chosen to live in the Black Hills. The simple beauty. The splendor. The fact we'd only met a dozen cars on this stretch of highway.

Rimrock Highway is a popular thoroughfare for tourists on the way to Deadwood. Rock cliffs in shades of cream and cinnamon jut to the sky, an expanse of blue the color of a newly laid robin's egg. Black Hills spruce, choke cherry bushes, and the occasional Aspen tree pepper the slanted shale ramparts. A stream meanders alongside clusters of houses. Most homes are situated on higher ground now, after the flood of 1972, when the mild-looking stream roared through the canyon, taking houses, boulders, cars, and many lives in its wake. Until that time, people had forgotten how Rapid Creek had gotten its name.

We passed the sign announcing the turnoff to Hisega.

Housing developments ruled here, with the occasional bed and breakfast, restaurant, or a tiny ranch thrown in for diversity. There was even an ostrich farm tucked in among the hills. "No trespassing" and "no hunting" signs were nailed to trees or rickety fence posts. Once we turned from the paved portion of the road, we entered the Black Hills National Forest. No wonder local law enforcement had trouble deciding jurisdiction. Even with a map of this quadrangle in my lap, the boundaries between public and private land blurred.

Kevin had driven his old two-seater Jeep, which he uses for off-road excursions. As far as unmanaged fire trails went, this one was close to a real road. Usually, I loved hanging on, bouncing around inside the cab, watching wildlife scatter in our wake. Not today. Every bump jarred my ribcage. Every turn had me grinding my teeth, expanding the ache in my swollen jaw. And every few minutes I glanced into the side mirror. But the trail behind us stayed empty. Still, I was spooked.

"I don't think Ray is going to come after us, if that's what you're worried about," Kevin said, downshifting to a crawl as the potholes in the rutted road became unbearable.

"I'm sure he's drowning his sorrows with his loser friends at Dusty's. But I've had this weird feeling since yesterday that someone is following me."

He muttered something and studied the envelope

clutched in his hand. We slowed and stopped. Kevin jammed the Jeep into reverse and parked in a fairly flat section close to the road. "Think I missed the turn."

"Isn't it marked?"

"What? The crime scene?"

I nodded.

"With yellow crime tape cautioning people to stay out?"

"Yeah. I mean on TV . . ."

"I'm unplugging your television. That might happen in LA or New York. Here most everything is handled in two hours unless they have to call in the DCI from Pierre. They don't even do that much any more." He rubbed the furrow between his eyes. "You up for a little hike?"

"Sure. How far?"

"Don't know."

I pulled on a jean jacket, leaving my cigarettes and lighter in the Jeep. As a lifelong resident of the Black Hills, I'd witnessed the devastation of forest fires firsthand. Smokey the Bear might be hokey to East Coasters, but I took his warnings seriously.

The overgrown road ended at the creek bed so we backtracked to search for a path along the water. The creek was high from melted snow and I knew from previous visits, bitterly cold. The water danced with life. Brown trout blended with the rocks, visible only by the barest flick of a mud-colored fin. Bright green algae teased from the river bottom as the water flowed patiently in places and rushed over boulders in others. The glumpy bank gave way to sheer expanses of flesh-colored rock, making navigating the spaces between the vastly different areas difficult.

But the view was worth it. The cliffs were higher back here than the ones close to the highway, with a pronounced rather than a gradual drop. Everything seemed better. Taller trees, fresher air, a brighter sun sparkling over the clear, icy blue river. I inhaled the cool scent of clean water and damp, loamy smells particular to a spring forest and closed my eyes. This reconnection with nature after my hellish week was exactly what I'd needed. Kevin had known. He always did.

He led the way, keeping an even pace. We hiked in solitude, as was pretty much our unwritten rule. I'd started to feel the burn in my thighs and calves when the creek banked right and disappeared between two grayish-black walls of rock. Darker splotches of moss discolored the stone; the formation looked like a diseased and discarded elephant.

Kevin stopped, uncapped his canteen and settled upon a log decaying in the small clearing.

I checked for bugs hidden in the bark and wood pulp before I joined him. "So, what do you think?"

"We should do this more often." He inhaled with great gusto and tipped his head back to enjoy the majestic cloudless sky, the unfettered air, allowing the spring rays to warm his face. "It's beautiful. I wouldn't mind building a house out here someday."

Kevin? Mr. No-maintenance-condo? Settling down and living in the woods like Ewell Gibbons? I cocked my head, taking a swig from his canteen. "Not many houses out here."

"I think that's why I like it."

Or, that's what Lilly likes. I kept the opinion to myself and grabbed a handful of pine needles, neatly snapping off the crisp brown ends before breaking the rest into little pieces and tossing them back on the chilly ground.

Kevin withdrew the envelope from his pocket. "Not sure if we're in the right place. Maybe we should head back. Follow the creek the other direction. We were supposed to pass a couple of houses. I didn't see any, did you?"

I lifted my chin to stare at the apex of towering trees. A pine-scented breeze sent my hair flying and my spirits soaring. Truthfully, I didn't want to move. This little clearing had temporarily patched the dark cracks in my spirit with peace. Not another soul was in sight to ruin it. Even the birds were songless and the turkey and deer were scarce. "Nope."

"Ritchie also said there were cabins along here for some kind of church camp."

"There's more than one camp." I remembered four or five different denominations claimed this area, each with a separate campsite. No "good will" camp games or tomfoolery was tolerated between Methodists and

Presbyterians. One year my father had threatened to send me to Catholic church camp for the whole summer. He never followed through, thank God.

"Let's try the other way."

Once again I trailed behind, but my blood tingled with energy and I wasn't huffing too loudly from normal physical activity. When we passed the Jeep and my stash of cigarettes, I looked longingly for a minute, but a sense of denial increased my feeling of nobility.

Kevin pointed out the vacant houses as our marker and we moved on. The thick underbrush gave way to a giant meadow speckled with pine trees. The creek made a couple of hairpin turns and vanished again.

I leaned against a large Black Hills Spruce to catch my breath, bending down to ease the stitch in my side. Something pinged above my shoulder; shattered tree bark dusted my hair like shrapnel. I stood, frantically brushing at the sticky sap, imagining pine beetles crawling across my scalp. "What the hell was that?"

Another loud crack hit somewhere above my head. Kevin dove for the ground, yanking me down into the tall grass beside him.

"Someone is shooting at us."

My body went rigid, except for my heart; it started beating like a unity drum at a Powwow. "Can you see who it is?"

He shook his head.

"Do you think it's kids?"

Another shake of Kevin's head.

The shots had been more potent than an air rifle or BB gun.

"Did you see any 'no trespassing' signs posted any-where?"

"I don't remember."

"Neither do I."

I wiggled back and the sound of gunfire sent another shot close enough to part my hair. I nearly screamed.

"Stop wiggling," Kevin hissed.

Motionless, I waited. No other blasts were fired.

"Where's your gun?" I whispered.

"In the Jeep."

"Have your cell phone?"

He signaled for quiet.

I lowered my voice and repeated, "Where's your cell?"

"Why? You plan on throwing it at them?"

"I was going to call 911."

"No service. That's why I left it in the Jeep."

Not a shock; most pockets of wilderness, especially those deep in the Black Hills had sporadic mobile phone service. So, what were we supposed to do with no weapons? I longed for my bow. Hell, I longed to be sitting in my living room watching this drama unfold on TV.

Two rounds were fired off in quick succession. I heard something splinter behind us, and crash, probably a tree branch, but didn't turn around for verification.

"We've got to get out of here," Kevin said.

"Do you have a white hankie we can wave? Then, maybe these people won't think we're poaching . . ."

"Most people don't shoot first and ask questions later, even in rural western South Dakota." He parted the grass slightly; his gaze darted to the ridge above us. "Whoever it is, they're only trying to scare us. Because if they were trying to kill us, we'd already be dead. We're basically sitting ducks."

This was one of those rare times Kevin wasn't real big on comfort. My heart pounded, my face flushed bright red as the dirt below us. Parts of my body that didn't even have glands started to sweat. And yet, we waited.

He pointed to the right. "Let's make a break for the tree line. On three." He eased to a push-up position.

I raised my butt off the ground, resting on my palms and toes, hoping my arms wouldn't give out before bone deep shakes wracked my body.

"One. Two. Three."

I scuttled blindly to the copse of trees, dropping to the earth behind the first stout trunk. My lungs were taxed, but I was surprised they still functioned; I'd fully expected to get shot in the back. I chanced a look around the gnarled roots of the big pine.

And saw Kevin sprawled in the grass.

Adrenaline kicked in. Without thinking, I belly

crawled to him.

Please, please, no, no, not Kevin.

Three shots, fired leisurely, kicked up chunks of vegetation. I hardly noticed. Kevin had curled into a ball. I shook him hard. He groaned and cursed. I wanted to drape my body over his and weep with gratitude. "Kevin? You get hit?"

"No."

"What's wrong?"

"Twisted my ankle. Must've slipped on a rock."

"Can you move?"

"Yeah, but forget it. Get your ass back in the trees where it's safe."

"Fuck that. I'm not leaving you." Four shots interrupted the ground around us, sending grass and dirt flying like confetti. I wanted to scream with outrage. Instead, I whispered, "Can you crawl backwards? Don't think I can carry you."

"I know you can't. Stay low. I'll go as fast as I can." We moved like turtles on the half shell. More shots were fired. Closer.

"We'd better kick into high gear. The fun is wearing thin for our shooter friend."

Crab-crawling backwards uphill was nearly impossible for me. Kevin's movements, with his bum ankle, made him look like a handicapped hopping spider, which normally would've sent me into gales of laughter. But normally, we didn't have bullets whizzing at us. I refused to get too far ahead of him, afraid he'd collapse while I was protected in the woods.

I'd never considered myself a tree hugger, but I latched onto the first pine in sight and wouldn't let go.

A rapid burst of gunfire echoed from the ridge above us.

Then it stopped.

We waited. Nothing.

The sounds of silence were music to my ears.

When I figured the coast was clear, I moved to where I'd propped Kevin against a large tree stump. Luckily his calf wasn't bent at a funky angle, a la' Joe Theismann. I lifted his pant leg; his hiking boot covered the ankle. At least the reinforced suede top would keep it from swelling too much for now. He needed to get out of here. I glanced at the path and around the trees but couldn't remember how far we were from the Jeep.

Kevin threaded his fingers through mine. "Thank you."

"Don't mention it." I fussed, picking pieces of grass from his hair, straightening his shirt with the casual touches he uses to calm me. "I'll probably be wishing I would have left you when I have to carry you all the way back to the damn Jeep."

He tilted my face back toward his. "Julie . . ."

Not now. "I know. Come on, let's get going."

"I can walk," he growled between clenched teeth. Even with my help, he fell back against the tree when he put weight on his foot.

"And I'll bet you can two-step to Dwight Yoakam too." Slinging his arm over my shoulder, I looked right into his eyes. "Lean on me, Kev. I mean it. You don't have to be tough with me."

"Same goes," he said softly, brushing an aspen leaf from my hair.

It was an agonizing journey. I took the brunt of Kevin's weight, and with my sore ribs, I knew I'd be in agony the moment I stopped moving. The Jeep was finally in sight and I'd quickened our pace to an excruciating rate when the flashing lights of a patrol car pulled around the bend and parked.

Pennington County Sheriff's Department. I recognized the officer easing out of the cruiser. Which meant he'd recognize me too. Better get the pleasantries out of the way first. "Hey, Bill," I called out cheerfully. "Are we glad to see you."

Kevin snorted.

I had the mean urge to let go of him. I crafted a small smile for Bill and refrained from further injuring Kevin. This Florence Nightingale stuff was harder than it looked.

"Julie Collins? I'd recognize that wild hair anywhere. What're you doing out here?" Deputy Bill Brownell walked over and helped me settle Kevin against the Jeep's front bumper. "You okay? You need an ambulance?"

"No, but thanks," Kevin said grimly, using that,

I'm-bleeding-but-it's-nothing attitude which cursed most men. Then, he blithely offered his dirt-covered hand and introduced himself. Hell, I was surprised he didn't whip out a business card.

"What are you doing out here?"

"We were looking for some land for sale but lost our way."

Bill's skeptical eyes moved from Kevin back to me. Zeroed in on my puffy jaw, then cruised up to study the gash on my cheek. "Christ. What the hell happened to you?"

"I ran into a pine tree," I laughed, touching the crusted scab, "which is why we ended up turned around."

"A couple of homeowners heard shots and called." His gaze accused Kevin, although his tone remained mild. "You weren't really out here for target practice, by any chance?"

"Only if we were the targets," I said, pointing to the path behind us. "Someone shot at *us*. We were headed back here to report it on Kevin's cell phone when he twisted his ankle."

"Did you shoot back?"

Kevin shook his head. "My gun is in the Jeep."

"Mind if I take a look at it?"

"Sure." Kevin dug his keys from his pocket and tossed them to me. "Permit to carry concealed is in the glove box."

I grabbed everything from the cab, including my cigarettes. I watched Bill scrutinize Kevin's license; he carefully handled his gun. He sniffed the barrel and handed it back to Kevin, butt first. "When was the last time you fired it?"

"At least three weeks ago. Why?"

"Don't need to get defensive, son. I figured as much since it looks and smells pretty clean. This your only one?"

"That I've got with me."

Bill shifted his bulk sideways, running a thick wrist under his jowl. "Got any idea who was shooting at you?"

I smoked and wandered around to the back of the Jeep while Kevin explained.

Deputy Bill sighed. "Probably just some ornery kids. We get that out here sometimes, although it usually happens closer to hunting season."

"I don't think it was kids," I said, grinding my cigarette beneath my boot heel and reaching down to pick up the spent butt. Beneath the wheel well, silver glinted in the afternoon sun. I crouched closer, noticing a bowie knife imbedded nearly to the hilt on the rear driver's side tire. "Especially not now. Deputy, come and look at this."

Bill sauntered back and squatted eye level with the knife. Several moments passed before he whistled. "I'll be damned. Doesn't look like you ran over it." To Kevin he said, "You carry a knife in your car?"

"No. Why? What's going on?"

"There's a knife sticking out of your tire." He stood and removed his hat, scratching his head. "Hang on. I've got a plastic bag in the car."

I dropped to the ground; Kevin hopped and grunted his way back around to see the action. We watched as Bill donned gloves and jockeyed the knife out, placing it in an evidence bag. The tire was totally ruined.

"Your spare any good?" Bill said to Kevin.

"Should be. I had it checked last month."

"I'll change it." Deputy Bill crawled under the Jeep and released the spare and the jack.

I scooted closer to offer my help, but Bill shooed me back.

"No sense in us both getting dirty. I'll have to take this tire in as evidence. Don't know what we'll find, but I'll give you a call when we're finished." Helping motorists must've paid off because he changed the tire with the speed of an Indy Car pit crew. The ruined tire was shoved in his trunk beside a blue plastic tarp.

After jotting down Kevin's statement, he turned to me. "I'll fax this to you at the office tomorrow, that okay?"

Crap. I couldn't very well say no. The fax machine was in Sheriff Richards' office, which meant he'd see it and read it, especially if my name was on the report. Then, he'd realize I hadn't been sick. He'd also realize that I'd been doing the one thing he'd warned me not to do, on a day I'd been scheduled to work for him. Too bad I couldn't blink like Jeannie and start this day over. "Sure. I'll be in tomorrow."

Bill helped me load Kevin in the Jeep and waited until

I'd pulled out to follow us back into Rapid. Neither Kevin nor I paid much attention to the scenery on the return trip.

In fact, Kevin acted paranoid, like the deputy had somehow bugged his car. We didn't discuss anything about the afternoon's events, which was another oddity. Normally, we'd dissect and compartmentalize every morsel we'd uncovered. My questions went unanswered because as soon as he got a clear cell signal, he called Lilly.

She was waiting outside Kevin's garage when we pulled up. Pacing, pale and wan, looking unlike the put-together Lilly I knew and loathed. I almost felt guilty because she was obviously worried about Kevin.

The second I'd shut off the engine, she yanked the passenger door open. She cooed at Kevin, stroking his face, cheeping her displeasure like an angry momma bird. When she demanded to examine his ankle in her soft, lilt-ing, puke-inducing voice, my faint stirrings of guilt turned into nausea. Especially after Kevin extracted an envelope from under the seat and handed it to me without a word.

I opened it. My paycheck.

Helpful Deputy Bill had parked behind us, insistent on helping Kevin inside and giving me a lift back to my vehicle. I stayed in his patrol car, sullen, sore, and surly. Lilly wanted to fuss and Kevin let her, but I'd be damned if I would watch. It hurt too damn bad.

Thursday afternoon, I answered the phone in my chirpiest voice, "Bear Butte County Sheriff's Office."

"Hey, Jules, Kevin. What time does your shift end?"

No, "How've you been", or "I missed you" softened his curt tone. I barely resisted sticking my tongue out at the receiver. "Three. Why?"

"Can you get off early?"

I hesitated. My butt was still sore from the ass chewing courtesy of Sheriff Richards. I'd crossed a line and the tension was extremely unpleasant for everyone that worked in the office. Especially for me. "I'm sorry, I can't," I said with a sniff.

"Have you heard from Meredith Friel?"

"Not since we saw her Sunday. Why?"

"Shelley hasn't contacted you either?"

"No. Why?"

"Because Meredith just stopped in and she was pretty frantic. Seems Shelley checked herself out of rehab."

My anger with Kevin immediately fled. "When?"

"The admin wouldn't tell her. Meredith only found out today when she went for visitation and Shelley wasn't there."

I chewed on the end of my pencil, ignoring the trickle of unease sneaking up my spine. "So, where is she?"

"That's the thing. No one knows. No one has seen her. It's like she just disappeared."

CHAPTER
NiNETEEN

MY TIRES NEARLY SMOKED as I made a mad dash for Kevin's office after my shift ended.

The door to his inner chamber was ajar and I slipped inside unnoticed. I knew better than to demand acknowledgement from him in his agitated state: deep frown lines knitted his brow, his hair was a parody of his normal tidy style, his Italian loafers beat a path in the carpet. I snagged a cold soda, fired up a smoke, and watched him pace. At least his pacing was more interesting when he limped.

"This doesn't make any sense," he said. "Why would Shelley check out of rehab now? Not after her daughter was murdered, but now? When she only had two weeks left?"

He glanced up, but I already knew it wasn't a rhetorical question. Kevin hobbled to the other office door. And back.

"Tell me again how she acted when you saw her

Monday."

"Upset, especially that I'd showed up again. Told me not to come back. But not like she wasn't going to be around if I did. More like she'd take pleasure in refusing to see me."

"I wonder if someone else visited her after you did. Think that person threatened her?"

"Thinking of anyone in particular?"

He added the small area in front of his desk between the visitors' chairs to his loop. "Dick or Charles LaChance."

Man, he was fidgety today. I counted on his calmness to keep me balanced. Usually, I was off balance enough for both of us. I stared at him pointedly until his feet stopped shuffling.

"Sorry."

"No problem. Who'd you talk to when you called out for confirmation?"

"Connected me right to the head administrator. Troy James? Remember him? Jock, captain of the football team, general pain in the ass?"

I wondered if was still a buck-toothed beanpole with the brain power of an acorn squash. "Yeah. Did he remember you?"

"Sort of. He was always way-too-cool to hang with lower classmen."

My cigarette stopped halfway to my mouth. "Wait a second. Troy James. As in the guy Nancy Rogers dated and married? Wasn't she the friend that ditched Shelley at the fair the night she was raped?"

Kevin affixed his butt to the edge of the desk. "God. Can't believe I missed that. He palled around with Charles LaChance too."

"And Dick Friel, Tim O'Reilly, Bobby Adair, Mike Lawrence, and Danny Christopherson."

"Remember, Jimmer hung around those guys for a while."

I hadn't forgotten. "No way was Jimmer involved in any of this shit, Kev. He may be a mean mother to guys, but he'd never hurt a woman. Besides, there's way too many of these connections for it to be just dumb luck."

"It may seem like a coincidence . . ."

"Is it a coincidence that Shelley checked into the treatment facility where her friend's husband is the head administrator?" I countered.

"Maybe. There are only two rehab centers in Rapid City. It's not like she had dozens to choose from."

"True, but remember Shelley claims that she hadn't seen Nancy in years?"

"Just because Nancy's husband runs the place doesn't mean she hangs out there or even knows what goes on." He shifted his weight off his ankle. "Probably because of all the confidentiality laws, he couldn't even tell her Shelley was a patient."

"So, what did Troy tell you?"

Kevin's face soured. "Not a thing, except she checked out on her own. Said if I wasn't listed as next of kin, they couldn't release any other information."

"Did Dick know she'd checked out?"

"Not according to Meredith. No one knew. That's why she freaked out." Pushing aside stacks of folders, he sighed. "Just what we needed. To be back at square one."

"We know Shelley didn't go make up with Dick. Bastard probably changed the locks."

He smiled slightly, bracing his palms along side his khaki-clad hips on the mahogany desk, staring thoughtfully at the Donald Montileaux litho above my head.

I watched the smoke curl up from the end of my fingers and mused, "So, where *would* Shelley go if she couldn't go home?"

A beat passed before our eyes met with perfect clarity. "I'll drive," he said.

The same quietness pervaded Rose Macintosh's neighborhood as it had on Sunday. Kevin parked on the street and killed the engine. Nothing looked different, but it felt different as we sat inspecting the house.

I opened my door.

Kevin's warm fingers slid up my arm. "If you want to stay here, that's okay."

"Why would I?" His reasons dawned on me and I bristled. "Because Shelley and I didn't leave on such friendly terms?" I pointed at his leg. "If anyone should be cooling their heels in the car, it should be you with that bum ankle, limpy."

His answering half-smile didn't reach his eyes. "Forget it, tough girl. Let's go."

We inched our way up the steep driveway and for once it wasn't my smoker's lungs impeding our progress. Kevin took a breather against the partition separating the glass windows in the garage door, resting his ankle. Face pallid, he closed his eyes against the simple exertion that had him sweating. I had stepped forward to offer comfort, when I noticed it. The sedan parked in the garage. With the lights on.

I pressed my nose to the glass, cupping my hands beside my face to block the glare. Taillights glowed a faint red and the window was rolled down. Someone had used the car recently. Or, intended to use it soon.

Or, was still in the car.

Nah. The shapes I noticed in the front seats were nothing more than headrests. I squinted. Except the headrest on the driver's side had long blond hair. And shoulders.

Shit.

I rubbed furiously on the dirty pane, thinking spit and polish would erase the image. *Not real, not real,* the mantra repeated in my head, trying to convince me the scene in front of me was an illusion. A distortion. A sick trick of light.

The glass damn near sparkled and nothing inside had changed.

I knew it was her. I knew Shelley was in the car.
I beat my fists on the wooden garage door panels until they stung, hoping to startle her. *Come on, Shelley, stop playing games and let us in.*

She didn't move. Kevin's ragged voice sounded distant even next to my ear.

The way her head was tilted it looked as if she were napping. Somehow, I knew this nap was one of the permanent variety. I jumped back, afraid my anger and fear might return the glass to its molten liquid state. In the process I lost my balance and fell ass first on concrete. Tears stung my eyes as I looked up at Kevin.

"Jules? What the hell are you . . ."

"It's her. Shelley's in there, Kevin, in the car . . ."

He didn't even blink. "Get my cell phone. Now. Call 911."

I leapt to my feet. "No. We have to help, we have to get her out of there. What if . . .?"

Kevin shook me hard, then held my head between his palms, forcing me to focus on his eyes. "Listen to me. We can't go in there. It won't help. Make the call, I promise, if she's alive that's the fastest way to help her." He nudged me. "Go on."

My run down the driveway was less than graceful. With fumbling fingers I dialed 911, somehow coherent enough to remember my name and a brief rundown of the situation. Luckily, the street number was listed on the mailbox or I would've struggled with the address. Now, I had firsthand experience on why people babbled when calling in an emergency.

I didn't venture back up the driveway until I heard the scream of sirens.

The fire department pried the garage door open and the faint odor of exhaust fumes drifted to the front steps, where Kevin and I had taken refuge. I plugged my nose when the sour smell of rot followed. After the fireman's all clear signal, the ambulance crew hurried in.

They needn't have bothered.

From the muttering and now slow movements coming from inside the garage, I assumed Shelley was dead. Radios squawked and a van from the Rapid City Police Department blocked the driveway. Cases of equipment were hauled in, probably for photos and cataloguing crime scene evidence.

Crime scene. I locked my jaw tightly against the automatic cry of denial. The numb, surreal feeling continued. I hated that feeling. Like I stood outside my own body watching the horror unfold for someone else. But, once again it was unfolding for me.

Cold cement stung my butt despite the relatively

balmy day. I wrapped my arms more securely around my knees to stave off the tremors. No way was I moving one foot off the cracked steps. I had no desire to see Shelley in her final moments.

An officer approached Kevin. Low tones drifted closer, but I didn't bother to eavesdrop. Kevin struggled to his feet and followed the officer inside the garage. He returned, minutes later, paler than the waning sunlight filtering through the treetops.

"Was it her?"

He nodded.

"Shit."

"You okay?" he asked.

Frustration and guilt gnawed at me, but this wasn't the time or the place to give in to it. I shook my head.

Kevin settled beside me. "Me, either. They've already sent a car out to Dick's repair shop. If he's not there they'll go to the house."

"Think he'll stay home tonight?" The idea of Meredith dealing with this blow alone set me back on the angry path. I desperately needed a cigarette but didn't want to walk back to Kevin's car on the off chance I'd get a glimpse of Shelley.

"I don't know."

Something thudded in the garage. I needed to hear myself talk to cover up the unsavory images in my mind of bloated bodies and rotting flesh. Probably, my mental images were worse than the actuality. Still, I didn't care to find out. "They're bringing Dick in for questioning, aren't they? I mean, come on, he's got to be a suspect."

"Probably not." He leaned over until I felt the comforting brush of his shoulder against mine. "They're treating this as a suicide."

I gaped at him. "A suicide? You can't be serious."

"Lower your voice. As soon as the preliminary report is done and they've taken your statement, we can go. Then, we'll talk about this."

The clatter of a metal stretcher clunking across cement made me press my forehead into my knees. Bile rose and I choked it down. I couldn't watch them load the body. My leather boots creaked as I rocked back and forth. The movement soothed my stomach and blocked most sounds. The blood rushing in my ears blocked the rest.

"They're gone," Kevin said.

I lifted my head, but Kevin wouldn't meet my eyes. A shadow fell over me. A man crouched down.

I didn't know the detective in charge, but he treated me delicately, as if this whole ordeal would send me further into shock. He was wrong. It sent me into a rage. I answered his carefully worded questions quickly, and we were both relieved when it was over. I didn't want to imagine how Sheriff Richards would react when he got wind of my part in this latest saga.

Kevin had barely pulled out of the cul-de-sac when I

exploded. "Suicide? How can they possibly think that? Is this entire police force inept on every case?"

He unwrapped a stick of Juicy Fruit gum and shoved it in his mouth, balling the tin foil wrapper and tossing it toward the ashtray. One hand stayed on the wheel while the other gestured wildly.

"Would you stop? What else are they supposed to think? They find her in a closed garage, ignition on, with the window rolled down and an empty bottle of Jack Daniels in the passenger seat?" He downshifted and turned on to Fifth Street, nearly rear-ending a garbage truck. "Her daughter has been murdered, her marriage is over, and she recently checked out of alcohol rehab. That would lead me to the same conclusion."

My mouth dropped open. I was used to Kevin taking the side of law enforcement. Hell, I usually took their side. But this was different. I struggled to tell him so but he beat me to the punch.

"Unless . . . one had spent time with Shelley recently and heard her very Catholic views on suicide, firsthand . . ."

He waited for me to fill in the blanks.

"And knew Jack Daniels is the only type of booze she refused to drink," I finished. I lit a cigarette, letting the smoke fill my lungs to the breaking point. Exhaled. "Do you believe she killed herself?"

"No." Kevin sped through a yellow light, cursing under his breath at a motor home clogging the passing lane before swerving into the driving lane. "I think someone went to a lot of trouble to make it look like she did."

I held my breath as we weaved in and out of traffic. I wanted to ask Kev if he had to piss really bad or something, as we were blatantly breaking half a dozen traffic laws. Odd behavior. He lived for following rules. As far as I knew, we had nothing as earth-shattering as discovering another dead body on our agenda for the rest of the day.

"The set-up was similar to the one involving her rape. So, who?"

"That's what we're going to find out." He whipped a U-turn into an empty lot behind his building and braked so hard at the last second my knees smacked into the dash. But, neither of us moved to exit the car. He was lost in thought; I was busy totaling up my bruises for the week.

"How?" I said finally, my voice still shaking from recent events. "We've spent the last two weeks unsuccessfully tracking the movements of one sixteen-year old girl. What makes you think we'll have any luck figuring out who killed Shelley? Especially when the cops think it was suicide?"

"For that reason." Kevin peeled his fingers from the death grip he had on the steering wheel before he faced me. "Look. If the person that killed her thinks they got away with faking her suicide, they won't be expecting anyone to investigate."

Anyone meaning us. And I'd hoped this was over.

I was puzzled by his fortitude, especially when this

wasn't our case. David LaChance's dime was up, not that Kevin had financial worries. He'd reminded me the thrill wasn't always in the chase but in small things, like the minute a client's check cleared the bank. David's check had cleared long ago. So, why his change of heart? "Kevin, no one is paying us to do this."

"I know. Let's just call this my version of a pro-bono case."

"Why?"

He stared at me for a long, long time, but not through me, which was a nice change of pace. "I can't stand the thought of someone getting away with it. Maybe someone we know."

"What do we do now?"

"I've been thinking. We talk to Troy James." A BMW pulled in next to us, momentarily distracting him. "Rather, while I'm talking I want you doing something else."

"What?"

"Remember those log books that everyone has to sign in at the rehab center? If someone visited Shelley after you did, there'd be a record."

I tapped my temple. "Good thinking. But I'm supposed to waltz in there and wrestle it from the TAR on duty?"

He frowned. "What's a TAR?"

"Trained Attack Receptionist. Come on, you know the type." I mimicked, " 'Do you have an appointment? Can I see some ID? Are you a member of the family?' The last woman whisked the book out of sight the minute I dotted the 'i' in Collins."

Kevin rolled his eyes. "Then, we'll go during lunch when they close the office down for an hour."

"How do you know that?" I demanded.

"Meredith told me she drove out there on her break from school and no one was around. The receptionist's office was locked and dark. She had to come back later in the afternoon."

"Hmm." I leaned against the car door; the plastic handle dug painfully into my back so I knew this wasn't yet another bizarre dream. "But I'm sure everything is locked up tight. No way could we get in there."

A small smile appeared and he shook his finger in front of my nose. "Never say never."

"You aren't proposing . . ."

He shrugged. "It can be done."

Kevin? *Planning* to break the law? My gasp rivaled that of a swooning gothic heroine. "You?"

"Yes, me," he mocked. "I'm not as squeaky clean as you imagine, Jules."

"Yeah, you're a real bad boy, all right, Kev."

"I certainly don't rival the type of badly behaved men you favor, but I haven't been a Boy Scout for one helluva long time."

Yikes. Be still my heart. Yet, I didn't care for the decidedly wicked gleam in his eyes. "Meaning?"

"I've got a few tricks up my sleeve that might impress even a cynic like you." His curious gaze studied my shaking fingers pleating a tiny crease in my rayon suit pants. "Besides, it's time I advanced your PI training. How are your fine motor skills?"

CHAPTER TWENTY

DING, DONG THE BITCH WAS DEAD. Which old bitch? The meddling bitch.

His spirits soared. He wasn't high on life, he was high on death.

The gun oil cleansed his rifle, and replenished the faith he'd lost. Following a kill, he philosophized; searched his soul for a deeper meaning of what compelled him. If he dug deep enough would he find a shred of his humanity?

Nah.

That well was dark, shallow, and bone dry. Just today he decided life wasn't a circle, but a dead-end. As he'd proved many times.

He laughed out loud at his own pop psychology, not caring who heard. The sound echoed in the small room, eerie, crazy as the forlorn cry of a loon. The last link to the past had been broken. Finally, things would return to the way they used to be, to the way they should have been these seventeen years past.

Waiting had been its own reward. Now was the time to reap the benefits of his divine intervention. He'd erased all links to that horrid night, save one. And he'd never tell.

He'd make certain.

Would he have to kill again?

God, he hoped so.

CHAPTER
TWENTY-ONE

THE NEXT MORNING WHILE Kevin charmed and distracted the TAR at the rehab center before his appointment with Troy James, I hid in the bathroom.

Sure enough, ten minutes later, the receptionist's heels clicked across the beige tile floor. I heard the soap dispenser pump before she washed her hands and turned off the lights. I waited another few minutes before jumping off the toilet seat.

I cracked the bathroom door open. The reception area was empty. Moving quickly in the dark toward the glass partition, I withdrew the slim lock-picking tool concealed in my sock. With the Muzak turned off, it was quiet. Too quiet.

My fingertips dug into the grooved glass window. I tried sliding it open, but it didn't budge. No big surprise, but I'd hoped for easy access. I made my breathing slow and deep, concentrating on the series of steps Kevin had taught me.

The lock clicked and the window slid open silently. It'd almost been too simple, but I wasn't about to dwell on my good luck; it could change any second. I hopped up on the imitation marble counter and duck-walked through the small opening into the office. Once my feet landed on the floor and no hidden alarms blared, I breathed again. A voice warned me that I'd finally crossed the last legal line.

The current log-in book was on the shelf below the window. I unfolded the paper from my back pocket and grabbed a pen. The dates were listed on the top column. I started at the beginning, noting visitors from each day filled as many as fifteen separate pages. Lotta people with substance abuse problems. Naturally, my body chose that moment for a nicotine craving. Noble of me to ignore it.

I flipped backwards in the logbook, counting to forty-five, scanning pages like a grocery store clerk until I was close. Bingo. My nearly illegible signature leapt out. I matched the visitor's names across the page to the patients they'd signed in to visit.

Charles LaChance. Shelley Friel. Gooseflesh broke out. The time noted on the entry showed he'd slunk in four hours after my visit. Coincidence? Or, had Shelley called him? With no time to consider, I jotted down the information and moved to the next page.

My hand stopped at the final entry for Monday. Father

Tim O'Reilly. Strange, he hadn't designated a patient. Or, had he seen more than one? Was Shelley on his list? The only way to find out now was to ask him outright. I wrote it down, replacing the pen and the book exactly where I'd found them.

The eerie stillness of the cramped space was getting to me. I kept looking to the front door. Still locked. That didn't fill me with a sense of security when what I was doing was completely illegal. No gray areas here. If it pissed off the sheriff that I'd faked illness and inadvertently discovered a body, what would he do if I got caught breaking and entering? Besides the obvious option of firing me?

I didn't want to think about it. I wanted to get the hell out of here before my bout of nerves caused me to throw up. Kevin had warned me not to leave any evidence behind and I figured a warm pile of barf was a dead giveaway.

A quick glimpse of the clock showed I had roughly fifteen minutes before I had to scurry back and hide in the bathroom. Hanging out in a stinky toilet wasn't appealing. What else could I find out while I had time to spare? My gaze landed on the discarded log-in books piled ten high alongside the filing cabinet. Since I'd figured out the system, and if I was fast, I could list everyone who'd visited Shelley in the last two months.

Crouching down, with one eye aimed at the front door, I skimmed through the most recent books. Sadness pooled in my chest when I noticed that Shelley had had very few visitors. Dick, in the beginning, but nothing in later weeks. Meredith.

My eyes narrowed at the calligraphy flares of Nancy James' handwriting. Nothing covert about that. Apparently she'd visited the first week of Shelley's admittance. But, Shelley had told us she hadn't kept in contact with Nancy. Another chance visit? Or, another one of Shelley's lies?

Dr. Mike Lawrence. Another pal of Troy James'. I added him to the list.

I kept coming across the name Charles LaChance. Few of the sign-in visits were with Shelley Friel. Seemed old Chuck got around. But, why would he be trolling for clients in a rehab center?

For fun, I double-checked the other entries. David LaChance. His father, again to see Shelley. Samantha.

Samantha. Her last, hopeful girlish scrawl caused sadness to tear my eyes and sear my soul. Enough. I snapped the book shut.

After restacking the logbooks, I shoved the paper back in my pocket. Did the duck-walk balancing act on the counter, squatting as my back cleared the window track. One small jump and I made it to safety on the other side. I'd barely relocked the window, when I heard voices. My pulse spiked and I sprinted to the bathroom.

Once back inside, I waited by the door.

A group of people entered and crowded around the office window. The minute the receptionist's back turned,

I slipped out unnoticed.

Kevin waited for me in the car. The feeling I'd gotten away with something left me high, buoyant, and giddy. Superior. Unfortunately I knew the addictive properties of that rush; jails full of criminals were proof enough. I couldn't help but grin when I waved the paper in Kevin's face. "Got it."

"Any problems?"

"No. What did you find out from Troy?"

"Not much. The guy is a fucking idiot." He scowled and turned down the chunky guitar riffs of "Man in the Box."

"We reminisced. O,r should I say *he* reminisced and I listened to all his previous bouts of athletic greatness. It was pathetic."

"He didn't say anything about Shelley?"

"No. Old Troy was pretty tightlipped when it came to that. Did mention it was unlikely the center would get the last installment for her treatment, now that she was dead."

My eyes widened. Kevin considered that nothing? "He said that out loud?" I knew places like this were money-hungry, but I'd always imagined they'd deny it and claim they'd provide the humanitarian service for free if it were financially feasible. Apparently not.

"Among other things. Also said he might be forced to sue Dick Friel for the remainder."

"Wanna take bets on who represents the clinic? Charles LaChance's name was everywhere out here." Revulsion dripped down my spine when I contemplated the man might have a clone. *One* of him was one too many.

"Anyway, I didn't get a chance to ask him much. He shooed me out right after the question about Shelley. Said he had a lunch date."

"With who?"

"His wife."

I grinned. "A nooner? With Nancy?"

Kevin looked at me as if I'd lost my mind. "Yeah, right. Don't think the Firehouse Restaurant encourages that kind of behavior."

"At least we know where *not* to have lunch." I fluttered the paper in front of his face. "Bonus. I found out Mrs. James had recently visited Shelley."

"Get out." He snatched the paper, managing to keep one hand on the wheel. "Let me see."

"Anyone else look familiar?"

"Mike Lawrence?" Kevin checked the road and the rearview mirror before redirecting his interest to the names. "I remember him. He hung out with Troy, Bobby, Tim, and Danny."

"And Jimmer," I said quietly, pointing to the name mid-page.

He glanced up. "Speak of the devil. Father Tim?"

"Don't you find it strange he was out here the day after our interview? Offering Shelley condolences? He didn't list her, but I'll bet she was the intended target. What do you think they talked about?"

Kevin tossed the paper in my lap. "Hell if I know, but I'm sick of guessing. I say we track Nancy down first and then Father Tim and find out."

We sped into town and parked on Main Street directly in front of the Firehouse Restaurant. I watched the door, wishing we were doing surveillance from the inside, while eating a buffalo burger and drinking a pint of their famous stout beer. My stomach rumbled. Seemed breaking and entering created a powerful hunger. Just as I was about to complain, a couple stepped out and paused in front of the red door.

"That's them," Kevin said.

After a brief kiss, the stout woman climbed into a gray Mercury Mystique parked six cars away and took off.

We followed. Luckily she didn't detour to Wal-Mart or the Country Club. She went straight home to a quarter-of-a-million-dollar house on West Boulevard. Did the rehab center offer treatment for addictions to ostentatious displays of wealth? Physician, heal thyself.

Kevin parked in the driveway, and we hurried to catch her as she hustled up the sidewalk.

She was unlocking the massive oak double front door when I called out, "Nancy?"

The keys dropped from the lock and she spun around. "Yes?"

"Hi. Sorry, I didn't mean to startle you."

"That's okay." She grunted as she bent over and picked up her keys, holding them like a weapon; her cold brown eyes zipped from Kevin to me. "Do I know you?"

"Maybe. I graduated a couple of years after you. Julie Collins?"

Her chin, just shy of double, raised a notch. "Sure, I remember you. Surprised you recognized me. Been a long time."

Truth be told, I wouldn't have recognized her. Nancy had plumped out more than was healthy. Instead of letting my eyes widen in horror at her ballooned shape, I smiled. "You haven't changed a bit."

She blushed with pleasure. "Thanks. Neither have you. So, what brings you here? Selling something?"

"No." I angled my head to Kevin. "Just want to ask you a few questions."

"Who's he?" Her hungry eyes raked him head-to-toe. I guessed she'd gorge on Kevin instead of food if he were on the menu.

"Kevin Wells," he answered with that knock 'em dead smile that made women seriously consider disrobing.

Nancy James was no exception. She moistened her pink lips; her fingers fiddled with the collar on her blouse. "I remember you. *You* sure have changed." Her coy smile turned into a frown. "Hey, wait a minute. Kevin Wells. Weren't you just out asking my husband a bunch of questions?"

Kevin shrugged and stuffed his hands into the front

pockets of his navy Dockers.

"We're working a case involving Shelley Friel," he said. "We wondered if you'd have time to answer a couple of questions."

"I don't know what you want to ask *me*. I was shocked as anyone else to read Shelley had died." She twisted the keys round and round her pudgy index finger. "Are you cops?"

"No," Kevin said, at the same time I said, "I work for the Bear Butte County Sheriff's Office."

Kevin grimaced, but it appeared Nancy hadn't heard me.

She stopped the nervous movement. A smug smile creased her wide face. "Then in all fairness, I don't know what to tell you."

Nancy hadn't known me well enough to remember I never played fair. "You could start by telling me how you live with yourself."

She blinked in confusion. "What?"

"Doesn't the guilt eat at you?" The tinny sounds of her keys echoed; twirl, clasp, twirl, clasp. "What guilt? What are you talking about?"

I leaned in, letting her read my repugnance. "The night at the fair. Seventeen years ago. You remember. You and Shelley, well, mostly you, whooping it up, having a good time?"

She tossed her shiny black hair, shaking her jowls. Eww. Dressed in a stretchy purple number, Nancy reminded me of Violet Beauregarde, from *Charlie and the Chocolate*

Factory, the snotty, privileged girl who'd swelled into an enormous blueberry after chewing forbidden gum. Maybe Nancy's super-sized body was an attempt to pack away that long ago guilt. It was hard, but I forced myself to give her the benefit of the doubt.

"I don't know what you mean."

And she blew my tiny show of faith with that one mocking sentence. No more playing nice.

"Sure you do, Nance. I wonder what kind of person just takes off when her friend is drunk to the point of unconsciousness? Just so she could go on some silly carnival rides with her boyfriend?"

She turned an interesting shade of green which clashed horribly with the purple.

"How were you supposed to know what happened to Shelley that night? You were too fucking busy getting dizzy on the Tilt-A-Whirl, right? I mean, we've all got our priorities." I stepped closer and dropped my voice to a conspiratorial whisper, "So, *did* you know that Shelley was abducted and brutally raped until she'd blacked out?"

"I didn't know . . ."

"No. I'll bet you didn't even notice," I snapped. "Did you wonder how she'd gotten home? Did you?" My voice rose. "Or were you glad to be rid of her since she was such an embarrassment to you and your friends?"

"Stop it," she begged, squeezing her eyes until they disappeared in her fat face.

"Or maybe you're the type that would've cared more if they would have killed her? Left her broken body to rot in that field until only forensics identified her? Then *you* could've gotten sympathy, playing the part of the victim's grieving friend . . ."

"Julie, that's enough," Kevin said.

I walked away, toward the skeletal hedge separating their property from the busy street. Anger burned; I knew my face looked like a ripe tomato about to burst. I couldn't stand next to Nancy; the urge to slap her overwhelmed me. I hated the violent streak I'd inherited from my father and did everything in my power to control it.

It didn't do any good that I blamed Nancy; apparently she didn't blame herself. How different would Shelley's life have turned out if Nancy would have done the right thing and taken Shelley home that night? Pointless to consider now, but it cut me to the quick anyway. Amazing, how one bad decision had the power to ruin so many lives. My hands shook as I lit a cigarette.

Kevin tapped me on the shoulder after I'd viciously ground the butt into Nancy's manicured lawn. "Come back. She wants to talk to you."

"Great. I can't wait."

Her enormous house was obscenely decorated Laura Ashley-style with flowers, ruffles, bows, and gleaming antiques. Nancy stood with her back to me, staring out the eight-foot tall bay window in the breakfast nook. I slid onto one of the leather barstools at the kitchen counter. An open bottle of Jack Daniels sat by the double sink.

She turned around, empty shot glass clutched in her hand. "You're right. What I did was wrong. I know I was a completely selfish shit. The only excuse I'll make was that I was eighteen. We were all self-centered back then."

I bit my tongue. Some of us more than others. My youthful selfishness hadn't harmed anyone beside myself. That wasn't the case with Nancy and Shelley.

"What I did was wrong," she repeated. "I know that now. Believe it or not, I even knew it at the time. But, it didn't matter. I didn't invite her with us that night because I was looking for her friendship."

Kevin said, "Why did you ask her?"

"Because I wanted her to fill in for me at the restaurant when Troy and I went camping in Yellowstone. Selfish? You bet, but she always annoyed the hell out of me. At the time I'd convinced myself I was doing her a favor. She'd complained all summer she hadn't gotten to do anything fun."

Her nostrils flared hostility.

"And what was the first fun thing she did? Got so drunk and obnoxious no one in our group could stand to be around her. So, yeah, maybe it was wrong, but when she went to the bathroom and didn't come back, I was relieved." Nancy planted her abundant backside against the polished oak table. "But, I swear I didn't know about the rape. It never even crossed my mind that something bad could've happened to her."

"But, it did."

Defiance shone in her brown eyes. "I didn't know that until later. Much later. I didn't find out until about four months ago."

"How?"

She ate the shell of lipstick off her bottom lip while she debated. "Shelley came to see me. Here at the house."

"She told us that you hadn't kept in contact."

"We hadn't. After that night at the fair she didn't come back to work at the restaurant. I left for college a few weeks later. I heard she and Dick had gotten married. Troy and I lived in Denver before moving back here five years ago."

"You didn't ever see her?" Kevin leaned casually against the wall papered with gaudy lavender cabbage roses. "Run into her occasionally?"

Nancy looked aghast. "We didn't exactly travel in the same social circles."

I bit my tongue. Hard.

"Anyway," she fluttered her hand, "she just showed up here one day."

"What did she want?"

"For me to convince Troy to let her into the treatment program." She crossed the room, setting the shot glass in the ceramic sink. "Apparently, Dick doesn't carry health insurance and she was denied access to treatment."

I shook my head. "Why would she assume that you could get her into the program?"

Nancy took a deep breath and looked right at me.

"By guilting me into it. She finally told me what happened that night. I heard all about the rape, the bad marriage, her drinking and drug problems. Said her mother was willing to pay for treatment, but only in a long-term facility, away from her kids and especially away from Dick. The Park Foundation is the only one locally which offers that option."

"What did you tell Troy?"

She was back to gnawing on her lip. I watched in fascination, meanly hoping blood would stain her whole mouth so I could see if red was more her color than Pepto-Bismol pink.

"Only that Shelley had money," she admitted. "I played up the fact it was lousy of the foundation to deny treatment when she obviously needed it. He presented her case to the Board and they agreed. But they wanted three quarters of the money up front, the remainder to be paid on her dismissal. Plus, she had to have a physical exam before entering the facility and after her ninety days ended."

"You didn't tell Troy anything else?"

She frowned. "No."

Kevin asked, "Where does Mike Lawrence fit into this?"

"Mike is the clinic's physician."

"Is he the one that examined Shelley prior to her admittance?"

Nancy nodded. "I asked him to do it as a favor to me. And to Troy."

"So, Troy is still friends with him?"

"Good friends. We've stayed in touch with most of the guys we hung around with in high school. Mostly because of Troy. We still do sporting events, and the guys hunt together."

Bully for them. "Does that group include Danny Christopherson?

She studied me for a minute, a mean tilt to her mouth. "How well did you know Mike and Danny?"

"Not well. It's not like I dated them or anything."

"No kidding?" Her sharp snort of laughter set my teeth on edge. "Yeah, I can see how that'd been tough since they're *gay.*"

I went utterly still. "Mike Lawrence and Danny Christopherson are gay?"

"They went from full-backs to full-fledged flaming fruits. Not that I care. They're great guys."

Did their largesse include stooping to rape and murder? My eyes met Kevin's. He wondered too. "How well do you know Charles LaChance?"

Nancy's gleeful face shuddered.

"Nancy?" Kevin prompted.

"I don't know him well, but he and Troy are acquainted."

"Anything else?" I pressed.

"Charles is our attorney."

With the explosion of frills decorating and defining her home, I suspected she'd have lousy taste. "According to my sources, Charles spends a lot of time out at the rehab center. Why?"

She lifted her chin and her eyes blazed. "How would I know? He's Troy's friend and business associate, not mine. He hired him because they've been pals for years. Not my first choice." Grabbing a crocheted dishrag from the sink, she scrubbed at a spot on the black marble countertop until it gleamed no brightly than before.

"How good of friends?" I asked.

Nancy whipped the rag back at the sink. "Look. No offense, but I don't see what any of this has to do with Shelley."

Kevin said, "We're looking at all angles. I think there's more to it than you're telling us."

"I don't want to get into this. It's personal."

I jumped in. "Would it be easier to tell us if I told you Shelley was considering hiring LaChance? He confronted her with the information that he knew who raped her."

Her horrified expression wasn't phony.

But, even that minor blip of humanity didn't soften my opinion of her. "Your husband's *pal* wanted to go after Samantha's biological father for back child support. Not because he wanted justice for the vicious rape or to help the cops find Samantha's killer. No. His only interest was his cut of the recovered money. Now, both Sam and Shelley are dead. I can see why *your* personal life is so goddamned important."

Her head swayed back and forth vehemently. "I can't tell you."

"Why would you want to protect scum like LaChance? Especially if you don't like him?"

The tears welling in her eyes had the reverse effect on me. I didn't feel sorry for her. I doubted she'd ever shed tears for anyone beside herself.

Kevin plucked a pink Kleenex from a dispenser and handed it over. "We aren't trying to get you in trouble. We're at a dead-end here. Anything you know that would put to rest this family tragedy would help us, Nancy. Please."

My partner deserved an Oscar for his moving performance of servitude, since his fury nearly bled from his reddened ears.

She dabbed her eyes and sniffled before directing her pitiful, hopeful gaze at Kevin the wonderful. "I'll tell you. But, if you think you're going to use this information in some case involving a drunken woman that's already dead, you're dead wrong. I'll deny everything."

"Whatever you tell us will be kept confidential," Kevin assured her.

Nancy clutched the Kleenex and stared straight ahead, neither meeting our eyes nor avoiding them. "Three years ago Troy had a serious gambling problem. Deadwood, video gambling, you name it, he owed money everywhere. He'd blown all of our savings and every penny of my inheritance. We were flat broke, had a second mortgage on the house and the bank was ready to foreclose. Every time I left my Mercedes I was afraid it'd be gone when I returned. Inspiring behavior for the head administrator in a business that deals with addictive behavior, huh?"

Her eyes narrowed and she twisted her mass deeper into the table, trying to get comfy.

"To make matters worse, Troy had done some funky paperwork dealing with referrals which put extra cash in his pocket. Charles is on the Board of Directors. He figured it out. So, magnanimous man that he is," she said snottily, "he approached Troy, offering to help him come clean with the Board. Even negotiated with our creditors. Troy agreed without discussing it with me. Troy has blinders on when it comes to Charles."

Kevin made sympathetic noises and murmured, "What did Troy agree to do?"

"Report any potential lawsuits from patients. I don't know the particulars. I don't want to know. And, they now split the referral kickbacks fifty-fifty."

"Referrals to whom?"

"Mike. Or Danny. He's a psychologist," Nancy said.

I couldn't imagine Danny Christopherson as an expert in the workings of the human mind. He'd always resembled a braying jackass that rivaled Charles LaChance for obnoxiousness. No wonder they were all still good buddies. No wonder Kevin and I had usually avoided them like the plague.

"So, did Danny counsel Shelley?"

"No. But he is in charge of assigning individual counselors."

It made perfect sense. That's how Charles LaChance knew the particulars about Shelley's rape. Danny boy probably gave him a whole play-by-play. It sickened me. It'd all been about money, never about healing or even helping Shelley. Or, poor Samantha.

Kevin frowned. "The Board doesn't know?"

Nancy shook her head. "On Charles' recommendation, they switched accounting firms. Now, the money Troy receives is considered a perk. And, the referrals are legitimate. The paperwork says what they're doing is completely legal."

"But unethical as hell," I pointed out.

She glared at me, eyes superior, bare, ugly mouth down-turned in condescension.

That was the last straw. We had what we needed and I had to get the hell out before I did something rash, like stab her to see if she bled vinegar. As I brushed past Kevin, he stepped forward and clasped her hands. "Thank you."

I didn't thank her. I was thankful I'd gotten through the interview without slugging her.

CHAPTER
TWENTY-TWO

WE LEFT THE JAMES' HOUSE and zipped down Main Street to Fifth. Luckily, Danny Christopherson and Mike Lawrence had set up shop in the same medical building. Unfortunately, their TAR wouldn't even let us know whether Danny and Mike were in the office, let alone allow us to talk to them. Since their appointments were booked solid for two weeks, Kevin left a business card, but we knew we wouldn't be hearing from them, especially when their pal Nancy shared her fun visit from us.

In desperation we headed to St. Augustine's to question Father Tim again. We didn't talk much, which was becoming the norm with us. I didn't like it and didn't like that Kevin seemed fine with the change. Usually, if I pissed him off he'd tell me. This silent treatment sucked.

At the Catholic church, the crabby receptionist motioned for us to stay back while she chastised some poor soul over the phone. Lord. It was a toss up which was more antiquated; her or her Danish Modern desk.

I studied her wrinkled skin under the layer of white powder she'd pounded to the top button of her high-necked blouse. Hah. A nun incognito. I wasn't fooled by the no-wimple attire; little wonder her disposition was lousy. If someone had told me I couldn't have sex, *ever*, I'd shrivel up and snarl at everyone too. Come to think of it, I had been pretty snappish lately. My gaze dropped to the skin on the back of my hand. Hey. Was I looking a bit prunish? While I didn't miss Ray, I missed the regular sex. God, I needed to get laid. Soon.

After cooling our jets for fifteen minutes in the no-smoking fire and brimstone zone, Miss Tight Mouth haughtily informed us Father Tim had taken a well de-served mini-sabbatical. He wasn't expected back until the following week.

She sent a lingering scowl to the man tracking concrete dust across the red-carpeted foyer. The construction con-tinued; unfortunately, I didn't catch a glimpse of Bobby Adair running around and barking out orders. He prob-ably avoided this woman too.

We left. I popped Stone Temple Pilots into the CD player, letting "Sex Type Thing" block the empty air in Kevin's car all the way to Kevin's office.

David LaChance leaned against the hallway wall out-side of Kevin's suite. Unshaven, sloppy clothes, dark circles under his eyes; he epitomized haggard. He pushed away and strode toward us.

"Hey, David," Kevin said as he punched in the access code for the alarm. After the green "ready" light flashed, he opened the door, motioning us inside the dark office. "Didn't expect to see you. Aren't you close to the end of the semester?"

"Meredith called me last night."

Kevin tossed his keys on the desk. "So, you know about Shelley."

"Yes. What the hell is going on? First Samantha is murdered and now Shelley kills herself?"

"Why don't you have a seat?"

David went rigid. "I don't want to have a seat. I want some answers."

I flipped my pack of cigarettes open, grabbed the ashtray, and settled into the buffalo-skin chair. This could be a long conversation.

Kevin remained composed, moved behind his desk, and eased into his chair. "Answers about what?"

"About all of this," David said. "I know you've told me where Sam spent those last two weeks."

"Which is what you paid us to do," Kevin pointed out.

"Yeah, so? I want to know who killed her."

Kevin shook his head. "That's something I can't do. It's strictly a police matter."

"Can't or won't?" David turned to me. "Why would

Shelley kill herself?"

"Why don't you ask your father?" I suggested sweetly. He blanched, sulking into the chair. "What does he have to do with anything?"

"Shelley had considered hiring him." I blew a series of tiny smoke rings. "Didn't he tell you?"

"No. Dad and I aren't exactly sharing confidences these days."

"Ah. So, your father didn't tell you he'd visited Sam at her house right before she disappeared?" Kevin said, watching David's reaction like a hawk circling a wayward prairie dog.

David leapt to his feet. "That's a lie. Why would he do that?"

Kevin held his hands out, palms up, and shrugged. "You tell us."

"Who told you this?"

"Meredith." I paused and exhaled. "She was there. She has no reason to lie, especially now."

Face red, hands clenched, David expelled a loud, "Goddammit!"

He looked ready to throw something or hit someone. I was tired of being on the receiving end of angry men's fists lately, so I scooted back.

"You aren't really surprised that he was warning Sam off, are you?"

I glanced up at Kevin's strange comment and waited

for him to strike. He knew something. But, since he and I hadn't been swapping confidences either, I felt like the proverbial mushroom.

"Tell me, David," Kevin said slowly, "why did you really hire us? What did you expect us to find out?"

David didn't move in mouth or body.

"Or, maybe a better question is: What were you afraid we'd uncover?"

He closed his eyes; his voice dropped to a gravelly whisper. "That my Dad was the one who raped Shelley."

I hadn't expected the deafening silence in the room to increase, but it did. Tenfold. Kevin and I exchanged a fleeting glance. That was one scenario we hadn't considered. Then again, no one willingly conjures up those abhorrent images.

"Why would you think that?" Kevin asked.

The thick laugh bubbling from David came mighty close to hysterical. "Because that bastard is capable of anything. When I first started dating Sam, he freaked, I mean totally freaked. Called her every name in the book and he hadn't even met her. I didn't understand why since he'd never acted like such an ass to any of my other girlfriends."

"When did you first think something was wrong?"

"When I found out he'd been at the fair that night all those years ago."

"How did you find out?"

"He didn't bother to hide it after I told him about

Shelley's rape."

"So, you jumped to the conclusion that you'd fallen in love with your sister?" Kevin said with skepticism.

"Half-sister," he corrected. "No, not right away. But, why would he be so adamant against me getting involved with her when he never gave a shit about anything I did, good or bad."

"Come on. That's soap opera farfetched," I said.

"You don't understand. He became obsessed with the details about what happened to Shelley. He kept hounding me for specifics; what Shelley remembered, and what she'd told Sam."

"Still, that's quite a stretch." Apparently his father's conversations with Danny Christopherson weren't giving him the dirt he needed and Charles wasn't opposed to using his own son as a shovel.

"Now, you tell me he went to see Sam? What would you think?"

"That even your father wouldn't stoop low enough to let you continue a sexual relationship with your half-sister," Kevin said.

But, I wasn't so sure.

"You'd wonder though, wouldn't you? Then Sam cut off all contact with me. It's like she found out something she was ashamed of."

"Something she couldn't tell you."

He nodded. "Or, knew I'd freak about. God. I've

never been close to my dad, but he acted in a way I'd never seen. It just got worse after Sam disappeared." David slumped against the back wall, knocking Kevin's picture askew. "Then he did a complete 180. He encouraged me to hire you."

Kevin's stillness sucked even more air out of the already oxygen-deprived room. "What?"

David's smug smile said it all. "You heard right. Dad suggested I hire you, knowing you'd never willingly work for him. Said you were probably a sucker for a sad story so he advised me to tell you that he was against me hiring you."

I choked on the last bit of smoke to leave my lungs. "David. There was no inheritance for the retainer, was there?"

He shook his head.

"Then, where'd you get the money?"

"From him."

Kevin stood abruptly, losing his balance on his bum ankle and knocking his chair into the window. The metal blind crashed to the floor.

David's questioning stare burned into my forehead, but my eyes were glued on the tensed line of Kevin's back. We'd been played. By Charles LaChance.

I recalled Shelley's last story, how her rapist used his violent actions against her to disprove his homosexuality. Charles LaChance hadn't remarried since his divorce. And, David's grandfather had threatened to have Charles arrested for rape after his daughter's pregnancy. Another coincidence? Or, was rape the only way Charles could get it up for a woman? And what about Charles' eagerness to help Troy James? Because they'd been lovers years ago? Is that why Nancy seemed panicked when I'd asked what else they were to each other? What was their relationship now? Embarrassing enough to kill for?

How did Danny Christopherson and Mike Lawrence fit in? Although they were openly gay now, it never would've been acceptable behavior in — or just out of high school. What had they wanted to prove?

Had that whole macho bullshit group of guys been covering up their homosexual activities?

I'd never seriously considered LaChance a suspect in Sam's death. Until now. In Shelley's last, desperate frame of mind, he could've coerced her into anything. Maybe she'd checked out early to meet him. In my mind's eye, I saw him pulling a gun, forcing her to drink until she passed out. He'd done it before with success. Except this time he guaranteed her death by leaving her body in a garage filled with carbon monoxide.

The scenario made perfect sense to me in some ways. And yet . . . in others, it didn't fit.

If Charles had raped Shelley, she knew all along he was Sam's father. Didn't think anything of it, lost in an alcoholic stupor. Until her daughter started dating David, her half-brother. So, had Shelley done something stupid when she'd sobered up, like blackmail Charles? Threaten to cement his bad reputation and reveal his sexual preferences? And their child? Had she thought up the back child support issue on her own? With him in the starring, paying role? Is that why he questioned Tony's lawyer? Wondering about his *own* legal options?

Shelley's financial choices were limited. Dick was divorcing her and she hadn't held down a paying job since high school. It'd probably seemed like easy money. I doubted she believed he'd kill both her and Sam to keep his business quiet.

It did seem farfetched. And, there wasn't a damn shred of proof.

Another horrible thought sneaked in. What if Shelley had told Samantha about her birth father, not knowing that Samantha had already been intimate with David? For some reason Catholics believed the chastity of their youth until faced with rounded bellies as contrary evidence. Samantha and David's relationship hadn't been platonic. Is that why Samantha had cut off all contact with him?

It didn't make sense, but the sick feeling in my stomach intensified. I was glad I hadn't eaten lunch because I'd be wiping the remnants of it off Kevin's desk.

David's weary sigh broke the icy silence.

Kevin's face was devoid of any expression when he turned around. "I'm sorry, David, I don't know what else to tell you." He reached into a manila folder, withdrew a sheet of paper and handed it to him. "I planned on mailing this, but now that you're here . . . I've itemized our time and charges. As you can see, your initial retainer is used up."

Dazed, David stared at him. "So, that's it?" He looked from me to Kevin helplessly. "How am I supposed to deal with not knowing what happened to Sam? Where am I supposed to go now?"

"I suggest you take that up with your father." I stood, opened the door, and leaned against the jamb, hardening my resolve in the face of his misery.

David LaChance's peace of mind was no longer our problem. But, I doubted Kevin or I would let this rest until we'd found ours.

I'd barely slammed the door when the phone rang. Kevin scooted his chair back to the proper position and picked up the receiver.

He signaled to me to sit, punching the speakerphone button. Jimmer's voice boomed. "Hey. You guys trying to piss off everyone in town?"

"What?"

"Heard from Harvey today, in person. He's still pissed off at you, little missy, because Helen up and quit."

I bit back a smile. "Not my fault."

"Actually, I should thank you because after he came in,

he left with not one, but two new, very expensive knives."

"See? I am good for business."

"But," he continued, as if I hadn't spoken, "it *is* your fault Tony Martinez called me, chewing my ass, wondering what it'd take to get you two to lay off this case."

My eyes locked with Kevin's. "We haven't done anything."

Jimmer snorted. "Yeah, right. Seems your names have been cursed all over town. Dick's head mechanic, Tommy Stahl, came in yesterday, supposedly looking for some Black Hills Gold earrings for his old lady, but I think he was fishing for info on you guys."

"Sounds like your day was as fun-filled as ours," Kevin muttered, reaching for his squishy stress reliever ball perched on top of the pile of manila file folders.

I took a wild guess. "Gotten a call from Danny Christopherson and Mike Lawrence yet?"

"No. Haven't seen those fags since last year's antelope season."

Apparently my "gaydar" hadn't been functioning at all if homophobe Jimmer knew the truth about them. "They customers of yours?"

"Yep. Their money ain't queer, even if they are."

I smiled and was about to ask about Charles LaChance and Troy James' buying habits when Jimmer groused, "Ready to hear conversation number *four* I had on your behalf today?"

"Bring it on."

"Interesting, you should bring up that group. I had a chat with another old friend of yours."

"Who?" Kevin asked.

"Bobby Adair."

"*We* weren't friends with him," I said, "you were."

"Don't matter. He's been in a lot lately, buying me out of damn near every kind of ammo. We got to shooting the shit and your names came up."

"In what context?"

"That's the weird thing. He asked me what the hell I was doing hanging around wannabe losers like you two."

"Seriously?" I said, watching Kevin.

He shrugged, tossing the ball in the air.

"Yeah," Jimmer continued, "then he went off on this tangent that you two shouldn't be running around playing cops. It oughta be left to the real pros. Went on and on that it was too bad everything wasn't run like the military." Jimmer hawked out something nasty and spit it close to the receiver. "That Bobby's turned into a freak show, regardless if he's a repeat customer."

I scowled at the phone. "Why does he think the military is so great?"

"Are you kidding? The man was like super-commando during the Gulf War. Got every medal imaginable. Friend of mine claimed Bobby had Saddam by the throat but they made him let Saddam go. Fucking pity."

Kevin said, "Jimmer, how do you know all this?"

"Guys talk. Like I said, he's a good customer. But, he ain't got a lotta good to say about you guys. What did you do to piss him off?"

I wracked my brain to think of something I said or did that might've offended him. Angering people seemed to be another of my special traits, but I'd been fuming over his racist comments and had barely said two words. He and Kevin and Father Tim had done all the talking.

"I don't know why," Kevin admitted. "He seemed fine on Sunday although he's never been real friendly. Might've been something that happened in high school. People around here carry grudges for a long time."

"Don't I know it. Well, I'd watch out. Rumor has it he got tossed out of the service for assault with a deadly weapon."

"What was the weapon?" I asked, picturing various tools.

"His hands."

"Honorable or dishonorable discharge?" Kevin asked, ever the consummate professional PI on top of scenarios I hadn't even considered.

"Honorable. Guess the only reason he didn't get the dishonorable was because the prostitute he beat the shit out of didn't die." Jimmer's voice lowered. "Julie, you'd better stay the hell away from him. And Harvey. Hell, Tony Martinez too. I'm not kidding. Sounds like all those fuckers are out for a piece of you."

A crash reverberated though the speaker. "Shit, those kids are skateboarding in here again. I gotta go."

The dial tone echoed until Kevin shut it off.

"That was interesting." He'd barely gotten the words out when the phone trilled again. Kevin answered, spinning his chair toward the window.

He needn't have bothered. I tuned him out, assuming the caller was Lilly. I couldn't stand to listen to him become all soft and sweet, especially when he hadn't been that way with me for days.

Instead, I righted the tiny picture on the back wall. While this piece would never be misconstrued as art, it was fascinating, one of those types of pictures you stared at until some hidden image emerged. The thing irritated the crap out of me, not only because it'd been a gift to Kevin from Lilly; it was highly embarrassing to admit I'd yet to see the supposed image. So, why did I bother looking? I chalked it up to another masochistic trait I inherited from my father.

I turned back and found Kevin staring through the picture. The receiver was back in the cradle. "What?"

He refocused on me. "That was Sergeant Schneider from the Rapid City Police Department. Seems they've had a break in Samantha's case."

My heart did a little happy roll. "Yeah? That's good news. What'd they find?"

"Strangely enough, we're the ones that found it. The

knife in my Jeep tire had traces of blood. Human blood, so they ran samples and matched it to Samantha's."

"No shit?"

"It gets better. They're pretty sure the knife belongs, or belonged to Dick Friel. One of his employees identified it. The sheriff's department brought Dick in for questioning."

"Is he still there?"

"No. He's under suspicion, not arrest. They let him go."

Okay, I should've been doing somersaults. A significant break in the case meant Samantha's death wouldn't go unsolved like Ben's. Which is what I wanted. Factor in the joyous fact that punch-happy Dick was the new suspect and I should've been flipping cartwheels. He'd held the top position on my list since day one.

So, why wasn't I cheering and planning a victory drunk?

Simple.

I no longer believed Dick Friel was guilty.

"Julie?"

I guessed my skepticism showed. "Doesn't it seem a little convenient that the missing murder weapon suddenly appears?"

"It happens more that you think. People get careless. Or lazy."

"I mean, come on, I'll admit Dick is lazy, but he's not *that* stupid. If he killed Sam, he'd basically gotten away with it. Why would he screw up now?"

Kevin placed his finger in his ear and wiggled it around.

"Excuse me? You're telling me now you *don't* believe Dick is guilty?"

"No way was Dick the one shooting at us that day."

"What makes you so sure?"

"You convinced me the person shooting at us was up on that ridge. Can you see Dick hauling his fat ass up that cliff in the middle of a workday? All the police have to do is check his alibi."

"They did. He was out of the shop all afternoon Monday. Besides, he could've hired someone to shoot at us and stick the knife in my tire."

I reached for my cigarettes. "Doesn't make sense. Shooting at us and planting evidence against himself is the last thing he'd do. Think about it."

Kevin's jaw tightened and his stress-relief ball bounced across the desk blotter. "Well, since you seem to have all the answers, who did it? Then, I can call Sergeant Schneider back and tell him you solved the case."

Heat rushed to my face. I'm not usually on the receiving end of Kevin's scathing comments. "I think we should look harder at the Charles LaChance-Mike Lawrence-Danny Christopher-Troy James angle." I exhaled, but didn't expound on my reasons. "Who do you think it is?"

"I don't know. That's not our job, remember? Let's leave it up to the experts."

"So, if Pennington County has FBI experts on hand, why is Sergeant Schneider giving you a heads up? Especially when your part of the case is done?"

"They *asked* the Feds on this case, so as a courtesy everyone has access to all information. Even a piss-ant like me."

I rolled my eyes when the phone rang again.

The call was brief and after it ended Kevin was on his feet. "Sorry. I've got to run. You going home?"

"Didn't plan on it."

"Why not? You're not working at the sheriff's office later?"

"No. I just . . ." I looked away, my embarrassment back. Kevin wouldn't understand my recent hatred of an empty house. He had the option of calling Lilly. I had the option of calling no one but him. And, he wasn't home often enough to suit my tastes anymore. I glanced back at him but couldn't force a smile or think of a snappy retort.

His gaze turned shrewd. "Ray hasn't been by again, has he?"

I shook my head. "Since I've got nothing going on, you want me to tag along?"

"No, that's fine. I can handle it."

I tried the tactic that always worked: "I could use the extra cash."

"Another time perhaps." He busied himself reorganizing his tidy desk.

Either his appointment involved Lilly or he didn't want me to meet some highbrow client. Either way, I felt like he'd taken another shot at me. Guess as a low level employee I was relegated to the shitty jobs that kept me up at night.

I tossed his lock pick on his desk and left.

CHAPTER TWENTY-THREE

SINCE THE INCIDENT WITH RAY, I'd avoided going into Dusty's. I needed a shot and was tired of drinking alone. On the spur of the moment, I drove to Fat Bob's. Four o'clock in the afternoon seemed the perfect time to find out what Tony knew about Dick's situation. Besides, I was probably safe from Harvey; the man couldn't work twenty-four/seven.

Wrong. The minute I stepped into the nearly empty bar, Harvey was on me like a bloodhound.

"Ms. Collins," he said without a hint of humor. "Lovely as it is to see you, you know you're not allowed in here."

"I need to talk to Tony."

"I think you're the last person he wants to see."

"Why?"

"You know why."

"Then, he knows about Dick?"

He nodded and took a step forward.

I stepped back, just as he'd intended. I tried a kewpie doll smile and an innocent shrug. I stopped short at batting my lashes. Didn't want to overdo it. "Come on. Have a heart. It's important that I explain some things to him."

"I don't."

Had my dazzling demeanor somehow confused him? Because he wasn't making sense. "You don't what?"

"Have a heart. Now, get out before I prove it."

"It's okay," Tony said from behind me. "I'll talk to her outside."

I blew Harvey a kiss but I wasn't stupid enough to turn my back on him as I shuffled out the door.

Tony walked to a rickety pine picnic table by the Dumpster. He didn't sit, or gesture for me to do so. He crossed his muscular arms over his chest, bit down on the toothpick in his mouth, and waited.

Big bravado. I suddenly lacked it. I shivered, not against the chilly afternoon, but from the contempt darkening Tony's eyes. "I just found out about Dick."

"I'm sure you're happy as shit. Got exactly what you wanted." He paused; his gaze raked over me sending another shudder down my spine. "Did you come here to gloat, blondie? Or, are you now trying to pin Shelley's suicide on him too?"

Not the time to mention Shelley's death hadn't been suicide. "No. But it doesn't make sense. Why would

Shelley . . ."

"Screw Shelley. It's her fault Dick is under suspicion for Samantha's murder. Like I said before, he didn't do it."

I held his eyes. "I know."

Tony thoughtfully chewed the toothpick, making it bounce up and down against his full lips. "Why the sudden change? Weren't you the one trying to convince me he killed Sam? Now, the cops buy your theory? And they've got evidence, found on your partner's vehicle, to back it up?"

"How do you know all this? We only heard a little while ago."

"You didn't come here for that information, did you?"

Part of me didn't want to know how Tony gleaned his knowledge. "I came here because I think Dick is being set up and I wondered what you were doing about it."

He gave me indignant. "Why would *I* do anything?"

"Because it'd be bad business not to. And, you told me everything with him was about business, remember? You really want him hanging in the cop shop, influenced by law enforcement officials who might convince him *they* could see to his interests better than you? They turn guys like Dick for kicks. I imagine the DEA would love the inside scoop on your operation."

Maybe that was why the Feds had been interested in this case. I leaned close enough that my hair fluttered against his black leather vest. "So, 'fess up on how you're handling this because you're not the stupid type to ignore it."

A car backfired, but I managed not to jump as Tony measured me in utter silence.

His teeth showed white against his copper skin; he rotated the toothpick to the other side of his mouth in a sexy, confident move which reminded me of a young Eastwood. "You are one ballsy broad. Few people in my life speak so freely." He reached out; his hand gathered my hair absentmindedly, stroking a golden section like the finest silken fabric. The eroticism increased when his calloused thumb lingered on the pulse beating wildly beneath my chin as he tucked the strands behind my ear. "You sure you don't want to come to work for me?"

Somehow, my voice sounded sure and steady. "I didn't realize riding around on the back of your bike was a paying position."

"It is for you."

I shrugged away his offer, pretending I declined them every day. "When I'm looking for something new, I'll let you know." It paid to keep my options open, especially when I understood Tony wasn't really blaming me for the latest development in the Dick saga. I offered up a little prayer to the patron saint of bars. Guess being in church *had* done me some good.

"The offer will stand." His black eyes zeroed in on the crusted gash on my cheek. "Who did that?"

I dropped my gaze to the gravel beneath my Doc

Martens and lifted a shoulder.

He lifted my face back toward his, smoothing his palm over the mark, demanding, "Tell me."

"It's been handled," I said, wary of the anger in his eyes and remembering too late Jimmer's warning about steering clear of Tony, his goons, and his brand of justice.

After brushing a feather-light kiss over it, he retreated. "I'll make sure of it. In the meantime, Dick is in good hands."

"Who's representing him?"

Tony gave me that killer grin. "Mark Adderton. Heard of him?"

Hell, everyone knew Mark Adderton. He was the Midwest equivalent of Gerry Spence. Dick Friel was in good hands, indeed.

"Be careful," he warned softly, smoothing his hand over my scalp one last time, letting his hand linger by my ear. The guy had a serious Jones for my hair.

"Of what?" The thing which seemed the most dangerous to me right now was why Tony Martinez appealed to my basal instincts. I needed sex. Pretty soon old Mr. Lambert from Dusty's would start looking good.

"I have a feeling you've only scratched the surface on this. It'll probably get nastier yet before it's over."

As I watched him swagger back into the bar, I had the feeling he was probably right.

Kevin called that night. "Shelley's funeral is Saturday."

"So soon?"

"Her mother came back and made all the arrangements."

At least Meredith wasn't handling this alone. "Where are the kids staying?"

"With her." He hesitated. "Want me to pick you up?"

He knew I hated funerals. Was he offering his support? Or, was this a duty I needed to perform as his employee? At this point I didn't care. I was glad he'd asked. I missed his company more than was healthy. "Sure."

As I hung up I realized I'd half-expected a phone call or a visit from Meredith. Once again, we had death in common. But the phone and the doorbell stayed quiet.

When I got home from work Friday, the light on my answering machine blinked red. First time this week someone actually wanted to talk to me. The excitement won out over fear it might be Ray calling to make additional threats.

I hit playback.

"Julie? This is Father Tim O'Reilly. My secretary told me you and Kevin stopped by. I tried calling him but his machine didn't pick up." He paused and his voice dropped an octave. "Look. I need to talk to you. I can't get into it over the phone and you can't reach me at the church camp. But would you let Kevin know I've been in touch and I'll call back later? God's blessings to you."

I didn't remember giving Father Tim my unlisted number, but that didn't concern me as much as the idea Kevin wasn't answering his office phone. I dialed the number and let it ring. No answer. Same thing at home. And his cell kicked to voice mail. Not only was it bad for business, it was bad for our friendship that whatever his problems, he wasn't confiding in me. At this point I so craved a connection with him that I'd even listen to him snivel about Lilly.

Car doors slamming and loud voices next door broke into my brooding. I lifted the curtain. Looked like Leanne was in the party mood again. Poor Kiyah. Would she seek refuge at my house? I mixed up a box of brownies just in case, nobly ignored the last can of beer, and sat down to watch TV.

I woke at 2 a.m., alone, my arm screaming in pain from the unnatural angle it'd been in when I'd fallen asleep on the couch. Feeling more bereft than I had in months, I didn't see it getting any better soon. Shelley's funeral wouldn't bring anyone closure. Especially me.

Funerals bothered me in principle. No matter how

uniquely a person lived their life, their final send-off remained predictable: hushed voices, standard black clothing, unscented flowers, and music usually consisting of a bad vocal rendition of "How Great Thou Art." Not to mention the printed programs chronicling a person's entire life in one tiny paragraph, and a guest book to sign, as if it were all some understated cocktail party. Add in traipsing to the cemetery, and back to the church for finger food, and it became a bizarre ritual I avoided.

I lodged my biggest complaint against how guests rubbernecked the grieving family to judge how well they were "holding up." Hysterics belonged at home. Those souls filled with grief and pain were expected to act like gracious hosts and accept meaningless phrases as comfort from those people that were basically voyeurs.

Catholic funerals are only slightly weirder than Baptist funerals. Pomp, circumstance, and incense are dignified compared to talk of hellfire, brimstone, and eternal damnation. Still, Baptist funerals are atypical and I'd pick wrath over decorum. Unfortunately, I didn't have a choice today.

The humidity on Saturday morning made the cold air outside feel like the inside of a meat locker. Kevin pulled up and Kiyah waved at me as she bounded down the road to the playground. I shivered against the synthetic fabric of my suit; the same one I'd worn when I first interviewed Shelley. Kevin's usual compliment was slow in coming.

The service was short. No need for the priest to drone on when there were so few people in attendance.

Dick Friel sat stiffly beside a stoop-shouldered, white-haired woman I assumed was Shelley's mother. She, Dick, Meredith, and RJ made up the entire front pew. When RJ turned to look at the soloist, his resemblance to Dick was uncanny. Dick would have a hard time proving RJ wasn't his kid.

The woman in the second row bore a striking similarity to Shelley, but in a refined way that led me to believe her life had turned out much different from her sister's.

I didn't recognize the two older women or the couple in front of us. Tony and Harvey had taken seats farthest from the pulpit. David and Charles LaChance sat on opposite ends of the same pew in the back.

We skipped the trip to the cemetery. The funeral director kept the family secluded, so I didn't get a chance to talk to Meredith. Part of me didn't know what to say; part of me knew exactly what she needed to hear. Tony and I exchanged a brief nod. The LaChances didn't acknowledge us at all.

Kevin cranked the heater to full blast on the drive back to my house. Once again we were silent. Kevin's distraction only heightened my misery. I didn't know how the day could get any worse.

As we slowed to make the corner of my street, I saw Kiyah, slumped on a sawed-off railroad tie, close to the same place I'd seen her more than two hours earlier. The ruffled purple parasol had stopped twirling, her shoes dug into the mud.

My stomach made a swooping tumble. "Stop the car."

Kevin hit the brakes and I jumped out and ran toward her, my heels slipping in the muck and slop.

Kiyah looked up at my approach, cowering against the cold. Her white arms were covered in gooseflesh, her jaw clenched against the shudders shaking her small body. On her slight frame she wore a skimpy yellow lace camisole, a long pink skirt and the sequined Mary Jane's I'd bought her last week. She didn't smile, didn't hold her arms out for a hug, didn't move beyond another shiver.

I shoved the rage down a layer and crouched eye level to her. "Hey. Little cold to be playing dress-up, isn't it?"

Her head drooped to her chest in misery and embarrassment.

My arms slipped underneath her. I lifted her easily; she weighed next to nothing. "Have you been out here all morning?"

Kiyah buried her chilled face against the heat rising in my neck.

"Where's your mom?"

"H-h-home."

"Does she know you're out here?"

She nodded.

I purposely kept my voice light, friendly. "Did she send

you outside to play?"

"S-she an' B-bobby wanted to b-be 'lone."

They'd sent a child out in the cold, barely dressed enough for a summer tea, so they could fuck. My insides pitched again and I clamped my teeth together to stop from screaming my outrage, focusing my attention on the little girl shivering in my arms. "Did you eat anything today?"

"Huh-uh."

I took a deep breath and stumbled back to Kevin's car. Damn Leanne. Her cavalier attitude toward Kiyah could get the child killed. I could kill her myself. Any sicko could've driven off the interstate and snatched her. How long would Kiyah have to be gone before Leanne noticed? I hugged her to my chest, pushing aside the comparisons between Kiyah and Samantha Friel. *Never*. I'd never allow it to happen.

"Julie."

Kevin had scrambled up the small hill and held his arms out, but I shook my head, reluctant to let go of my charge. "She's frozen. I'll warm her up at my house before I take her home." We slid in, and her arms tightened like frozen ropes around my neck. "How about some hot soup Yippee Ki-Yi-Yay?" My pet name for her didn't even bring a smile. I smoothed her dirty hair, humming softly again her temple.

At home I filled the tub with warm water and dug out the extra clothes I keep on hand. Kevin heated tomato soup, whipped up a couple of grilled cheese sandwichesn and we watched Kiyah eat. She made no pretense of daintiness; she shoveled in every morsel and drank two glasses of milk. I had to leave the kitchen; I couldn't stomach that sweet, sweet child eating like a starving Ethiopian.

I smoked and stared out through the bluish haze covering my front window. Nearly every house on my block was broken down to some degree. How many other kids were like Kiyah? Like Samantha? Waiting for someone, anyone to notice them? The tears I wouldn't give into earlier this week fell unheeded.

I heard Kevin move in behind me, felt his gentle hands cup my shoulders, felt his warmth digging for purchase inside that dark place inside me where I'd retreated. "You hungry?" he murmured.

"No."

"Me, either." His palms slid down my arms to clutch my hands.

I left my cigarette smoking in the ashtray and leaned back into him. "I hate this."

"I know."

"What am I going to do?"

"You need to call Social Services."

My gut tightened. "I can't do that."

"Jules, you have to. You're too close to this. Kiyah needs someone like you, but not necessarily *you*."

The cigarette smoke rose in a straight line from the

ashtray until our words caused it to waver and curl again. "She's only six."

"That's all the more reason for you to make the call."

"Kevin . . ."

He turned me around, his face so soft another bout of tears arose. "You can't make this your problem anymore. Don't you think I know how much she means to you? This is killing you. God, it's hard enough with you still dealing with Ben's death . . . I can't stand to watch you hurt, babe. She isn't your child, but she might have a chance if you let the system handle it."

"The system sucks." I sniffled. "She'll get shuffled off to some foster home where she'll be subjected to kids that've been through much worse situations. And they'll teach her all sorts of new, bad tricks."

"Or," he countered as he smoothed his fingertips over my wet cheeks. "Maybe some nice family will give her the love she deserves."

I bristled against his well meaning platitudes. "Do you know the statistics on sexual abuse in those places?"

"No." Kevin placed a tender kiss on my temple. "But, maybe her mother will wise up when the social workers appear on her doorstep."

"Yeah, right. The only way Leanne is gonna wake up and smell the sour milk is when her ADC and WIC checks stop coming."

"Julie?"

Kiyah's small voice interrupted our fierce whispers. Kevin and I moved apart. "Yeah, sweet pea? You still hungry?" I wiped away a sandwich crumb from the corner of her mouth and she flinched.

"No. I'm tired."

"Why don't you lie down in the little bedroom? The Barbie jammies are clean. I'll come and tuck you in a sec."

Kiyah hesitated, staring at her tiny pink toes. "I wanna go home."

I couldn't meet Kevin's gaze. Home. She wanted to go home; regardless of what I'd done for her, or could do for her, it'd never be enough. She wanted her mother; even bad mothers have more appeal than non-mothers. I gulped the chunk of my heart that had stuck in my throat. "Sure, whatever you want. I'll walk you over."

Her wet clothes were a pitifully small bundle in her arms as we trekked over the sludge and soggy, decaying leaves. The area separating our houses was a sad patch of ground, strewn with litter, which I occasionally picked up. God knows if I left it to Leanne, it'd look like a landfill had sprouted between us. One year I threw a handful of grass seed around, hoping crisp patches of green would magically appear. Nothing. Not a weed, not a single dandelion or even hard-to-kill Creeping Jenny bothered to take root. That spot of earth is determined to stay infertile and desolate.

The front steps had cracked away from the foundation

of Leanne's house, leaving a ten-inch gap. I peered down at the collection of candy wrappers, plastic grocery bags, and crushed beer cans gathered there while Kiyah kicked aside the broken aluminum storm door and knocked.

I frowned and ruffled her damp hair. "Why don't you just go in? I don't think you need to knock at your own house, silly."

"The door is locked." Even the package of clothes tucked under her chin hadn't muffled her words.

Kevin's sharp intake of breath echoed mine. Leanne had actually locked Kiyah out of the house. I reached over Kiyah's head and rapped with enough force to bruise my knuckles.

Nothing happened for several cold minutes. I knocked harder and gave Kiyah an encouraging smile.

"She's gonna be mad." Kiyah bit her trembling lip and spoke to the concrete.

"At me?" I asked.

"Yeah, but at me too."

I'd started to bend down when the door was flung open. We were treated to Leanne's flimsy cover-up that actually covered nothing. She hadn't bothered with underwear, either. Her erect nipples poked through the pink chiffon robe, fresh red suction marks trailed down her neck and circled her breast. And I'd believed intentional hickeys went out after high school.

Leanne scowled at Kiyah, then me. "What now?"

Kiyah moved forward to circle her reedy arms around Leanne's flabby waist. "I was cold."

"You should've worn your coat." Leanne pushed Kiyah's arms aside and glared at me. "What are *you* doing here?"

"Walking her home."

"Well, she's home now."

My gaze remained on her bloodshot eyes. I forced myself not to lunge for her hickey-laden neck. "Just making sure she could get in this time."

"What were you doin' at her house anyway, Ki?" Leanne jerked a thumb toward me. "You ain't 'sposed to be goin' over there."

"And, just where is she supposed to go?" I asked in a tone she couldn't misinterpret as friendly.

"That ain't none of your business."

"It is my business when she's half-frozen and practically starved. What were you thinking when you locked her out of the house?"

Leanne lifted her chin. "Get off my step."

"No. I'm sick of this." I leaned in, catching the sweet scent of pot on her bedclothes and the booze on her breath. "She sat in the rain for two hours, two hours, cold, alone and hungry while you, and whatever man tripped your trigger this week, rolled around on your mattress in the warm house."

"Is that what this is about? Who I fuck and when I fuck? That ain't any of your fucking business." The spacious gap in her front teeth flashed as she smiled at her own perceived cleverness.

"This isn't about you, this is about Kiyah. When will you start treating her like something more than a trick pony? I don't care who you're sleeping with, but she shouldn't get locked out of her house because of it. She's only six."

Kiyah stared morosely at her feet.

Shifting in the doorframe, Leanne scoffed, "I know how old *my* kid is. I don't answer to you even when you think you're so high and mighty 'cause you work for the sheriff."

"No, you don't answer to me. But, I could see to it you answer to Social Services."

Leanne's mouth opened and closed like an air-starved trout. "You bitch, you wouldn't dare."

"Why don't you try me? I've had a lousy day and I come home and see Kiyah freezing outside in the same place she was hours ago." I slanted over the doorjamb, pleased when she appeared to recoil. "Push me today, Leanne, 'cause I'm looking for a fight."

Leanne grabbed Kiyah. Kiyah stumbled but didn't look up. "Where didja get them clothes?" she demanded.

"Julie gave them to me."

"Now, I see what your interest is in her." Leanne placed a hand on her hip and sneered. "You buy her clothes, play games with her, and hope she'll turn out as queer as you.

You like little girls, don't you? I know you give her a bath. Do you like to watch? Do you get off on it?"

Kevin stepped in. "That's enough."

"I tell you what. Maybe I oughta put a call into the sheriff's office myself. Wonder how long you'd keep that job if they found out their pet lesbian preferred 'em young."

"I'm not a lesbian and you're avoiding the issue. I'm calling Social Services. Count on it. Kiyah deserves better than this."

"Think so? If you come within ten feet of her again, I'll have you arrested." Leanne leaned down, the slit in her robe widened, and her breasts spilled completely out. "Kiyah, honey? Never talk to her again, got that?"

Kiyah glanced at me quickly and I saw a hint of sorrow before she shuffled closer to Leanne. "Yes, Momma."

Leanne stroked the top of her head and crooned, "That's my angel, that's my angel girl." Leanne glared at me and said to Kiyah, "Give her back them ugly clothes."

Kiyah tried to slip around Leanne but was stopped when Leanne's fingers banded around her stick-like arm. She winced.

I took a step forward but Kevin's firm hand on my shoulder held me back.

"No. Take them off right there," Leanne said. "I don't want her filthy ideas or clothes in my house."

Panic-stricken, Kiyah looked up. "But, Momma, we're outside . . ."

"Take 'em off now. Them clothes don't belong to you."

Kiyah hedged and a man, Bobby, I assumed, appeared in the foyer. He'd managed to put on jeans, but they were unbuttoned and his sunken, hairless chest was bare. His blurry eyes landed first on Kevin, and then without interest on me. "What the fuck is going on?"

"Nothing," Leanne trilled. When she turned toward him, her grip on Kiyah loosened. Kiyah seized the opportunity to scramble up the inside stairs.

I expelled a relieved breath. Leanne would've actually made her daughter publicly strip down in order to avoid backing down from me. At that point I didn't know whose behavior was more juvenile, hers or mine. Kevin was right. I had to be the adult; I had to make that call.

Kevin tugged on my sleeve. "Come on, let's go."

"That's right, you'd better go," Leanne said, her voice rising with renewed confidence now that Bobby had entered the scene. "And, you'd better remember what I said. Stay away from my daughter."

Never could stand women who gleaned their courage when trying to impress a man. "You'd better remember what I said too. Expect a visit from my official friends very soon."

"What friends?" Bobby asked on a huge yawn. Leanne's fingers slipped though the greasy strands before she flipped her hair over her shoulder. "Lesbo bitch here has threatened to call Social Services . . ."

"Whoa." Laid-back Bobby vanished. He yanked his 'Big Johnson' T-shirt over his head, buttoned his Wranglers and extracted a set of keys from the skin-tight front pocket. Once the teal-colored flip-flops covered his narrow, pale feet, rubber squeaked across the linoleum, nearly leaving burn marks. "I'm out of here." He shouldered us aside without a backward glance.

Leanne whined, "But, Bobby . . ."

Kevin yanked me off the steps and had us back inside my house before I could respond. After sliding the dead-bolt home, he faced me. "I really wish you'd move."

"To where?"

"Anywhere besides this low rent 'Melrose Place'."

"How can you make jokes?"

"I'm not joking. Move in with me until you find something else. For Chrissake, this place would make anyone crazy."

I closed my eyes. For once his take-charge role wasn't helping, no matter how much I'd longed for it in the last week. But, when I considered how pissed off Callous Lilly would be if I took up residence with Kevin even temporarily . . . Scratch that. My mood was too grim to consider that scenario, although I had fantasized about it.

Maybe he was right; how could I live next door to Kiyah and not interfere? It seemed every person I connected with was touched by misery. The black plague following me around spread to others when I wasn't busy beating i back, keeping them safe.

Samantha. Shelley. Meredith. And now Kiyah. Who was next?

A tear escaped and Kevin wrapped me in his arms before it dripped from my chin. In the last few weeks my life had gone to complete shit. Evidently, my tears had the effect I'd desired because Kevin made no move to leave me alone, yet again, with only my despair for company.

CHAPTER
Twenty-Four

I'D FALLEN ASLEEP ON THE couch sometime through my crying jag. I glanced over to Kevin, lounging in my second-hand tweed recliner, flipping through channels, a half-empty twelve-pack of Coors at his feet. He smiled a bit loopily, stood, then ducked into the kitchen, stumbling slightly when he returned, and placed the bottle of tequila and all the accoutrements on the glass coffee table.

Gotta love a man who knows the best way to heal me.

After the second shot of Don Julio, I'd regained my bearings and lost my embarrassment. I'd bawled like a sissy girl and passed out from sheer mental exhaustion. Still couldn't think about Kiyah, or Samantha, without the feeling a pair of vise grips had been clamped onto my heart.

The tequila loosened my tongue enough that I felt ready to tackle Kevin's problems. "So. You gonna tell me why you've been acting like such a moody jerk?"

Kevin tossed back a shot and poured another. "This case hasn't exactly been easy on me."

"But, it's over, right? Even the cops believe Shelley's death was suicide."

He shook his head. "Shelley lied to us more than once."

I wet my finger and pressed it down on the salty plate. "True. But of all the things she told us, her belief in eternal damnation after suicide seemed the most sincere." I sucked the salt off and drained the shot, finishing with a wedge of lime.

During a drag of my cigarette I realized the only vice missing was sex. I swept a quick glance to Kev. Doubted he was up for that, although his mood to drink was rare of late. I decided not to push my luck.

The dull snick of aluminum drifted across the table as Kevin popped open a Coors. He didn't sip. He guzzled. The empty can took its place on the second rung of an impromptu pyramid. Through a muffled a belch, he said, "Didn't expect Dick to show up today."

"Probably only saving face."

"You don't think he had anything to do with either death, do you?"

I opened a beer. "Nope." The yeasty tang of barley and hops mixed perfectly with the salt, citrus and tequila.

"Me, either. I think Shelley was the last link in whatever happened at the fair that night. Whoever killed her probably feels safe whatever secrets she held, died with her."

I puffed on my cigarette. "Even if Charles LaChance, who's sworn to uphold the law, is guilty? I thought you couldn't stand the idea someone is getting away with this."

"There's no proof. Just speculation. We aren't getting paid to continue delving into this fucked up mess. It's not doing either of us any good."

Glad he finally admitted things had been strained between us. "So, we're done with this case?"

"As far as I'm concerned."

"Thank God." I held my can aloft and toasted him. Kevin downed another shot without the frills. "What's going on with you and Tony Martinez?"

I took a sip of beer. "Nothing. Why?"

"I saw him eyeing you at the funeral."

"Giving me the evil eye probably," I lied. Things were going so swimmingly with Kevin I didn't want to piss him off. And, my choices in men seemed to be a trigger. "I'm banned from Fat Bob's, remember?"

"He wasn't looking at you like a potential customer. He was looking at you like lunch." Fizz exploded across the arm of the recliner as he popped another Coors. "You sleeping with him?"

"Wish I was sleeping with someone." I rested my elbows on my knees, and waggled my eyebrows. "Got anyone in mind, baby doll?"

He shrugged. "After the Ray fiasco I thought maybe you'd be more selective."

"More selective?" I repeated, humor gone. "You really want to get into this right now?"

"Yes. No." The beer can dented under his grip. At least he hadn't crushed it on his head Jimmer style. "Hell, I don't know."

I counted to ten, willing my temper to ebb. "Kevin, what's going on?"

For a minute I thought he'd pull his evasive trick, but he didn't. He studied me with curiosity or hostility. I wasn't sure which was worse.

"Lilly," he said.

It figured. "What about her?"

"She wants to talk."

"About what?"

"I don't know."

"Come on, I'm in no mood for this cryptic shit. Surely, after all the time you've been spending with her you have some idea what the hell she wants to talk about."

He wiggled off the can's metal tab and flicked it at me; *ping*, it nailed me right in the chest. "I haven't seen her in two days."

That stopped me cold. "Really? So, where have you been? Not hanging by any of your three phones. I assumed you were with her." Then, it clicked. "You've been avoiding her, too, haven't you?"

"Too?"

"Yes, *too*." I stabbed my cigarette at him. "You haven't

exactly been eager to hang with me."

"I've been working strange hours on a surveillance case involving employee theft."

"Why didn't you ask for my help?"

He lifted a brow. "You willing to come to work for me full-time?"

"We've talked about this." I paused, wondering how things would change between us if we were in each other's faces every day. This one case had caused unbearable strain on our friendship. God, I couldn't deal with more failure in my life. Especially not where Kevin was concerned.

"Jules?" he said softly.

I dragged my gaze back to his. "I'm not sure."

"I know." He angled the crumpled Coors can at me. "I'll remind you I pay better than the county."

"True." I ran my finger around the rim of my shot glass. "But, I'm not the most even-tempered person in the world. I'd hate for . . ."

"For God's sake, I'm not one of those stupid guys you sucker in with your promise of unlimited sex but run at first sign of your crappy temperament." He cracked open yet another beer. "I'm used to your mood swings. I need your office expertise, you know, basic stuff I don't have time to sort out, but fortunately, you excel at."

I shook my head. "Understand this. *If* I work for you, it won't be in a secretarial capacity."

He paused, letting his gaze bore into me. "At this

point, I'll take whatever I can get from you."

The implication was there, but unclear. Was it wishful thinking? Or, the alcohol talking?

Kevin didn't comment further, but his eyes flicked to the star quilt drooping off the couch, then to the RC Gorman lithograph and gigantic dream catcher hanging side-by-side on the wall. He pointed to the lopsided clay bowl on the chrome end table. "Where'd you get that?"

"Antique store in Keystone. Why?"

"It looks like . . ." He waved abstractedly. "Never mind."

"So, you've been busy. Is that why you didn't tell me what's been going on with you and Lilly?"

"Partially. You've had your own problems with this case and with Ray." He drained the rest of his beer and grimaced. "I have a pretty good idea of what Lilly wants to discuss. I just don't know what I'll do."

I braced myself with another shot. "What do you think she wants?"

"A commitment."

"Seriously?" I sucked a lime, but the bitterness lingering in my mouth wasn't from the overpowering citrus. "Truthfully, you haven't been together that long."

"A year is a lot longer than *you've* managed to last with any guy."

"True." But, we both knew length of time didn't have shit to do with the value of the relationship.

"Anyway, she's been making those noises lately."

There wasn't enough booze in the world to dull the sharp pain stabbing near my heart. I figured I'd test that theory plenty of times if he and Lilly became a permanent item. "Is that what you want?"

No answer.

"Do you love her?"

He shoved both hands through his hair and threw his arms over his head. "I don't know."

"Who am I supposed to ask?"

Kevin glowered at me and I felt more ashamed than when I'd sobbed in his arms. It hurt to think he cared so much for her. I'd wanted to hurt him back, but I hadn't expected the ricochet effect.

"It's not that easy to answer. Some days I think, yes, I love her. Some days she's so clingy and needy I almost hate her." He refilled his shot glass. "Bottom line? She's not you." His laugh held a knife edge. He lifted the golden liquid to his mouth in a mock salute. "Then again, you're not her." Once he'd emptied the glass, he slammed it back on the glass table with a sickening crack.

Loud, thick, silence developed that scared me to the bone.

When he swayed to his feet, I stumbled to mine in an effort to steady him. I wasn't exactly unaffected by the amount of liquor we'd consumed in such a short time, but he'd had a head start. We looked like some drunken losers as I half-pulled, half-fell onto the couch with him.

"I think I'm drunk," he groaned.

"You're allowed." I grabbed his hand when he made to reach for the bottle of tequila. "But, enough for a while, okay? You can crash here."

His eyes opened when I entwined our fingers, like I'd done a million times before.

But this time was different.

Sitting hip-to-thigh, I shifted forward to escape. His hand slid up my arm to stop the departure. The gentle motion brought me back around to face him. He swept the hair from my bruised cheek, watching my reaction.

His gaze wasn't the blurry, bloodshot one of a drunken man. His green eyes were completely focused on me.

Warm hands traveled up my neck and lightly cupped my face. "Julie," he said softly.

"Kevin." I resisted closing my eyes at the odd sensation of his caresses. "Don't."

"I can't help it."

His fingers smoothed over my temple, slipped into my hair, gripped my head, keeping it in place. For once, I let myself get lost in his eyes.

He lowered his mouth, brushing tender kisses over my lips, over my cheekbones, my chin, muttering unintelligible words against my flushed skin.

I forgot to breathe and the dizzy sensation wasn't from the overindulgence of tequila.

Kevin settled his lips over mine, sweeping his tongue inside.

I sank into his mouth without hesitation.

An occasional friendly peck was all we'd allowed ourselves. We'd never kissed like this. The loving strokes of his hands didn't veer out of control. I'd imagined his reverent touches, but those fantasies paled against the erotic, yet familiar feel of him. I tasted tequila, beer, and the faint flavor of my tobacco as our mouths, our souls, everything we were mingled and seemed to synchronize into one being.

In one movement, he lifted me to his lap. Hands once gentle explored with determination. I touched his chest, urging him to take what we both wanted. The sweet kiss turned hungry and insistent.

I pressed my body to his and arched back when he broke away. I opened my eyes, afraid of what I'd see in his. Afraid of what he'd see in mine.

Kevin's head was slumped against the back of the couch. His eyes remained shut, yet one hand was clasped with mine while the other twined in my hair, his knuckles grazing my breast in an offhand manner that didn't feel casual. It was comforting and disconcerting as hell. I didn't want the moment to end. I was sorry it'd ever begun.

Leaning forward, I rested my sweaty forehead to his, ignoring the warnings flashing in my brain. "What?"

He rubbed his face over my temple, my cheek, my ear, until his breath expelled as an exhausted sigh. "What am I going to do?"

Not *we*. I.

I refrained from blurting out the obvious answer. Realistically, this had nothing to do with me. I couldn't offer him whatever it was he got from being with Lilly. I didn't know if whatever it was I offered him was enough. Or ever would be. Kevin needed to make a decision and I had no business handing out advice. So, I didn't. I kissed him softly, equal parts regret and yearning as I untangled from his embrace. He didn't stop me. His eyes stayed closed when I stretched out his limbs and tucked the quilt around him. "Sleep on it. We'll talk later."

He nodded off instantly.

We didn't talk later.

"Kevin." I shook him. "Kevin. Wake up. You gotta see this."

"What?" His feet dropped to the floor. "Where am I?"

How much would he remember from before he passed out? By the blank expression on his face, probably not much. I didn't know whether or not I should feel relieved. "The news." I turned up the volume.

"What are you babbl . . ."

"Ssh. Here it is."

The raven-haired newscaster's eyes took on a somber look. "Tragedy struck a local Catholic church today upon the discovery of the body of Father Tim O'Reilly. According to authorities, the church is undergoing an extensive remodeling project and it appears Father Tim fell from the balcony choir loft some time last night. The protective railing had been removed earlier in the week. In light of this accident, all Sunday services at St. Augustine's are cancelled. A candlelight vigil is planned for tomorrow night at the cathedral. Services are pending and any memorial funds may be sent directly to the main diocese office."

I flipped to the other local news station and caught the tail end of the interview with a couple of priests who expounded on Father Tim's virtues.

Horror leached into my bones and they felt brittle enough to shatter. Another death of someone involved in this case. Someone we knew. I shut the TV off and fumbled for my cigarettes.

"Is this another coincidence?" I asked Kevin, his face an unreadable mask.

"No." He grunted, swinging his legs to the floor. "Sounds like an accident. They do happen."

I looked at him. He wasn't referring to what had transpired between us a few hours ago. But, my sense of relief morphed into another bout of gloom: Father Tim was dead. Why?

"I thought he was on mini-sabbatical at the camp. Did he ever get a hold of you?"

"No."

"Don't you think this is related to Sam and Shelley's deaths?"

He shook his head and stood with caution. "If it'll make you feel better, I'll call Ritchie at the Rapid City PD and ask him if they suspect foul play."

"But, she said . . ."

"Don't believe everything you hear on TV."

At the door Kevin placed a chaste kiss on my forehead. "I'll call you tomorrow." He disappeared into the darkness without a backwards glance.

Trying to sleep was a cruel joke.

When I pulled into the parking lot at the sheriff's office the next morning, it surprised me to see Missy's car parked next to the sheriff's Ford Explorer. Odd. We rotated Sundays. Since I'd spent last Sunday working for Kevin, the shift this week fell to me. A strange sense of disquiet twisted my gut, but I breezed into the building anyway.

Missy sat quietly at the desk, *my* desk, but wouldn't meet my eyes. She mumbled, "Umm . . . The Sheriff's waiting for you in his office."

My feet moved normally even when they seemed thick, heavy, and encased in mud. At the sheriff's half-open door I knocked.

He barked, "Come in."

I made little noise as I crossed the threshold and gave him a curious look.

Sheriff Richard's gaze didn't waver. "Shut the door." He pointed to the chair in front of his desk. "Sit."

I sat.

He opened a manila folder, scanned it, closed it with a decisive snap. Without preamble, he said, "Leanne Dobrowski requested a restraining order against you yesterday afternoon. Why?"

Shit. "Did you grant it?"

"That's beside the point. Why would your next door neighbor file a complaint?"

"I told her I was calling Social Services."

"Because . . ." He waited.

"Because her daughter is borderline malnourished, abused, and neglected," I recited.

"Did you tell her that as a representative of this office you could guarantee her daughter would be placed in foster care? That you'd personally see to it?"

Every pretense of calm rationality I maintained fled. "Leanne said that? She's a fucking liar. All I said was Social Services would be interested to know she'd locked Kiyah out of the house in the cold for hours yesterday. Without food, without proper clothing. And, that's not the first time."

Screw his intimidation tactics. *I* was not in the wrong here.

"I saw her grab Kiyah, hell, Kevin was there and he saw it too. I'll bet if you sent someone over there right now, you'd find bruises on her arms. I doubt there's a god-damned thing to eat in the house. The place is pigsty and Leanne has men traipsing in and out at all hours. You tell me if that's a healthy environment for a child."

"Not my call, nor is it yours." He stared at me, border-line incredulous, and shook his head. "And, it is your word against hers. She's also claiming you have an 'unnatural' attachment to her daughter."

"Fuck that. She'd think it was unnatural since she doesn't seem to give a shit about Kiyah one way or another. As long as the ADC checks keep coming."

"Watch your mouth." He tossed the folder on his desk. "Look. I understand where you're coming from. This kind of situation isn't unique, but it isn't your job. It'll probably just make it worse for the child."

"I don't see how."

"With the complaint on file, we both know Social Services will make a visit as soon as possible. Even if Ms. Dobrowski isn't aware that *her* phone call, not your threats, are what's setting the ball in motion. If the situation is as bad as you claim, they'll handle it."

"So, where does that leave me?"

Sheriff Tom stood and refilled his coffee. His tan cotton shirt tightened across his back, but he didn't turn around immediately. "That's the reason I've called you in here."

I wrapped my purse straps around my fingers and waited.

"Banner couple of weeks for you, Julie. You've involved yourself in a murder case, a bar fight, discovered a body, and been used for target practice." He turned around and ambled toward the front of his desk, settling his backside against it. Less than two feet separated us, yet I knew we were miles apart. "Missy let it slip how your breakup with that fella came about."

I started to protest, but it died on my lips at his harsh look.

"You should've pressed charges. But instead, I'm called and find out some woman wants to press charges against *you*."

"I didn't choose for all that to happen."

"Yes, you did." He glared at me over the rim of his cup. "I've never been crazy about you working in the private sector. If I had my way, the county commissioners would overturn that law. Almost every other county in the state has that particular conflict of interest situation handled with specific legal parameters. Up until last week, I knew you hadn't used your position in this office to gather information for whatever cases you were investigating."

"Up until last week?" I repeated. "What are you talking about?"

"I had two interesting calls yesterday. One from Ms. Dobrowski, one from attorney Charles LaChance."

He paused and watched my reaction. I gave him none.

"Seems Mr. LaChance's client, Nancy James? Believes

you deliberately misrepresented yourself as an agent of this office when you and your partner accosted her in her home to question her about the past relationship with the suicide victim, Shelley Friel." He blew a stream of air across his coffee. "Is that true?"

I shrugged. Rage was pointless now. Nancy was covering her ass. In all honesty, I didn't blame her. I blamed LaChance and his buddies. No doubt they were afraid I'd blow their sweet set-up. Charles had warned me not to mess with him. Wished I'd listened.

"So, Mr. LaChance informed me if you reveal anything of what she discussed with you in confidence, he'll file suit against this office for your false impersonation of an officer of the court."

"But . . ."

His large hand stopped my objection. "You've done the one thing I warned you not to do. And, you leave me no choice." He moved around to his chair and extracted a sheet of paper from the corner of his desk.

I took the missive, but didn't bother looking at it. I knew what it was, what it said.

His voice was firm but held that same "you've-disappointed-me" tone I'd heard from my father my entire life. For a split second I almost believed it was Dad's voice intoning, "You're suspended indefinitely, without pay, pending investigation."

Blood rushed to my face. I swallowed, but said nothing

in return.

"Julie?" he prompted.

"You can't do this."

"I just did," he said.

"No, you can't." I crumpled up the paper and threw it on his desk. "You can't. Because I quit."

CHAPTER
TWENTY-FIVE

OUTSIDE THE SHERIFF'S OFFICE the cloudless blue sky mocked me. I'd wished for warm, bright, balmy weather all week. Now, as I seethed, the black maw of anger threatened to consume me. I longed for gray, black, and bleak; lightning storms, crashes of thunder, sheets of relentless, cold rain. Once again, what I ended up with was completely different from what I wanted.

At loose ends, I went home and changed into jeans and a ratty Van Halen T-shirt. I didn't march over to Leanne's door to tell her off. With the week I'd had, the situation with the sheriff would've blown up in my face even if Leanne's phone call hadn't added to my woes. Besides, Social Services would visit her, without warning, guaranteed. That thought offered me little consolation.

I paced. I smoked. I stared longingly at the bottle of tequila, empty shot glasses and beer cans still cluttering my coffee table. True, it was only ten in the morning, but it was noon somewhere. I scowled at the clock. Dusty's didn't even open for another two hours.

So, what the hell was I supposed to do with myself? Call Kevin and tell him my not-so-good news? He was probably ass-deep in alligators with Lilly. I didn't want to contemplate how he'd handle it or how I'd react in the aftermath. No job, no best friend, no bar, no boyfriend. What was a girl bent on destruction supposed to do?

I grabbed my bow and headed out to my dad's ranch. The meandering drive through the county which usually soothed me, didn't. Confrontation with Dad was inevitable; he loved to point out my shortcomings and right now, my life was spectacularly shitty.

With the chilly wind blowing my hair, the clean smell of spring wafting through the car, sunlight warming my forearm on the window frame, I calmed down. The dead last place I wanted to be was with my father. After the way I'd seen family treat one another lately, I'd be better off with strangers. The back end of my car fishtailed on the gravel road, kicking up a dust-devil when I whipped a U-turn and drove back into Rapid City.

Kevin's car wasn't on the street or in the lot near his office. I punched in the security code and entered the dark suite. Weird, being in his office alone. I shut and locked the door behind me.

The idea of playing the brooding PI, smoking and

considering my lost prospects appealed to me. I imagined a broad-shouldered hunk with a beefcake body showing up to offer me a case only I could solve. All I needed was a hip flask and Kevin's gun shoved in an ankle holster, and my spectacle would be complete. The tactic to deal with disturbing events by drifting into fantasyland was better than the habit I'd picked up lately of drinking myself into a trance.

I'd barely propped my Timberland hikers on the desk when the phone rang.

I cocked my head and took another quick drag of my cigarette. Maybe it was my potential fantasy client. Maybe it was Kevin. I exhaled and picked up the phone.

"Wells Investigations."

A clipped tone demanded, "Is this the answering service?"

"No. This is Julie Collins. Who is this?"

His greasy chuckle jabbed every nerve in my body. I knew who he was before the words oozed from his forked tongue.

"This is Charles LaChance. So, you really *do* work for Kevin?"

"Why are you surprised?"

"Thought he liked having gorgeous, blond, arm-candy hanging around, not that I blame him."

"You didn't call to slime me with compliments, La-Chance. What do you want?"

"We need to talk."

The first response dangling on the tip of my tongue was "fuck you." But this was Kevin's office and I knew that wasn't his preferred method of message taking. I sighed. With forced sweetness I said, "I'm sorry. Mr. Wells is unavailable right now."

"That's fine. You're the one I wanted to talk to anyway."

Hooray. So much for my stud fantasy. "About what?"

"I just passed Halley Park. I'll be there in five minutes to tell you in person."

He hung up.

A niggling fear replaced the indignation; I wasn't subject to the demands of one Charles LaChance, especially after he was responsible for getting me canned.

Why did he want to talk to me? To warn me his threats to the sheriff were real? Or confess he'd been responsible for all the recent deaths? A shudder worked loose. Smart move. I might've invited a killer into Kevin's domain and I was here alone. Guess I failed Detective 101.

Still, I doubted Chuck would kill me here. He didn't take chances. I didn't either. I called Kevin's home and cell numbers, left messages at both places, and called Jimmer. I smoked, hoping my bout of nerves would subside. At this rate I'd be buying Mylanta by the gallon.

Two impatient raps. "Julie. I know you're in there."

"Hang on." Through the door I warned, "I've got a gun."

"Not necessary. Look, I really need to talk to you."

I flipped the locks and opened the door.

LaChance hustled in and tried slamming the door behind him.

"Leave it open."

"Don't trust me?"

"No."

He lifted his elfin shoulder in a half-shrug and dropped into the new leather chair across from Kevin's desk. Now, we'd definitely have to fumigate it. I stretched into Kevin's usual position; mighty pleased LaChance looked insignificant and ill at ease sitting across from me. "What do you want?"

Annoyance distorted his mouth. "David told me."

"Told you what?"

"About your conversation the other day."

"Oh." I waved my cigarette indifferently. "The one where he let it slip you were the one who'd paid for our services? Kevin is very unhappy."

"I imagine. But it's difficult to pay the rent with your principles, isn't it?"

I shrugged. "Not my call."

"Let's get something else straight." He pressed forward, hands on knees. "I did not rape Shelley. Samantha was not my daughter."

"So, I can assume you've reassured your son that he hadn't been sleeping with his half-sister?"

"Of course. I can't understand who put those ideas in his

head in the first place."

"Kind of like why I can't understand why you'd secretly hire Kevin through your son." I took a drag, blew smoke in his face, and waited.

He coughed, hand flailing through the gray cloud. "Although it pains me to admit, Kevin is the best investigator in town. I knew he'd never work for me, no matter how noble the cause."

"True. But you made contact with Samantha *before* she disappeared, before she got kicked out of her house. So, we're not exactly sure you didn't have something to do with her disappearance. And then hired Kevin through David after the fact to cover up your tracks."

He recovered his initial shock almost immediately. His slick hand smoothed his tie; I was surprised he hadn't left an oil stain.

"My, my, Ms. Collins. Seems Kevin has taught you well. Unfortunately, you are missing some facts. I had no reason to want Samantha dead, in spite of my feelings about her relationship with my son. I was trying to help her and her mother. Dead clients don't pay."

"And that's what this was all about, wasn't it? Money?" Charles laughed. "And, if I tell you it wasn't, would you believe me?"

I shook my head.

"I thought so. Regardless. When David told me the story about Shelley and Sam, I realized I'd been at the fair that night. I also realized Shelley had probably known her attacker, most likely someone in her group. Maybe she'd even gotten a ride home with him. That's why she hadn't come forward." His rapt expression didn't hide the dollar signs in his beady eyes. "It's statistically proven brutal rapes rarely go unreported. That's why I never believed it was a gang rape."

Because he knew the gang in question? No one believes someone close to them is capable of atrocities; I knew differently. My brow lifted in question but I let him continue.

"I approached Danny Christopherson at the rehab center and asked him for his professional interpretation of Shelley's case. He agreed with the counselor. Shelley was withholding the identity of her attacker."

"Did either counselor understand why?"

"No. Fear was no longer logical. If she'd have turned him in back then, no question he would've been locked up."

I snorted. "Yeah. Ever heard of a man getting away with rape because the woman 'asked for it'? Get real. She was scared shitless. Try again."

He settled back in his chair. "Fine. She was frightened then, but when this came to light, years later, she had legal recourse . . ."

"Even I know there is a statute of limitations on rape . . ."

"Your knowledge of the law is impressive, Ms. Collins" — his shark teeth gleamed briefly — "but so is mine. Let me finish. There is no limitation on proving paternity. Or, using that knowledge to get the financial support Shelley and her daughter were due. Dick Friel planned on washing his hands of Shelley and Samantha. It seemed logical to take the matter to civil court."

A chill settled in my bones. "With you representing her as her attorney."

No response.

"I don't get it. There can't have been much money in this case. So, why would you be so anxious to take it on?" I had a light bulb moment; the flash exploded but my throat seemed to fill with crushed glass. "You weren't in it for the money, after all, were you? It was for the publicity. You wanted to smear this guy's reputation."

"See?" He lifted his palms in supplication. "I'm not all about the cash. You have to agree this rapist, masquerading as a normal guy, deserves some legal repercussions. My concern was: If Shelley couldn't get justice from her horrible ordeal, she'd receive monetary compensation."

"Then, you know who raped her."

He nodded. "I'd narrowed it down. She finally told me the last time I saw her, but it's a moot point."

"Who?"

"Who what?"

Man, we really weren't going to spiral into the "Who's on First" comedy routine, were we?

"Who raped her?"

The drama built; I knew he used the same tactic in court.

"Why, Father Tim O'Reilly. Ironic isn't it, the good Father didn't even know he was a father?"

He locked his gleeful gaze to mine.

"We both know why it is a moot point now."

Because Father Tim was dead.

Shelley was dead and Samantha was dead. Moot fucking point, indeed. My stomach turned. I leaned over to hide my face, now devoid of blood. I lit another cigarette and decided I'd keep him talking. He'd come here to gloat. And, something still didn't fit.

"How did you find out?"

Charles gave me smug.

"Shelley had a change of heart with you? She told me Monday morning she'd never tell anyone else."

"I guessed," he said. "She didn't deny it. She accepted even though Tim was a priest, he killed Samantha."

"But, how would he know?" I squeezed my eyes shut but the revulsion remained. *Anyone else*, Shelley's words echoed. "My God, Shelley told Samantha that Father Tim was her biological father."

"Afraid so. And, with Father Tim's vocation, I doubted he wanted that information broadcast. Or, the manner in which he'd sired that child. His life was about to be ruined and no matter how the diocese would try to spin it, well, everyone would know, wouldn't they? More fuel to the fire, not good PR with the bonfire of controversy burning the Catholic church's coffers the last couple of years."

I stared at the open door afraid I'd be stuck sitting in the same place hours from now, jaw hanging open, my throat dry as jerky.

"Julie?"

I refocused on LaChance. He didn't seem any worse for the wear. He dealt with murderers and rapists all the time. This was probably just another breezy day at the office for him. "Why tell me? Why not the police and turn Father Tim in?"

"I did call them after Shelley was found. But, they assured me they had already questioned the suspect in Sam's death."

"But, they'd been questioning Dick Friel," I protested, "not Father Tim."

He shook his fat finger at me. "Ah-ah-ah. I didn't know that. I said I had information and they weren't interested. I performed my legal obligation."

Shelley had told me there were two men. Another lie? No, she'd told the truth. But, in pieces. Part to me, part to Charles LaChance. Had she really believed we couldn't put two and two together? The sick feeling subsided when I realized I had figured it out, but Charles was still one piece shy of the puzzle.

My immediate, cat-who-ate-the-canary smile was well received. "Maybe you should hang up your juris doctorate and hang out a PI shingle. You narrowed it down to two guys? Hell, Kevin and I hadn't come that close." I sucked in a lungful of smoke. Blew it out. "Who was the other guy you initially checked out?"

A skeptical look tightened his eyes to steel BBs. For a second I was afraid he wouldn't tell me, but his ego reared its ugly head. "Bobby Adair."

"Bobby Adair?" I manufactured a confused look.

"Remember him? Big guy, drank like a fish? Played center senior year when they won the state football championship?"

"Vaguely. Don't remember Bobby and Tim being that tight."

"Are you kidding me?" LaChance twisted his index and middle fingers together, holding them up. "Those two were inseparable. Surprised the hell out of all of us when Tim up and joined the seminary. Soon after, Bobby headed for basic training with the Marines."

What event precipitated an abrupt life change in both their lives? Graduation? No light bulb this time, but I knew.

Shelley's rape.

Father Tim had joined the priesthood out of guilt. Or, because of the shame of his relationship with Bobby. It made sense. It also made sense on why he skirted the issue about Samantha. She had confronted him. But, I didn't see him slicing her throat. Or, killing Shelley. I said casually, "So, what is Bobby up to these days?"

"Not much after his discharge."

"He hang out with you guys?"

"Not much. We hunt prairie dogs occasionally. Keeps to himself, mostly. Volunteers at Tim's church a bunch and at the mission. Though, I don't think that's his first choice. Tim can be pretty pushy when it comes to helping the less fortunate."

My lungs wouldn't work. I grabbed a Bic pen and chewed on it instead of lighting another smoke. "He seems a little young to be retired from the military."

Charles' oily laugh boomed as he slicked his palm over his balding pate. "Bobby was *forcibly* retired. The Marines don't take kindly to his behavior."

I blinked my eyes wide open with apparent shock. "Really? What for?"

"He was tried for sexual assault."

"And, you discounted him as a suspect in Sam's murder?" I couldn't help the dig. "With a conviction for sexual assault?"

The lawyer in him countered, "He wasn't convicted. Big difference. And Samantha wasn't sexually assaulted."

"Ah. But, Shelley had been."

"He seemed the logical choice, until . . ." LaChance cleared his throat and pressed his thin, wet lips together.

"Come on Chuck," I cajoled with false good humor. "Don't go all coy on me now."

His smile beamed confidence born of a nasty secret.

"Bobby was off the list when I discovered the prostitute he'd assaulted was male."

I resisted jumping up and yelling, Bingo! Instead, I said, "Really?"

"Everything is pretty hush-hush with the 'don't ask, don't tell' policy."

"Yet, *you* found out," I fairly gushed.

He preened again, oblivious to my sarcasm. "Yes, well, anyway, I found out only because Bobby hired me when he bought his land. I do extensive background checks on all clients."

"Where's he live?"

"Out off of Rimrock Highway near the 385 junction. Father Tim got the Catholic church to donate this rustic log cabin they'd planned on tearing down. Their church camp is a couple of miles downstream. Apparently, Bobby is living that whole 'back to nature' lifestyle."

Evidently Charles paid more attention to the amount of zeros on the check than the address on it. Now, armed with the information I needed, I'd had enough of being nice. "So, did you do an extensive background check on Nancy James too, when you took on her case?"

"I wondered when you'd bring that up."

"That why you're here? To make sure I know you'll make good on your threats to Sheriff Richards?"

"No. I won't press charges as long as you understand the consequences of your attempt to terrorize my client."

I resisted rolling my eyes. "Terrorize?"

"Yes. You frightened Mrs. James when you boasted about your involvement and position with the Bear Butte County Sheriff's Office. Fear is a powerful motivator. Any answers to your questions were obtained illegally. No Miranda warning, no chance that anything Mrs. James allegedly disclosed is admissible in court."

"A secretary doesn't have the power of Miranda. You know that."

"Mrs. James didn't know that," he said slyly. "But, I think you've finally come to understand my threats are rarely idle."

"Is there anything else?"

"No. As long as we understand each other." He smiled, stood, and reached his hand over the desk.

I understood perfectly. I shook my head and his pale fingers withdrew.

His smile dried up like a spring puddle. "Lovely to see you again, Ms. Collins. Give my regards to Kevin. I'll show myself out."

The second he slinked out the door I booted up Kevin's computer. No rural route box numbers in Pennington County, all addresses, no matter how far out of town, had street designations for emergency services and fire protection. Thank you, Smokey the Bear. I nearly kissed the screen when Bobby's address popped up in a matter of seconds.

After leaving updated messages on Kevin and Jimmer's phones, I went off in pursuit of Bobby Adair.

CHAPTER TWENTY-SIX

IN MY OBSESSION TO SEEK JUSTICE for Shelley and Samantha Friel, it didn't occur that I was alone until I'd reached the road leading to Bobby's house.

I parked in a clearing off Rimrock Highway and took stock of the situation. Few cars zipped past me. Here I was, alone in the woods, about to confront a man I guessed had killed three people. No cell phone, no training in guerrilla tactics, no clue what I'd do if I crossed paths with Bobby. Run? Climb a tree? Hide? What the hell had I been thinking? I doubted that if I got caught I could talk my way out of it.

The tough girl in me assured me I wouldn't get caught.

The chickenshit, weepy girl almost threw the Sentra in reverse and sped away.

The surreal scene brought to mind low-budget horror flicks from my drive-in days. I hated those slasher movies where the barely-dressed heroine confronts the killer alone, at night, armed with nothing more than a blood-curdling scream and a great pair of breasts. I believed nobody would be that stupid. Yet, here I was, running off half-cocked and indignant. Except, it wasn't night. And I wasn't exactly unarmed.

I grabbed my bow from the backseat, wishing I had the foresight to load my arrows with tips more lethal than target tips.

Okay. I revised the plan; I'd take a quick look around, hop back in the car, and head to the office to wait for Kevin and Jimmer. We'd call the cops, the FBI, the CIA, and the NPS.

A deep breath later, I slipped through the rusted barbed wire fence strung across the rock-strewn road. "No trespassing" had been painted in huge white letters on a gargantuan tractor tire hanging from a telephone pole. Wires swooped down through the mix of pine and oak trees lining the driveway.

Opting to stay off the glorified goat path, I trod lightly on the pine needles and ground cover of decayed organic material which made up the forest floor. With the soaring pine trees, scant patches of watery sun shed little light on the uneven terrain. I shivered and walked steadily, stopping every so often to listen for noises, crunching pinecones, snapping twigs, rustling dead leaves, a dead give away of another presence.

A murder of crows cawed, squirrels chattered discontent, but I seemed to be alone. I hadn't any idea of how far I'd walked when my burdened smoker's lungs needed a break. I set my bow on the ground, resting against a towering Black Hills Spruce, flexing my cramped fingers.

The sharp snap of a rope broke the silence. Before I recognized what the sound meant, my body was flush with the tree by way of a canvas cord. Wound tight around my center first, then my shoulders, then hips, and then calves. This person had roping skills the envy of a rodeo circuit cowboy. Before I took another breath, I'd been rendered powerless. In a bewildered kind of fascination, I watched the rope digging into my upper arms as it was cinched taut. My vocal cords finally made sound when those same ropes ripped away the first layer of my skin.

A man stepped in front of me, face camouflaged with paint, body covered in military fatigues. Part of me hoped I'd accidentally stumbled onto the National Guard training grounds. I knew better. That site was ten miles from here. The sensible side of me knew it was Bobby Adair.

"Well, well." He picked up my bow. "If it isn't Xena."

I didn't scream since my entrails were clogging in my throat.

"What are you doing here?"

Fear loosened the hold my teeth had on my tongue. I yelled, "Jimmer, Kevin, I found him. About a thousand yards to your left."

Bobby slapped me hard across the face. "Shut up. I know you're out here by your little lonesome."

Through the stinging sensation on my cheek and the pain roaring in my head, I couldn't move or ask how he knew. It was almost as if he'd sensed my question.

"Got cameras hidden in the trees up by the gate. Keeps away unexpected visitors. I saw you get out of your car. Alone."

He kicked my bow, then picked it up. "Just what do you expect to do with this itty bitty thing?" His fingers stroked nylon cord up to the cam. "Nice. Though I'm surprised it isn't pink. What's your draw weight?"

The tangy taste of blood filled my mouth but I managed to gulp it down. "Forty pounds."

Bobby scoffed, "Can't hardly kill a squirrel with that. I pull seventy-five." He withdrew an arrow and studied it. "Target tips? You came out here loaded with target tips? Why?"

"They're handy for shooting targets."

"You're out here for target practice?"

I let a look of horror cross my face that wasn't entirely faked. "You mean Jimmer didn't call and tell you I was coming?"

He slapped me again, same side, same bruise. Same open spot inside my mouth squirted blood onto my tongue.

"You've got a big mouth. Always did. Didn't like it then, don't like it now. Let's see what other goodies you're carrying."

I closed my eyes, revolted by the feel of his thick hands skimming my body, patting me down through the ropes. "I'm clean," I choked as his fingers inched toward my crotch. "I don't have anything else."

"No matter."

"Just let me go."

The right backhand split my lip; the left backhand reopened the cut on my cheek Ray had given me that had finally started to heal.

"Now, I'm sure this isn't a social visit. Playing Nancy Drew, you must've figured it out, so you get marks for that. But," he tsked, tsked, "Not so smart coming up here by yourself, are you?"

I played dumb. "What?"

"*What*? She says."

He whacked me on the collarbone with the cam of the bow. Sharp, agonizing pain, followed by a red-hot flash of heat; a poker searing my flesh. I shrieked and shut my eyes.

He laughed and smacked the other side of my clavicle. "I'm gonna enjoy watching the smart remarks drain out with your blood."

My eyes flew open. I expected to see a knife perched near my throat. "Like you killed Samantha?" I managed.

"No." He gestured with my bow. "Something different this time. It's always different. Same old same old gets boring."

"Why did you kill her?"

"She got in my way."

"How?" I let my gaze track the woods surrounding us. "What was she doing out here?"

"Not out here. God, you are stupid." Bobby extracted another arrow, studied it. "I was working in the back room off Tim's office when she accused Tim of being her sperm donor. Said Shelley told her about the rape. Tim didn't know what to do so I handled it for him."

Father Tim had given the edict to off Samantha? "He told you to do that?"

"No. He didn't need to. I always know what's best for him, even when he doesn't recognize it."

He sighed.

"Take those prairie niggers down at the Mission. They'd suck up every bit of his free time, if Tim let them. Gotta tell ya, it was a helluva lot more fun getting them drunk, and holding their bodies under the water than it was playing basketball with them. They have no sense of sportsmanship. Hell, I thought they might scalp me."

He nearly busted a gut, laughing at his own humor.

I gulped down another sticky mass of blood, spit, and fear. Had Bobby slashed Ben's throat too? "So, you killed them? All the ones they found in Rapid Creek?"

"Yeah. Another dead injun don't make much difference, does it. Besides, gave them my own kind of last rites." He crossed himself and laughed again.

"What about the one in Bear Butte Creek a few years back?"

"Don't know nothing about that one. Too much hassle when I've got plenty to choose from here." His eyes narrowed. "Why?"

My momentary relief Bobby hadn't killed Ben evaporated when I realized Bobby would be *my* killer. But, if I kept him talking, maybe Kevin or Jimmer would rush in and save me. "Just wondered how you got Samantha to come with you."

"Why should I tell you?"

With the ropes wound so tight, I couldn't shrug. "Since I tracked you down, it'd be unsportsmanslike for you to let me die not knowing how you pulled it off."

He nodded like it made perfect sense. "She'd seen me around, knew Tim and I were buddies. Stopped her inside the church before her counseling session. Told her he'd been called to the church camp. Said if she wanted to see him we'd have to head up here."

My eyes bugged. "And, she just went with you?"

"Jesus, you are stupid. I just *told* you Tim and I are best friends. She didn't suspect a thing." His mouth turned into a grotesque frown beneath the war paint. "Didn't expect her to have that knife."

"Dick's knife?"

"Didn't know it was his at the time." He stared at the gash across the back of his hand. "Little bitch pulled it out of her purse when she realized Father Tim wasn't coming. Can you believe she cut me?"

I gagged at the idea of Samantha taking on, and ultimately losing to Bobby Adair. But, I kept up the flow of conversation; it took my mind off the fact I was tied to a tree, completely at his mercy. And, I knew he hadn't showed any mercy to any of his victims. "Why did you stick it in Kevin's tire?"

"That day in Tim's office, I knew you suspected Friel. I'd kept the knife, but when I saw you and Wells . . . seemed obvious to leave it and let the cops connect it with that loser, Friel. Fucker deserves to go to jail. Screwed me over on the last bike I'd brought in for repair."

I didn't care about Dick's bad business practices because it hadn't led to Samantha's death. But, it'd nearly led to ours. "So, you were the one trying to kill us that day?"

He scowled at me. "Not kill you. If I was, you'd be dead. This is better; I might even let you run before I shoot you."

Underneath the ropes my body started to shake. From my toes, up to my shoulders, to my head. I clamped my teeth together to keep them from chattering. I was going to die. Violently. Alone. No way around it.

He caressed the carbon fiber arrow shaft, fingering the orange nock.

Bobby's sudden silence unnerved me. I blurted, "You killed Shelley, didn't you? Left her just like you did after the rape."

The arrow tips unscrewed easily under his deft fingers and he reached in his pocket. "I had nothing to do with raping her. Dumb cunt thought Tim killed her bastard girl. Told Tim she planned on checking out of rehab and going to the police. Tim panicked and went off to the church camp to hide and *pray* about it. Fuck." He tossed his head back and laughed. "Stupid asshole, praying. Like God himself was gonna come down and save him. *I* saved him."

"By getting rid of her?"

His eyes never left the bow. "So? I followed her. My gun, a bottle of Jack, made it easy. She passed out." His shoulders rolled casually. "Tossed her in the car and started it. Not much challenge, but she deserved it. Shelley had already fucked up my and Tim's lives enough."

"Then, why did you kill Tim?"

Jaw tight, he blew across the blunt tip of the arrow. "He was an ungrateful, pious prick."

The ropes had started to cut off my circulation. If I moved, they chafed my forearms. Without a knife there was no way I was getting loose, but I wasn't going down without a fight. "Not a good way to describe your lover."

"We hadn't been that for a long time," he nearly crooned, husky voice replete with longing. "I almost had Tim convinced no one would know about us . . . then that girl showed up and ruined everything."

Not one ounce of regret. He wasn't sorry that he'd

killed, just pissed off that his former boyfriend had moved on. To God, apparently. I'd heard of carrying a torch for your high school sweetheart, but this was carrying it too far. Fucking crazy loon. His dulcet tone scared me worse than his silence. I took a shuddery breath.

"But you'd tried to change things to the way they used to be? By taking care of Samantha and Shelley? No one knew what happened seventeen-years ago."

I tried moving my hand, but it wouldn't budge. The rope burned like it'd gone through skin and was grinding on bone. "Bobby, were you hoping that Tim would show his gratitude by . . " I searched for a delicate phrase. "By resuming your relationship?"

Bobby jerked upright and sneered, "He said what we'd done, what we'd been to each other for *years* was an abomination. What he did to Shelley was an abomination."

"So, he hadn't been with other men?"

"Shut up." He edged closer. "I don't want to hear another sound."

From the inside pocket of a flak jacket identical to Jimmer's, he pulled out a small tin box. I craned my neck; Bobby lifted the arrow to my line of vision. He'd replaced the target tips. With broadhead tips.

Shit. Everything inside me went liquid hot with fear.

Broadhead tips are essentially flying razor blades. Diamond-shaped steel on a stick, zooming at 180 mph and can drop a three-hundred pound fully racked buck in seconds.

Through hide, through bone, sometimes even straight through the body until it's stopped from coming out the other side by meaty tissue or the vanes on the arrow. Hunters use a variety of types and sizes of these deadly tips, mostly determined by the prey. All broadheads have one thing in common. They are lethal.

Depending on the accuracy of the hunter, death can be quick, but not always. Some deer have been known to run twoo-hundred yards or farther with the arrow intact. Or, spend years with an arrow showcasing a hunter's lousy aim. Any animal drops to their haunches when a pierced lung collapses and fills with blood. Or, their heart explodes from a combination of the arrow and fear. Bad shots are not pretty, but slow and incredibly painful. And, I knew that's what Bobby planned for me.

I pressed closer to the tree, as if I could melt into the bark. "Even if you kill me, they'll know it was you."

"I know. Don't care." He screwed another broadhead into the second arrow. "I won't be around."

He'd slaughter me like some animal and leave my carcass out here to rot as fodder for wildlife. Anger welled in me and I spit, "Places to be? Other people to kill?"

"Just you."

I screamed as loud as I could.

The quick slice of the arrow across my chest cut the flow of sound. Huge spots of blood appeared on the edges of my T-shirt before I felt the fiery pain.

"I told you to shut up." Bobby dragged the side of the arrow across my forearm, leaving a thin red line that turned thick with blood. Then, he offered the same treatment to the other arm.

He watched the blood gather. Using his finger, he traced a circular pattern before pressing his thumb into the cut, and then rubbed the paint off his forehead. He'd made a singular dot. With my blood. Like some kind of warrior. My stomach convulsed and I dry heaved.

Watching me, he dropped to his knees by my other arm. "Remember when you made your first deer kill? And you drank the warm blood?"

Frozen in terror, with cuts throbbing and bruises swelling, I couldn't move. I hadn't taken part in that particular ritual, although it was standard practice and I'd seen it done with first kills.

"I'm gonna do it beforehand this time. Mix things up a bit." His wet tongue licked a path up my arm, lapping up blood. He stood and smiled, lips and teeth red.

Everything inside me revolted. I screamed, "Fuck you, Bobby. You are a fucking deviant. You can go straight to fucking hell."

Rage twisted his features as he reached down and picked up the bow and arrow. "Shut the fuck up."

I whimpered when he stomped closer and pressed the sharp side against the pulse hammering in my throat. His angry, hot breath gusted over the chill of my exposed skin.

His prickly beard brushed my cheek, chin and neck, repeatedly. He was marking me as his kill. My subconscious kicked back to my rape, the sensation of strange hair burning my flesh, and I wanted to pass out from sheer terror.

"Feel like screaming now? Talking some more? Or, are you finally scared?" he goaded, digging the tip into my skin until it gave way under the pressure.

Liquid trickled down my neck, sticky, warm like sweat, but I knew it wasn't. I didn't look. I didn't answer.

He stepped back and loaded the arrow in my bow. Aimed it at my head. Lowered it to my heart. Sighted my abdomen. His eyes were wild, out of control. "This isn't going to be any fun," he complained. "I can probably shoot you one-handed."

"Then, let me go. I'll run. I swear."

Bobby cuffed me again. "Shut up."

I bled.

A dog howled in the distance; angry, loud snapping barks followed by growls. Bobby cocked his head, lowering the bow to his side.

Silence peculiar to woods answered.

"Something is going on with Max. I'm gonna check it out." He backed up and looked at me attentively, placing the bow and second arrow fifteen feet in front of me on the ground. Taunting me, knowing I couldn't reach it, but that I'd try.

An unnatural grin split his face. "Don't go anywhere.

I'll be right back."

He disappeared into the trees.

I thrashed against the ropes, muttering, the flow of frustrated tears mixed with the blood on my chest until I was too tired or weak from the blood loss to move.

Then I heard it.

A twig snapped behind the tree. I went completely still. Was this some kind of psychological game of terror Bobby played? Sneak up behind the quarry, make me wonder how long I had to live until the knife glinted and I watched as it slit my own throat?

Just like Ben. Would my body end up in the creek too?

But Bobby didn't step out from behind me.

Meredith Friel did.

I blinked. Couldn't be. I blinked again. Not an apparition; her tiny form stood there, not ten feet from my bow. I whispered, "What are you doing here?"

"I've been following you."

"That was you? Why?"

"I knew you wouldn't let Sam down. That you'd find whoever did this to her."

"I did and look what happened." I took a quick look around. "Meredith, he's going to kill me *and* you if he finds you here." I calmed my hopeful breathing. "Run. Run to the road and get help."

"Is that yours?" she said, pointing at my bow. Crouching down, she picked it and the extra arrow up before slinking back to me.

I didn't pay much attention to her demeanor, busy as I was thanking every god in the universe for not letting me die. "Use the sharp side to cut the ropes."

She studied the arrow and raised her limpid glance to mine.

"Meredith? Come on. He'll be back any second. Cut me free."

"No." She calmly stepped behind the tree. Her whisper drifted out, "He's mine."

I didn't think my heart could jackhammer faster. It did. Meredith was dooming us both by her need for vengeance. I understood it, but knew she'd never get a kill shot off with my bow. As it was, a forty-pound pull weight was difficult for me to maintain, even with my added muscle. With my years of experience, I doubted I could best Bobby Adair. Unskilled Meredith had no chance. I had no chance unless she cut me free.

"Meredith, please. Listen to me. Let me take care of this. You trust me, don't you?"

"Ssh. He's coming."

I heard nothing. No wind whistling through the trees, no chirping birds, no plodding footsteps. Nothing but my own ragged inhalations and the sound of my heart swelling in my ears.

Then, there he was. Fear had sharpened my senses and I made out his form even as he blended into the tree line.

Bobby appeared with the stealth of a mountain lion. Stalking his prey. Fifty-yards out. Then twenty. At fifteen feet, he stopped and scoped out the empty ground where he'd left the bow. He looked up at me, puzzled.

His eyes slid to my right side as Meredith stepped out from behind the tree.

Planting her tiny feet, she drew back, aimed, and let it fly.

Stunned, Bobby didn't move.

The spinning arrow made no sound as it sunk into the middle of Bobby's chest. Neither did Bobby, save for the surprised *uff* when he glanced down in disbelief at the pink and orange vane sticking out of the center of his body. No dying words or additional last minute confessions spewed from his mouth. Blood geysered out from the wound in a thin stream onto the forest floor.

Meredith stepped closer and reloaded.

Bobby dropped to his knees when the blood started pouring out of his lips, over his chin, and onto his neck, discoloring his fatigues.

Meredith sighted one last time. Eased up. And let go.

The second shot, the kill shot, hit him right between the eyes. Right where he'd used my blood to mark a perfect bull's-eye.

The final blow knocked him backwards. I didn't need an up close and personal look at the bits and pieces littering the terrain; Bobby's head had all but exploded upon impact. I'd seen it happen once before. Not on a human, however.

The sick feeling I expected never came.

Meredith tossed the bow aside before she fell to her knees. When she faced me, she had that same deer-in-the-crosshairs look I witnessed when I'd killed my first and only buck. Body wracked with convulsions, she wrapped her arms around her up-drawn knees and rocked back and forth, her sobs lost in the black void of the forest. Nothing would ever fill the blackened section of her heart. But, maybe now she'd heal.

Finally, I said, "Meredith. You need to cut me loose."

She stopped rocking to raise her tear-stained face toward me. "Are you going to turn me in?"

I shook my head.

She crawled closer, pulling out a switchblade. She studied it with confusion and I tamped down on renewed fear. Meredith wouldn't hurt me. I'd given her the only thing she'd ever wanted: justice for the unjust death of her sister. Behind the pine I heard sawing sounds and my legs broke free first. "I'm not sorry," she said.

"I know."

"I followed you because I knew you'd find him. No matter what."

The jerking motion against my hips stopped and her voice became a rattled whisper.

"Thank you."

My hands broke free to the sensation of pins and needles and raw pain. "How did you know?"

"I heard them in the church. Him. Bobby."

She pointed to the crumpled form in front of us.

"And Father Tim. Arguing. Father Tim asked him if he killed Sam and Shelley. Bobby didn't deny it. Said he was doing them all a favor. Father Tim threatened to call the police. Bobby picked him up and tossed him off the balcony, right onto the pews below."

I angled toward her face, but couldn't see anything beyond the tree bark and golden rivulets of pine sap. "You saw this happen? Why didn't you call 911?"

"The drop was at least twenty feet, so I knew Father Tim was dead. I figured I would be too, if I gave myself away."

"What were you doing in the church in the first place?" My shoulders were blessedly free and I slowly inched to the ground.

"He'd counseled Sam. I snuck into his office, thinking I'd find a file or something. Then, I saw her rosary hanging on the back wall. I thought Father Tim had killed her and kept her rosary as a trophy, like those serial killers on TV. Then, I heard them arguing."

She scowled at Bobby's body.

"Am I gonna go to jail?"

Juvenile detention would ruin Meredith. She didn't pose a danger to society. The real menace to society was drawing flies and an interesting circle of buzzards overhead.

Meredith needed a chance at a normal life and it was within my power to give it to her. "Not if I can help it."

"But . . ."

"You trust me, right?"

She nodded.

"So, when the cops get here, let me do the talking, all right? Promise?"

She nodded again, and then lowered her head until her hair brushed the dead spots on the forest floor like pale strands of wheat.

"Good. Here's what we're going to do." I explained it, drilled her, and when I was satisfied she knew her part, sent her up the road to flag down a car.

I removed my ripped T-shirt and wiped her prints off my bow.

The wail of sirens, footfalls destroying underbrush, loud male voices; I heard it all, yet I heard nothing. Police swarmed from every direction. I didn't move until I saw the one thing that set my feet to running.

Kevin.

I vaguely remembered shouldering Lilly aside as I limped toward him, throwing my bleeding and battered body right into his widespread arms.

CHAPTER
TWENTY-SEVEN

DEPUTY BROWNELL FROM the Pennington County Sheriff's Department interviewed me at the hospital while a nurse tended my wounds. The ligature marks on my arms throbbed, made worse when they picked fibers out of the open lesions with what felt like a wire scrub brush.

Kevin assured me the torturous device was an ordinary pair of tweezers. I didn't buy it, but was glad he stayed by my side, holding my hand through the excruciating pain. I'd have scars. The invisible ones were ten times worse than those requiring sutures.

Meredith and I were questioned separately. She'd backed up my story claiming I'd been tied to the tree and she freed me just as Bobby re-entered the clearing. No one doubted it was self-defense. No one questioned whether I'd been responsible for the kill shots.

I hadn't asked Meredith if she'd ever picked up a bow

before she aimed one at Bobby. Part of me didn't want to know. I chalked it up to an adrenaline surge because I knew it wasn't about skill. It was about guts. And Meredith Friel had plenty. She'd had no choice; she had nothing else to lose.

I heard about Meredith's statement detailing her secret visit to St. Augustine's secondhand. Her removal of Samantha's rosary and the fact she hadn't reported Father Tim's murder were overlooked when Deputy Brownell called Sergeant Schneider of the Rapid City Police Department and they tactfully pointed out to the powers-that-be she'd saved my life. And, been the only witness to Bobby and Tim's enlightening conversation.

But, I got the third degree from the Deputy Brownell for my one-woman showdown. He backed off when I told him that Bobby, in the interest of maintaining his off-season hunting skills, had confessed to me he'd been responsible for drowning transient Indians from the mission.

Kevin didn't comment. Or, ask if I'd confronted Bobby about Ben's murder.

No charges were pressed against me. Or Meredith.

Once the news broke to the general populace of our racially divided city, about the final closure of those unresolved drowning cases, would Renee Brings Plenty plan a reconciliation march? Probably not.

There'd be no parade for the remaining members of the Friel family.

With time, I hoped to be a distant memory to Meredith. She deserved a normal life as much as Kiyah did.

Jimmer showed up right after the cops left, bulling his way by my side. He promised me a new bow the minute I wanted it. Since he'd spent hours with me choosing that particular model, he alone understood how much I'd loved it. He also understood I'd never use it again. Although his strange proclamation would've shocked some, it flowed over me like warm brandy.

I refused to let Kevin call my father. His brand of comfort I could do without.

After several agonizing hours of observation, the hospital released me into Kevin's care. He seemed reluctant to let me out of his sight. We'd have to deal with what had happened between us sometime, but not now. At his condo I downed painkillers, following them with a chaser of antibiotics. Then, fell into a blessedly dreamless sleep.

The sunlight warming my face sent my pulse skipping with joy. Had the last two weeks been a bad dream and I was waking in a tropical paradise? I stretched and pain reverberated through my body.

"Easy," Kevin warned. The bed creaked when he parked himself beside me. His face, severely drawn in fine lines with stubble covering his jaw, showed he hadn't slept a wink. Still, I realized his tentative smile was my own slice of paradise.

"What time is it?"

"Noon." Tangles of my hair fell back from my forehead with the gentle stroking of his cool fingers. "I think the sheriff will understand if you take the day off."

Damn. With the way events had blurred together in the past twenty-four hours, he hadn't heard about my current unemployed status.

"I no longer work for the sheriff."

I explained Leanne's restraining order and LaChance's lawsuit threats.

"So, he suspended me, indefinitely, without pay. Pissed me off, so I quit." My fingers smoothed over the crisp cotton sheet and I inquired stiffly, "That job offer still open?"

Kevin grabbed my hand, placing a kiss on the palm. "Always." Then, he sighed and stood, giving me a view of his back. "Actually, I'm glad. I wanted to talk to you about something."

Lilly. He didn't say her name, but I knew. He'd made a decision. Somehow, the denim comforter ended up clutched tightly in my fist. "About what?"

He fiddled with the plastic stick controlling the blinds. In one quick movement the blinds closed, blocking fulgent light and plunging us back into near darkness.

"Lilly's cancer is back," he said.

Not what I'd expected. "*Back*? When did she have cancer?"

"Five years ago. Way before I ever knew her."

"I didn't know."

"No one knows, she doesn't exactly broadcast it. Anyway, she couldn't shake her cold and it freaked her out, considering her history. They ran a bunch of tests."

"What did they find?"

"Cancer. It's metastasized. Nothing they can do."

I rose from the bed like a ninety-year-old invalid and hugged him from behind, every part of my body aching. "Kevin. I'm so sorry. What can I do?"

"I don't know. Right now she doesn't look or act any different, she's just dying inside. Since there's no hope of surviving it this go around, she's decided against treatment."

His sarcastic chuckle scorched the airless room.

"Much scarier than a commitment, don't you think?"

"I don't understand."

"They gave her a couple of months, at best. She refuses to spend all of them confined to a hospital bed."

When he paused, I realized that's why Lilly had disappeared when I was being treated at the hospital. For once I didn't blame her.

Kevin said, "She wants to travel, do and see everything before she can't. Spend all the money she's been saving for a rainy day. She's asked me to come along."

"In what capacity?"

"As her companion."

"Where?"

"Wherever she decides."

"Make-a-Wish for grownups?" I said lightly.

"Something like that."

"What did you tell her?"

"What do you think I told her?"

I rubbed my chin into his shoulder blade, inhaling the clean scent of him. He leaned back into me and I held on. I should get used to this role reversal; he'd need my strength in the coming months. "When?"

"As soon as I can convince you to come to work for me as my partner."

I let that sentence hang. "Are you sure you can do this?"

"What? Have you as my partner?"

"No. This thing with Lilly."

The shades flicked open again. "I don't have any choice."

He wouldn't see it as a choice. Kevin always did the right thing, wore the white hat, galloped in at the last second to save the day. He wasn't the type of man to deny a dying woman her last wish.

But at what cost? He'd never been subjected to the gut-wrenching grief that marred my life. As much as I'd bemoaned that fact, I'd never wished it on him or anyone else. Watching his lover die was the worst sort of initiation into the club. But, he didn't have to do it. This time with Lilly wouldn't resemble a free vacation, no matter how neatly she packaged it. Part of me hated she'd even asked this of him.

"You always have a choice," I said.

He shook his head. "There's only one way I wouldn't go."

My heart thumped. I knew where this was headed. To an area we'd avoided since we'd renewed our friendship three years ago. I wanted to stop right then, but found myself asking, "How?"

"If you asked me not to."

Feelings neither of us wanted to admit were hidden in his simple set of words. I knew a selfish answer on my part would complicate things more than either of us was prepared to acknowledge.

I slowly stepped back away from him. "I wouldn't."

"Wouldn't what?"

"Ask you not to go."

"I know that." He sighed. "Why do you think I've got no choice?"

The silence was suffocating. I'd never wanted to cry as badly as I did right then. For him. For me. For us. For everything we'd been through in the last few weeks and the denial we'd been playing our entire lives. I sucked it up. Tough girls didn't cry. I'd survived worse, but it sure didn't feel like it. I had a choice to make too.

And, I'd always believed choices were what you made of them.

Shelley's choice years ago ultimately destroyed her. Father Tim's guilt over an appalling choice had created a monster in Bobby Adair. David would grieve, but at some point he'd choose to go on. I doubted anything would change Dick's decision to spend his life on a barstool at

Fat Bob's. Or, cause Charles LaChance to quit offering his clients outrageous options in the lawsuit lottery.

Poor Samantha Friel had had no choice.

Meredith's choice was the wisest of all. She'd decided to cut ties, blood and all, and move to Lincoln and start her life over.

Smart girl.

But then again, so was I.

Nothing about this case had provided me closure. Even when I wasn't any closer to finding out who'd killed Ben, I knew I'd never stop looking.

Still, I'd changed, Kevin had changed, and that had changed us. For the better? Only time would tell. For now I was able to return the support he'd freely given me. This was the opportunity to pick a different direction in my life; maybe the right one, for the first time, in a long, long time.

Kevin had made his choice.

I made mine.

He turned. His eyes bespoke a wariness he'd masked from his face.

"So, what do you say?"

"I say, bring it on, baby." I smiled and stuck out my hand.

"So partner . . . When do I start?"

"Now?" He clasped both my hands in his and pulled me close for a hug to seal the deal.

"On one condition."

"What's that?"

"I get that new buffalo skin chair in my office. Oh," I added as an afterthought, "And a gun. A really big gun."

"Deal," he said, resting his chin atop my head. "But I have a condition too."

"Yeah?"

"No sex in that chair. It's a real bitch to remove body fluids from leather."

I eased back and asked, "How do you know that, *Heloise*?"

His wicked, bad boy grin spoke volumes.

My doubts fled, at least temporarily. My ties with Kevin weren't forged in blood, but were stronger because we'd chosen to root them in friendship. No matter what the future held for us, I had a feeling we were in for a helluva wild ride.

THE END

BREEDING EVIL

Liz Wolfe

Someone is breeding superhumans . . .

. . . beings who possess extreme psychic abilities. Now they have implanted the ultimate seed in the perfect womb. They are a heartbeat away from successfully breeding a species of meta-humans, who will be raised in laboratories and conditioned to obey the orders of their owners, governments and large multi-national corporations.

Then Shelby Parker, a former black ops agent for the government, is asked to locate a missing woman. Her quest takes her to The Center for Bio-Psychological Research. Masquerading as a computer programmer, she gets inside the Center's inner workings. What she discovers is almost too horrible to comprehend.

Dr. Mac McRae, working for The Center, administers a lie-detector test to the perspective employee for his very cautious employers. Although she passes, the handsome Australian suspects Shelby is not what she appears. But then, neither is he.

Caught up in a nightmare of unspeakable malevolence, the unlikely duo is forced to team up to save a young woman and her very special child. And destroy a program that could change the face of nations.

But first they must unmask the mole that has infiltrated Shelby's agency and stalks their every move. They must stay alive and keep one step ahead of the pernicious forces who are intent on . . .

BREEDING EVIL

ISBN #1932815058
Gold Imprint: Available now
$6.99
www.lizwolfe.net

SUMMER OF FIRE

LINDA JACOBS

It is 1988, and Yellowstone Park is on fire.

Among the thousands of summer warriors battling to save America's crown jewel, is single mother Clare Chance. Having just watched her best friend, a fellow Texas firefighter, die in a roof collapse, she has fled to Montana to try and put the memory behind her. She's not the only one fighting personal demons as well as the fiery dragon threatening to consume the park.

There's Chris Deering, a Vietnam veteran helicopter pilot, seeking his next adrenaline high and a good time that doesn't include his wife, and Ranger Steve Haywood, a man scarred by the loss of his wife and baby in a plane crash. They rally 'round Clare when tragedy strikes yet again, and she loses a young soldier to a firestorm.

Three flawed, wounded people; one horrific blaze. Its tentacles are encircling the park, coming ever closer, threatening to cut them off. The landmark Old Faithful Inn and Park Headquarters at Mammoth are under siege, and now there's a helicopter down, missing, somewhere in the path of the conflagration. And Clare's daughter is on it . . .

Gold Imprint
June 2005
$6.99

SIREN'S CALL

MARY ANN MITCHELL

Sirena is a beautiful young woman. By night she strips at Silky Femmes, enticing large tips from conventioneers and salesmen passing through the small Florida city where she lives.

Sirena is also a loyal and compassionate friend to the denizens of Silky Femmes. There's Chrissie, who is a fellow dancer as well as the boss's abused and beleaguered girlfriend. And Ross, the bartender, who spends a lot of time worrying about the petite, delicate, and lovely Sirena. Maybe too much time.

There's also Detective Williams. He's looking for a missing man and his investigation takes him to Silky's. Like so many others, he finds Sirena irresistible. But again, like so many others, he's underestimated Sirena.

Because Sirena has a hobby. Not just any hobby. From the stage she searches out men with the solid bone structure she requires. The ones she picks get to go home with her where she will perform one last private strip for them. They can't believe their luck. They simply don't realize it's just run out.

ISBN #1932815163
Gold
$6.99
Fiction
Available Now

www.sff.net/people/maryann.mitchell

LIFE SENTENCES
TEKLA DENNISON MILLER

There are men who take women's lives. There are
men who kill their souls. . . .

Celeste Brookstone has the perfect life. On the
surface when her daughter takes a job with the Michi-
gan Prison System, she fears for Pilar's safety.

But she's glad she's away from the hell on earth
Marcus Brookstone has created within his own home.
Pilar Brookstone is an idealist. She thinks she can
change things, Make inmates' lives a little better. And
ever, ever make the mistake her mother made. Chad
Wilbanks is a serial killer. He is serving life. Eight young
women were his victims.

Is he about to take his ninth?

Men who kill.

The women who love them.

LIFE SENTENCES

ISBN #1932815252
Gold
$6.99
Fiction
Coming 2005

www.teklamiller.com

For more information

about other great titles from

Medallion Press, visit

www.medallionpress.co█